Praise for *Follow Me*

"*Follow Me Back* is the perfect mix of fandom with just the right amount of suspense. An enthralling page-turner from beginning to end."

—Anna Todd, *New York Times* bestselling
author of the After series

"Dark and suspenseful, *Follow Me Back* is sure to be the next big thing in YA thrillers."

—Ali Novak, author of The Heartbreak
Chronicles and *My Life with the Walter Boys*

"Timely, twisty, and totally thrilling. *Follow Me Back* will have readers wondering about the identity of every online friend and follower they've got. A riveting read that will keep you up late and keep you guessing!"

—Paula Stokes, author of
Liars, Inc. and *Vicarious*

"*Follow Me Back* is an unforgettable page-turner and a cautionary tale for any fan who's ever wished their favorite celebrity followed them on social media."

—Sandy Hall, author of *Signs Point to Yes*
and *A Little Something Different*

"*Follow Me Back* is a mystery/thriller/suspense roller coaster ride that keeps readers on their toes. Jaw-droppingly twisty and continually surprising."

—Laurie Elizabeth Flynn, author of *Firsts*

FOLLOW
ME
BACK

FOLLOW ME BACK

A.V. GEIGER

sourcebooks
fire

Published by Sourcebooks Fire, an imprint of Sourcebooks, Inc.
P.O. Box 4410, Naperville, Illinois 60567-4410
(630) 961-3900
Fax: (630) 961-2168
www.sourcebooks.com

Library of Congress Cataloging-in-Publication data is on file with the publisher.

Printed and bound in the United States of America.
VP 10 9 8 7 6 5 4 3 2 1

To David, for reminding me to breathe.

THE INTERROGATION
(FRAGMENT 1)

December 31, 2016, 8:42 p.m.
Case #: 124.678.21–001
OFFICIAL TRANSCRIPTION OF POLICE INTERVIEW

—START PAGE 1—

INVESTIGATOR: Sorry to keep you waiting, Mr. Thorn. We'd like to ask you a few questions.

THORN: Where's Tessa?

INVESTIGATOR: I'm Lieutenant Charles Foster. This is Detective Terence Newman. For the record, today is December 31 at 8:42 p.m. This interview is being recorded.

THORN: Is she here? Is she in the building?

INVESTIGATOR: Mr. Thorn, please sit down. This is an ongoing criminal investigation.

THORN: Tell me where she is!

INVESTIGATOR: We can't discuss that until we've taken your statement.

THORN: She's safe though, right? Will you tell me that much?

INVESTIGATOR: Son, the sooner you cooperate, the sooner we'll get this whole thing sorted out.

THORN: OK. OK. What do you want to know?

INVESTIGATOR: Thank you. Please state your full name, date of birth, and occupation for the record.

THORN: Eric Taylor Thorn. Date of birth, March 18, 1998. What was the third thing?

INVESTIGATOR: Occupation.

THORN: I don't...I don't even know anymore. Take your pick. Singer. Songwriter. Actor. Underwear model. Professional media whore? Does that qualify as an occupation?

INVESTIGATOR: That's fine, Mr. Thorn. Take it easy. This should only take a few minutes.

THORN: Should I have a lawyer?

INVESTIGATOR: You have the right to call an attorney at any time.

THORN: Am I under arrest?

INVESTIGATOR: We just have some questions. As I said, the sooner we have your statement, the sooner—

THORN: OK. Forget it. Tell me what you want to know.

INVESTIGATOR: Let's start at the beginning.

THORN: The beginning. What's the beginning? The day I got my record deal? The day I first picked up a guitar? I was about four years old.

INVESTIGATOR: We're talking about Tessa Hart. Tell us how you and Ms. Hart first became involved.

THORN: Over Twitter. Last summer. I think it was some-time in August. It started before that though. Before I even set up the account... [pause]

INVESTIGATOR: Please continue.

THORN: I guess... [pause] I guess if you have to start the story somewhere, I'd say the whole thing actually started in June with Dorian Cromwell. You know, from the boy band.

INVESTIGATOR: Are you saying this case is connected to what happened to Dorian Cromwell?

THORN: No, not really. Sorry, I'm not making any sense. I just meant the story was all over the news. And then the trial with that messed-up girl. All because he followed her back.

INVESTIGATOR: I'm afraid I'm still not following. How does the Dorian Cromwell case relate to your relationship with Tessa Hart?

THORN: It's funny. I knew it the moment I heard the story. I knew in my gut what must have happened to him. People say they'll always remember where they were when Kennedy was shot. Or where they were on 9/11. That's kind of how it was for me. I was driving down the Santa Monica Freeway with the top down, listening to the Top 40 on the radio. And the announcer broke in, right in the middle of number twelve. I wasn't even paying attention, but that was weird. You knew it was something big because they stopped in the middle of the song. They didn't know exactly what had happened yet. It took a few days to get to the bottom of it. About that girl, that fan. They didn't even know for sure it was a murder at that point. They only knew that it was Dorian Cromwell. That's what they said. Those were the exact words: Dorian Cromwell, lead singer of Fourth Dimension, was found dead this morning in London, floating facedown in the Thames.

1

PROJECTING

August 12, 2016

"YOU'RE NOT OBSESSED. You're projecting."

"Projecting?" Tessa looked up from the thick coil of long, brown hair that she'd been braiding and unbraiding for the past half hour. She met eyes uncertainly with her psychotherapist, Dr. Regan, sitting on the other side of the bedroom.

"It's a common defense mechanism," Dr. Regan said. Her tone remained emotionless as usual—the human equivalent of a white noise machine—but she shifted uncomfortably as she spoke. She sat perched in a low-slung, pink beanbag chair with her legs crossed at the ankles, striving to maintain a professional demeanor. Normally, she only met with clients in her office, but she made an exception for Tessa.

Tessa's gaze dropped to the older woman's panty hose, bunching at the knees, and she couldn't help but feel a grudging admiration. It took serious mental fortitude to brave the heat of the West Texas summer dressed in nylons. Tessa herself wore nothing but a tank top and cotton sleep shorts that barely skimmed the tops of her slender thighs.

"Projection," Dr. Regan said. "We use that term when an individual takes her own thoughts and feelings and attributes them to another person—in your case, to a celebrity."

"But I've never met Eric Thorn. I've never even been to one of his concerts."

Dr. Regan picked up Tessa's thought journal and flipped to the beginning. She made no comment on the drawings scribbled across the cover: a hodgepodge of hearts, woodland creatures, and eyeless human faces. *Forget projection*, Tessa thought, wrinkling her nose. They should probably discuss the fact that she couldn't even stand her own doodle-people looking at her.

Dr. Regan indicated one of Tessa's early entries. "Tell me about this. What piqued your interest enough to write something down about him?"

"About Eric?" Tessa reached for the spiral-bound journal, and her eyes swept over the page. "I was watching TMZ, I guess. They'd caught him walking around New York City with some actress from *Pretty Little Liars*. So naturally they assumed he was dating her."

"But that's not what you wrote down."

"Of course not. Have you seen TMZ? It's like fan fiction but less believable."

One of Dr. Regan's brows quirked upward, the closest she ever came to a real facial expression. She pushed her horn-rimmed glasses up her nose. "Tell me what you wrote instead."

Tessa pulled her knees against her chest. She felt a vague unease as she remembered how the grainy paparazzi footage had held her transfixed. Eric and that girl… He hadn't looked like he was on a date. Not even close. The video showed him walking briskly, with a furtive glance over his shoulder as he picked up the pace. Then the camera zoomed in close. Those piercing blue eyes of his had looked straight out of the screen. And the look on his face…

"He didn't look like some happy guy with a new girlfriend," Tessa told her therapist. "Not to me."

"What did he look like to you?"

Tessa closed her eyes. "Like he was scared out of his mind."

"Good, Tessa." Dr. Regan rewarded her with a nod. "And what do you think that might say about your own state of mind?"

"You mean I just imagined it? *I'm* actually the one who's scared out of my mind?"

Dr. Regan leaned forward intently. She tucked a strand of graying hair behind her ear.

"I suppose that's possible," Tessa said slowly. "That's one of my worst fears, I guess. Walking around some crowded city sidewalk, not knowing if I'm being followed…"

Dr. Regan took the thought journal and flipped it closed. "Excellent. Keep going."

"It wasn't just that one time though," Tessa said, thinking aloud. "Every time he looks straight into the camera, you can see this glimmer of fear."

"Fear of what?"

"Like he feels haunted by something. Haunted or—" Tessa broke off, searching for the right word. Her eyes slid over the journal cover and landed on one of the baby deer she'd drawn, running for its life. "Hunted, maybe? I don't know."

"That's very interesting, Tessa."

"Really? It's interesting?" Tessa couldn't help but laugh. *Interesting.* That must be one of those obscure psych terms for when the patient has a total one-track mind.

Every time she sat down to do her mindfulness exercises, she just ended up writing stories about Eric Thorn. Tessa had already filled two whole journals with all the elaborate plots she'd imagined. "It can't be healthy, right?"

Dr. Regan pulled out a yellow legal pad and recorded a quick note. "You may feel safer exploring your own anxieties by assigning them to someone else. That can be quite useful, actually, as long as you recognize what you're doing. Try to think how your theories about this celebrity might connect to what happened in June."

Tessa responded with a choked noise, hugging her knees even tighter. She'd spent the month of June in New Orleans, part of an eight-week creative writing program for teens—or it was supposed to last eight weeks at any rate. Tessa had left the program halfway through and fled back home to the safety of her childhood bedroom. Now the whole summer had nearly come and gone, and she still couldn't bring herself to talk about why she'd left. "No... You said I didn't have to...not until I was ready—"

"OK, Tessa." Dr. Regan raised a calming hand. "Remember your breathing. That's it."

Tessa swallowed. The rising anxiety threatened to engulf her, but she focused her mind on her one most trusted distraction. *Eric. Eric Thorn.* Tessa chanted his name inside her head as she sucked air deep into her lungs. She was supposed to hold her breath for a five count, but she had her own little spin on this particular relaxation technique. *Eric one... Eric two... Eric three...* Tessa watched her chest slowly rise and fall until the tension in her shoulders ebbed.

"Good, Tessa," Dr. Regan said. "We can keep the conversation framed on Eric Thorn if that's where you feel most comfortable."

"I just don't understand why I chose him. Why Eric Thorn of all people?"

"You tell me. Why do you think you've fixated on him?"

Tessa felt her face heat up. She'd considered herself a fan since his debut album a few years ago, but her fascination lately had reached a whole new level. It went way beyond the stories in her thought journal. Every time she came across a new picture of him, she felt this overwhelming compulsion to save it to her cell phone camera roll. She had more images of Eric Thorn squirreled away than anyone she'd ever known in real life. Here in her bedroom, Tessa had taken down all the other photographs that used to decorate the pale-yellow walls, but she'd left her Eric Thorn concert poster in its place of honor above her bed.

"I don't know," Tessa said. "Maybe because he's hot?" She

glanced over her shoulder at the poster, and her eyes lingered on the familiar scene: Eric performing onstage, with an electric guitar slung across the sculpted muscles of his chest. He had his head thrown back, eyes closed, lost in the music…

Dr. Regan peered over the rim of her glasses at Eric's sweaty torso. "I'm guessing there's a little more to it than that," she said. "But let's leave it as something for you to think about for our next session. Now, what about your desensitization exercises? How did it go this week?"

Tessa bit at her thumbnail, already chewed down to the nub. Her therapist filled the silence as she hesitated.

"Last week, you were able to sit downstairs in the living room with your mom and your boyfriend, Scott, for half an hour."

"Yeah," Tessa muttered.

"And your goal for this week was to try touching the front doorknob of the house."

"That didn't exactly happen." Tessa bit down on her cuticle, tearing it with her teeth. She knew that she'd messed up. It had taken her more than a month of therapy just to summon the courage to set foot outside her bedroom door, but the past few days had felt like a huge step backward. "I've just been really overwhelmed this week," she said. "There's this…thing…happening. It's stupid."

Dr. Regan frowned. "What thing?"

"Nothing. It's just something that happened on Twitter."

The therapist stopped scribbling notes and looked up. "You're on Twitter?"

"I'm really sorry," Tessa said. She hadn't mentioned her Twitter account before. It hadn't seemed relevant. She rarely ever tweeted nowadays. But this past week, Twitter had somehow managed to occupy most of her waking thoughts. "I know what you're going to say. I should probably deactivate so I can focus on my exercises better."

"No, Tessa. That would only isolate you further." Dr. Regan jotted furiously as she spoke. "Any kind of social interaction can potentially hold therapeutic value."

"Really?" Tessa glanced skeptically at her phone, resting on the bedside table in a red leather cell phone case. She'd left it there, facedown, so she wouldn't be distracted by any new Twitter notifications during the hour-long session.

Dr. Regan nodded. "Our goal is for you to interact with other people in the outside world of course, but social media can serve as a positive first step."

"OK. Well, that's pretty much all I did all week, so…"

"Do you have followers? People with whom you interact?"

Tessa laughed. What a question. If anyone had asked her a few days ago, the answer would have been different: a couple hundred followers, who mostly ignored her existence. But when Tessa last checked her account today, the follower count stood at 30K. Tessa still felt a little dizzy, thinking of it. Thirty thousand followers. Thirty thousand sets of eyes watching her every tweet. Her emotions kept swinging back and forth like a pendulum, from terror at the thought of them all to an irrational desire for more. Her fingers itched to check her phone again. How many more had she gained in the time since she and Dr. Regan started talking?

"It's kind of intense," she said, as she picked up the phone and glanced down.

Tessa H @TessaHeartsEric

FOLLOWERS:
30.1K

She showed the screen to her therapist.

"Very interesting." Dr. Regan pressed her pen against her lips, considering. She wrote something else on her pad.

"My account kind of blew up this week."

"What happened?"

Tessa ducked her head. She avoided Dr. Regan's gaze, fiddling with the frayed hem of her bedspread. "It started with a story I've been writing. About Eric. I posted one online last weekend." Tessa watched a row of stitching come undone as she pulled at a loose thread. "I called it 'Obsessed.' It was supposed to be a little joke at my own expense, you know?"

"And what happened?"

"I started this hashtag, #EricThornObsessed. Do you know what a hashtag is?"

"I'm familiar with the concept." Dr. Regan's tone remained perfectly deadpan but her eyes lit with amusement, and Tessa bit her lip. She generally assumed that anyone Dr. Regan's age didn't even know how to download an app, but she must have misjudged her therapist. Tessa's mouth curved into a shy smile as she continued.

"I was trying to get other fans to read it. So I made all these tweets with sexy pictures of him and the link to my story. And it just…blew up somehow. It happened so fast. First one of the bigger Eric Thorn fan accounts retweeted me. And then @Relatable retweeted. And then @Flirtationship retweeted. And then… I forget after that. I think it was @GirlPosts? Or maybe @SoDamnTrue? One of those big accounts that everyone follows. And then it was everywhere after that. I think it hit number one on Wednesday? Maybe Thursday? Look." Tessa swiped across the screen of her phone and held it out to Dr. Regan again. "See? These are all the hashtags trending worldwide."

And there, still hovering third on the list, were the words Tessa had first typed into her phone six days ago, now amplified by more voices than she even dared to fathom:

#EricThornObsessed
21.8 million tweets

#ERICTHORNOBSESSED

ERIC OPENED TWITTER and pulled up the list of trending topics.

#EricThornObsessed
21.8 million tweets

"Shit," he swore softly, chucking his phone down on the bed beside him. Still third on the list. The damn thing refused to die. Couldn't all those stalker-iffic parasites find anything better to obsess about?

At least he wasn't first anymore.

He slumped back against the velvet-upholstered headboard of the hotel bed. A lock of his shaggy, dark-brown hair fell over his eyes, and he raked it away in annoyance, grimacing at the crunchy texture of leftover hair gel. He should have showered before turning in last night. He'd put in another sixteen-hour day of interviews yesterday, and he'd been too tired to do much more than kick off his clothes and pass out on top of the covers by the time he made it back to his hotel room.

No point showering now anyway. His morning workout regimen began in twenty minutes, and his trainer would give him hell if he showed up late. Then again, his hairstylist would give him hell if he showed up in the makeup chair afterward with a tangle of sweaty, hair-gel-caked disgustingness. Maybe he should hop in the shower just for a sec…

A faint creak sounded from the other side of the bedroom door, and Eric paused, his spine stiffening. Someone was in his suite. Maid service? No. They knew better. Did he forget to turn the deadbolt before he passed out last night? But then it could only be—

He shrank back against the pillows as the bedroom doorknob turned.

"*Who's there?*" His lips formed the shape of the words, but there wasn't enough air in his lungs to make a sound. He grabbed a bedsheet to cover himself—undressed except for yesterday's pair of boxer briefs—while his eyes made a quick scan of the room. Anything he could use as a weapon? Bedside lamp? No. Just wall sconces in here. No ashtrays either. *Shit!* Maybe that ceramic vase over there—

"Hey, kid, you decent?"

Eric squeezed his eyes shut at the sound of the familiar voice. He relaxed his death grip on the bedsheet as his manager, Maury, sauntered into the room.

"Dude!" Eric exclaimed, his heart fluttering like a caught bird inside his chest. "You don't even knock anymore?"

"Sorry, kid. Were you sleeping?" Maury looked like he'd been up for hours. Eric couldn't remember the last time he'd seen his manager dressed in anything other than polished wingtip shoes and designer-label suits. The man deserved a *GQ* fashion spread—probably could've landed one for himself, if he hadn't been so short and fat and bald.

"No, I wasn't sleeping," Eric said. "That's not the point. This is my bedroom!"

Maury roved his eyes appreciatively around the well-appointed room. "Technically, this is a hotel suite paid for by your record label," he said, brushing a hand against the duvet cover. "What is this, Egyptian cotton? Probably eight hundred thread count. Did you sleep cozy?" His manager didn't bother to mention the room rate, and Eric knew better than to ask.

"So we're not even going to pretend I have privacy anymore?"

Maury poked a toe at the pile of dirty clothes that lay discarded on the hand-loomed carpeting. "Maybe hang a sock on the door if you're gonna have a girl in here," he said, his eyes twinkling with mischief. Eric made no response. He punched his fist into one of the overstuffed pillows.

"Oh, come on, kid. Lighten up. It's a joke!"

"You're hilarious, Maury."

"Relax! I'll knock next time. I promise."

"Thank you. Can I get dressed now?" Eric clasped the

bedsheet tighter around his shoulders, but his manager didn't take the hint. "What?" Eric asked. "Is there something you needed?"

Maury reached for Eric's cell phone. "Yeah, I just got off the horn with social media. The #EricThornObsessed trend fell to number three overnight, so they want you to give it a little shot in the arm—"

"No!" Eric swatted the phone out of reach before his manager could get his paws on it.

"They just want you to do a little follow spree," Maury said. "Follow a few fan accounts. You know the drill."

Eric thought he might throw up. Seriously? Did those words *seriously* just come out of Maury's mouth? Didn't anyone at his record label watch the news?

Eric buried his head in his hands. He knew he must sound like a broken record, the way he brought up the murder case on a daily basis, but he couldn't put the ugly story out of his mind. His manager's words had summoned up all the sordid details once again. A follow spree… Eric let out a low moan.

Maury cast his eyes upward. "Oh, for the love of God," he said. "Let me guess. Dorian Cromwell?"

"Maury, don't you get it? That's *exactly* what happened to him! He did a follow spree!"

"Kid, I understand you're freaked out, but—"

"He followed some obsessed teenager, and she got all carried away. Convinced herself that they were soul mates. Star-crossed lovers. Some bullshit like that. So she found out where he was staying and waited for him to come out of his hotel. And when he didn't quite see it the same way?" Eric tilted back his head and slashed a hand across his throat.

"Listen to me, kiddo." Maury shuffled over to the side of the bed and dropped a fatherly hand on Eric's shoulder. "That girl had issues. You understand that, right? They locked her up. It was a one-in-a-million thing—"

"See, that would be a lot more reassuring if I didn't have fourteen million Twitter followers."

"Eric—"

"So, by that math, I only have fourteen potential ax murderers following me. No big deal."

Maury laughed. "You need to stop watching the news, my friend, and maybe try showing your followers some gratitude." His manager reached again for the cell phone resting on the mattress. "Here," Maury said, tapping at the phone. "Do the follow spree. You can pick the fans yourself. You just have to include this one."

Eric glanced at the Twitter account that Maury pulled up on the screen.

Tessa H @TessaHeartsEric

FOLLOWERS
30.1K

"Why her?" Eric asked. He ran his eyes down her recent

tweets—all various pictures of him, shirtless, with a link to some website called Wattpad and the hashtag #EricThornObsessed.

"She's the one who started the trend. She wrote a fanfic story about you called 'Obsessed.'"

"Oh, perfect." Eric snorted. "That sounds healthy."

Maury waved away the sarcasm without taking his eyes off the screen. "It's actually not half-bad, as these things go. The label's thinking about publishing it and bundling it with the next deluxe album—"

Eric stuck a finger down his throat and pretended to gag.

"They're just keeping an eye on it for now. But if you follow her, that story will explode—"

"Which is exactly why I'm not doing it!" Eric snatched the phone away. "I'm not encouraging these people to be any more obsessed than they already are."

Maury didn't answer. He merely shrugged and looked away, studying the tips of his shoes. Eric had worked with him long enough to know what the gesture meant. He could fume all he wanted, but when it came to the edicts of his record label, he didn't really have much choice.

Eric pinched the bridge of his nose. He could feel a tension headache coming on. He'd been having them far too often lately—especially when his manager was in the room. "Did the label get back to you yet about beefing up security?"

"Let's just tackle one thing at a time, shall we?"

"Did you even talk to them?" Eric asked.

"Kid, you're their number-one earner. I promise you,

they're not going to let you get hacked to bits by some serial killer..." Maury shot him a sly grin. "Just as long your ticket sales don't slump."

Eric rolled his eyes. "Great, Maury. I'm so glad you're amused. Now do you think you could knock it off with the bad stand-up routine?"

"Whoa, big guy!" Maury threw up his hands. "I asked. They answered."

"And?"

"And your liaison said yes. But then publicity got wind and nixed it."

Publicity, Eric thought. He should've known. It always came down to those bottom-feeders, didn't it? The geniuses at his record label didn't care if he ended up dead.

No, they might consider it a stroke of luck. Look at Dorian Cromwell. Fourth Dimension had been starting to fade before it happened. Sales were soft on their latest album, but it had popped back up to the top of the charts the moment the murder story broke. The PR folks at Dorian's label probably all stood up and cheered when they heard the news. Probably started the #RIPDorian hashtag themselves, just to spur the feeding frenzy a little longer. No such thing as bad publicity, right?

Eric clenched his jaw. There was no point trying to argue. He knew what the publicists would say—what Maury would say too—if Eric dared to voice a complaint: that he should be flattered. He had the entire Twitterverse obsessed with him. Literally. He should take it as a compliment.

Yeah, Eric thought, meeting Maury's eyes with a sullen glare. *Dorian must've been super flattered, right up to the moment that fangirl slit his throat.*

"It's just a little follow spree," Maury said, cajoling. "You've done it a million times."

Eric shook his head.

"Eric, if you don't do it, the label's going to take your Twitter account and let some publicist over there run it. Then you won't have any control at all."

"They can't do that—can they?"

"You know what it says in your contract."

Right. His contract. Eric folded his arms across his chest. Honestly, his manager had a lot of nerve, bringing up the subject. Eric had been on Maury's case for months to renegotiate that sorry excuse for a record deal. Signing it in the first place was probably the biggest mistake of his career.

Maury cleared his throat. "I know what you're going to ask, Eric, and the answer is I'm trying."

"How much longer is it going to take?"

Maury didn't answer. He turned to straighten his tie in the gold-framed mirror that hung opposite the bed. For a moment, Eric thought he didn't hear the question, but Maury spoke in a confidential tone as he adjusted the points of his shirt collar. "Listen to me, kid. They weren't born yesterday."

Eric met his manager's eyes, reflected in the glass. "What does that mean?"

"It means they realize you're not happy. They see what you're trying to do. As long as your parents are cosigners on that contract, they've got you by the balls. They'll wipe out your whole family's life savings, just like *that*"—Maury snapped his fingers for emphasis—"if you try to walk away."

"But I'm not a minor anymore! I'm eighteen years old!"

"And you're almost out from under it." Maury raised a hand to silence him. "Just hang in there a little longer. Two more album cycles and you're free. You can go indie. You can retire. You can do anything you want."

Eric's shoulders sagged.

"Three years, tops," Maury said. "Maybe two and a half if we hustle."

"Oh, so I'll get out early for good behavior?"

Maury laughed. "If this is prison, kid, then sign me up." His eyes made another circuit around the opulent hotel suite. "You wanted this, Eric. You worked your ass off to get discovered. Remember? What happened to that pimply-faced kid I found posting cover songs on YouTube?"

"I know, Maury," Eric said. "I just didn't totally understand what I was signing up for."

Maury sat on the edge of the bed and punched him in the arm. "Come on. Get up. Go do your workout. You'll feel better. Then you can do the follow spree after that."

Eric groaned at the reminder. His workout… As if he had any choice about that either. Three hours a day of cardio and weights, overseen by the personal trainer of his record label's choosing. It was all right there in the contract. And lo and behold, pictures of his perfectly chiseled pecs and abs featured prominently in every one of those #EricThornObsessed tweets.

"Fine," he grumbled. "Just give me a few minutes to myself first. Can I have that at least?"

"Of course." Maury stood and made his way toward the door. "You smell like a zoo animal, by the way. Did you shower?"

"Body odor isn't in the contract," Eric said dryly. He wrapped the sheet around himself, toga style, and followed his manager to the main door of the suite.

"Actually it is, my friend," Maury said over his shoulder. "I hate to break it to you."

"What? Since when?"

"Personal hygiene clause."

"That's ridiculous. Like anyone can smell me over Twitter!"

Maury didn't answer. He already had his cell phone pressed to his ear, and he waved to Eric offhandedly as he made his way out.

Eric poked his head out the front door of the suite and swept his eyes down the length of the corridor. Empty except for a maid pushing a housekeeping cart. She spotted him, and Eric tensed as her eyes widened with recognition. A fan, he could tell, from the way her face flushed crimson.

Eric looked away, praying she wouldn't make a fuss. She wouldn't scream, would she? Or, worse yet, snap a cell phone video to sell to TMZ? But the maid lowered her gaze discreetly as she pushed the cart around the corner. Eric took a breath. For a moment, he considered going after her. Maybe he should offer to sign an autograph. He used to take such pleasure from little things like that. It only took a second of his time to make some fan's whole day…

But that was all at the beginning of his career—back when his Twitter followers counted in the thousands, not the millions. Now he didn't dare leave the safety of his room. Anyone could be lying in wait around the corner. Publicists…photographers…fourteen-year-olds with knives…

Eric hastily returned the Do Not Disturb sign to the door handle. He flipped the heavy deadbolt and checked it twice to make sure it was secure. Then he padded back toward the bathroom and turned on the shower.

"Personal hygiene clause," he muttered under his breath. He turned his phone back on as he stood waiting for the water to heat.

Twitter app.

Trending topics.

#EricThornObsessed
21.9M tweets

In the half hour since he woke this morning, another hundred thousand people had added their voices to the chorus.

3

THE FOLLOW SPREE

ERIC SAT DOWN on the toilet with a white hotel towel draped around his neck. He glanced down at the tweet he'd sent ten minutes ago before stepping into the shower.

Eric Thorn @EricThorn
Wow! Thanks for the #EricThornObsessed thing. How bout a follow spree? Retweet for a follow!
🔁 18.7K   ♥ 20.1K

He'd immediately followed the first twenty fans who responded, but the retweets and replies were still rolling in by the thousands. He flicked back over to the trending list. Oh goodie. Up to the number-two spot. No doubt #EricThornObsessed would climb back to number one worldwide soon enough.

The label should be satisfied, even if he didn't follow that one fan in particular: Tessa H, the most obsessed one of all, who'd managed to get the rest of them whipped up into this latest frenzy. Frankly, they could kiss his ass with that idea.

It would be a cold night in hell before he followed her.

"Enough," Eric muttered to himself. "Put the phone down." He knew he shouldn't read the replies. It would only irritate him further—all those thousands of fangirls, tweeting their undying love to him. Not like in the old days, when they used to praise him for his music or his voice. He still appreciated tweets like that, but they were few and far between. Most of these fans had never even been to one of his concerts. They'd made it all too clear what they loved about him when he released his most recent album a few months back. He'd conducted a little experiment at the time.

First, he'd tweeted a link to buy the lead single on iTunes:

    🔁 4.1K   ♥ 10.2K

Then he tweeted a selfie, shirtless, from the set of the music video:

    🔁 42.6K   ♥ 86.3K

The numbers only confirmed what he already knew in his gut. His so-called fans would much rather stare at silent pictures of his body than listen to any song he bothered to record. Ever since then, he hadn't sent a single tweet unless commanded by his handlers. His Twitter app remained unopened and untouched for weeks at a time.

And I should close it again right now, he told himself. He'd done his duty. Move along.

Eric let out a weary sigh. He needed to get on with his day, but the thought of the workout looming before him kept him planted to the toilet. Just a few more minutes, he thought. They couldn't give him a hard time for being late, right? Everyone needed to take a dump once in a while. Even pretty-boy pop stars.

He switched over to the notifications tab and rolled his eyes in disgust as he read the first one:

Eric Thorn Lover @EricLuv982
I LOVE UUUUUUUUUUU ERIC PLS
FOLLOW ME I'M CRYING!!!!!!!!!!!!!!!!!!!!!!!!!!!!!

She loved him? He'd wager good money that she barely listened to his music. Who had time, with all those pictures of him in his underpants to tweet about? But she loved him. Sure. If she only knew what he really thought.

It was so tempting to tell them. He could just imagine how that tweet would read:

@EricLuv982 You don't love me. You don't
even know me.

Yes, he thought. How amazing would it feel to get it all off his chest? But why restrict it to that one when there were millions of others just like her?

Eric punched at his keypad, embellishing as he went:

> Attention fans. You don't love me. You don't
> even know me. I'll never, ever love you
> back. So put down the phone, go outside,
> and get a life

Not bad for 140 characters. He could go on, of course, but he'd reached the maximum length.

Eric wondered what would happen if he sent it. What would all the fangirls do? Would #EricThornObsessed grind to a screeching halt? He closed his eyes and pictured it, his lips forming a crooked grin.

Pure fantasy, of course. There'd be hell to pay if his finger slipped and hit the Tweet button. His publicists would rake him over the coals—and that would be the least of his problems.

Eric shifted his weight uneasily against the cold, hard surface of the toilet seat. He couldn't risk it. He couldn't antagonize the fans. He only needed one of them to flip out and come after him with a butcher knife. How many were hovering on the brink, just waiting for one wrong move to push them over the edge?

He tipped back his head and ran his hand up and down his throat, rough with stubble. Did Dorian see it coming? Eric wondered. Or did that girl surprise him from behind?

No, he could never tell his followers what he really thought of them. Way too dangerous. In fact, he should probably tweet the opposite right then, just to be on the safe side—something to soothe the raging disappointment for all the ones he just passed over.

He hastily wrote a new message and hit Tweet.

Tessa clicked the bedroom door closed behind Dr. Regan's retreating form. She dove across her bed to grab the cell phone on her nightstand. The Twitter notifications had been going off like fireworks for the past ten minutes, and Tessa had watched helplessly out of the corner of her eye, waiting for her therapy session to end so she could read them.

She looked eagerly at the screen and saw the cause of the commotion: a new tweet from Eric Thorn.

"No!" she exclaimed as she read it. A follow spree? Now? He never did those anymore. He barely even tweeted these days. People said he must be too busy with his hectic promo sched-ule, but Tessa didn't buy it. It only took a moment to send a tweet. Something else had changed with him lately, although she seemed to be the only one who thought so. She saw it all over his face in the underwear campaign he just shot. He'd tried for his usual smoldering stare, gazing straight into the camera as he lounged around a bowling alley in nothing but his boxer briefs. But in his eyes she saw only a mixture of anger and sadness—and fear.

Projecting. Just projecting. Dr. Regan probably knew what she was talking about. Tessa hadn't felt totally convinced during the therapy session, but she saw now that it must be true. He wasn't avoiding Twitter on purpose, out of some deep-seated inner turmoil. He was just busy, like everyone said. He just did a follow spree after all.

And she had missed it.

Tessa read the time stamp on Eric's tweet with a stab of disappointment. Eleven minutes ago now—a lifetime in the Twitter game. No doubt the fans he followed had all replied within the first thirty seconds.

She couldn't believe her bad luck. Here she was, cooped up twenty-four-seven in this self-imposed prison cell of a bedroom with nothing to do but look at her phone...and he chose the *one* hour she had therapy to do a follow spree. It would probably be days, if not weeks, before he had time to tweet again.

With a groan, she began composing a halfhearted reply:

@EricThorn FOLLOW ME! I LOVE YOU! I'm
so upset I missed this! Grrrr :(

Her finger hovered over the Tweet button, when another notification flashed onto her screen:

New tweet from Eric Thorn (@EricThorn)

Follow spree complete. Don't be upset if I
missed you. I love each and every one of
you more than you could ever know.

She couldn't help but smile as she read the words, soothing
her disappointment like a…like a healing balm on a nasty burn
after falling asleep in the sun…

Tessa chuckled softly to herself. She really was obsessed with
him, wasn't she? That whole metaphor came from his latest
single, of course. He called it "Aloe Vera."

> *Come on and soothe this sunburn.*
> *Baby, take away my pain.*
> *The light, it lured me under*
> *On a perfect, sunny day.*

He'd supposedly written it while vacationing in Cozumel
at some fabulous beach resort. And he made the same self-
deprecating joke about it, over and over, on all the late-night
talk shows afterward: *Yes, Jimmy. I wrote a love song to my skin-
care regimen. I'm working on another one about my aftershave
now. Not that I'm obsessed with my looks or anything…*

Tessa had felt a bit worried about him when she first heard
the song. He could joke all he wanted, but she knew that
song wasn't really about a day at the beach. It was about
getting burned.

She flicked on a bedside lamp. If only better lighting could chase away the gloomy thoughts. Obviously, she was reading way too much into things. There was nothing wrong with Eric Thorn's mental state. This tweet just now didn't come from someone dealing with depression and anxiety. No, those words came from a guy who was sensitive. Thoughtful. Someone who really cared about his fans' feelings. Most celebrities wouldn't have bothered.

She could just picture him typing it out and then watching his phone light up with the replies. All those words of love pouring back at him. No doubt he wore that crooked grin of his plastered on his face as he basked in the adoration. He deserved it too. Every word.

Tessa wondered where he was right now. Maybe lounging in the backseat of a limo with cushy leather seats. Was he watching his phone, right at that moment? Her cheeks flushed at the thought. She abandoned the tweet she'd been composing and hastily wrote out a new one:

@EricThorn You sweetie pie. SMILE IF YOU
SEE THIS! #EricThornObsessed

With that, Tessa flicked over to her music app and slipped in her earphones, unwilling to let her mental image die. She closed her eyes with satisfaction at the sound of Eric's voice singing the catchy opening hook to "Aloe Vera."

Come on and soothe this sunburn.
Baby, take away my pain...

She could almost see him now—looking at his phone when her reply came up. The grin on his face growing a shade brighter as he read it.

Eric scowled down at the tweet he'd just sent. Did they actually buy it when he put on his sugary-sweet I-love-my-fans act? Apparently so, by the looks of his notifications tab, lighting up with thousands of new replies.

His scowl grew a shade deeper as he watched them rolling in.

Maybe he should write a song about it, he thought bitterly. A nice, sappy ballad about how much he loved his fans. Call it…"Snowflakes." Yeah, that was good. "Special Snowflakes."

> *I watch the snowflakes falling,*
> *Too many for me to see.*
> *But I know each one is beautiful,*
> *Special and unique.*

God, that was awful. The label would probably love it though. They could release it in time for Christmas, and the fans would eat it up with a spoon. Well, assuming anyone actually listened to his music anymore…and had the mental capacity to understand a simple metaphor.

He snorted. Who was he kidding? Anyway, a song like that would only serve to spur their obsession further. Just

like this tweet of his. He ran his eyes over it again with a trace
of regret.

I love each and every one of you…

Why had he just sent that? It would only egg them on.

But he had to do it. It was a matter of survival at this point.
No telling what kind of homicidal tendencies they might be
harboring out there. He had to keep leading them on, telling them what they wanted to hear—even if it meant lying
through his teeth.

OLD HABITS

THE SOUND OF Eric's voice faded in Tessa's ears as the song came to an end. With a sigh, she lifted her finger to hit Replay.

She'd developed a habit lately of listening to the same song three or four times in a row—so different from the way she used to consume music in the past. Before this summer, her playlists always contained hundreds of songs by different artists, all set to random shuffle. It was only since returning home from New Orleans that she'd fallen into this new pattern, listening and re-listening, over and over. It put her in a kind of trance. She could let her mind drift free from any thoughts of her own life and picture Eric Thorn singing the familiar words for her ears alone.

Now she lay with her head at the foot of the bed, gazing up at her concert poster. She imagined herself pressed against the railing at the edge of a stage, watching the whole show live. Someday, she vowed. Someday, somehow, she would find a way to attend an Eric Thorn concert for real…

Tessa closed her eyes and hummed along with his clear, smooth tenor voice. She remained completely still except for the gentle rhythm of her heels against the mattress. Her tank top hitched up to expose her bare midriff, and she didn't bother to fix it. She didn't hear the scrape of the bedroom door behind her or the soft footsteps creeping toward the bed. She had no inkling of any other presence in the room until a shadow fell over her shoulder and a hand from out of nowhere grasped her on the knee.

Tessa's eyes flew open. Her head snapped up so hard that she bit her tongue. Her daydream of Eric vanished, replaced by the sound of her own pulse pounding in her ears. She yanked out her headphones with a gasp.

Scott, her boyfriend since sophomore year of high school, loomed above her.

"Hey, hot stuff. Whatcha doing?"

Tessa stared at him blankly. His hand rested heavily on her leg, and his eyes were glued to the exposed portion of her stomach. Tessa jerked her disheveled tank top back in place.

Scott, she told herself, forcing a deep breath. *Just Scott.*

It didn't help that he'd changed his appearance lately—no longer the baby-faced teenager that she'd first grown to know and love. He'd cut off his mop of curly, brown hair, opting instead for a close-cropped buzz cut, and he kept his jawline shadowed with a fringe of dark stubble. Tessa knew he was going for a more mature look in honor of high school graduation, but she wasn't sure she liked the change. His face looked more masculine but also more unfamiliar. She couldn't help but find the stranger who stood before her vaguely sinister.

Scott smirked, completely oblivious to her discomfort. His eyes wandered down the length of her legs. "Busy, huh? Don't tell me I missed visiting hours again."

"You scared me!" Tessa tucked her feet beneath her. She clenched a fist and pressed it to her chest. "Do you have any idea what that does to me?"

"Sorry. I knocked. I wasn't sure you were in here."

She frowned at him. Not in here? Was that supposed to be a joke? And how many times did she have to tell him not to sneak up on her? Every time he did it, she had nightmares for days.

"Just listening to music," she said. With her hands still trembling, she flicked the music app closed. She didn't want him to see whose song she'd been playing.

He nodded, his gaze now moving restlessly around the cramped room. He sounded distracted as he spoke. "Honestly, Tess. I don't know how you stay cooped up in here all day. I would lose my friggin' mind."

Tessa's mouth fell open. Had he really said that to her? Was he even trying to understand what she was going through? No wonder she spent all her time fantasizing about a celebrity. Eric Thorn didn't even know she existed, and yet he showed more consideration for her feelings than the guy who supposedly loved her.

Wow, Scott, she wanted to say. *And the award for world's most insensitive boyfriend goes to...*

But she swallowed the words. She shouldn't snap at Scott. At least he still came to see her. She couldn't afford to alienate him—one of three people in the universe that she trusted inside her bedroom door. Aside from her mother and her therapist, Scott was the only person Tessa had spoken to since June.

She knew it couldn't be much fun for him either, having a girlfriend with severe agoraphobia. His life kept moving forward the whole time she remained locked up in her room. He was about to enter his freshman year of college, with a whole new set of friends that Tessa would probably never meet. She knew some of them would be female. Some of them would be cute. He could easily leave her behind for greener pastures, but so far he'd remained by her side throughout the whole ordeal. She needed to remember that.

He grinned at her and kicked off his shoes. Tessa forced herself to smile in return as he came to sit beside her on the bed. She set her phone back on the nightstand, facedown—any new notifications for @TessaHeartsEric safely out of her boyfriend's line of sight. Then she rested her head on his shoulder and wrapped an arm around his waist.

Scott gave her shoulders a friendly squeeze. "Seriously, Tess. It's got to be a hundred degrees in here. Let me crack a window or something—"

"No!" She felt his weight shift beside her, and she grabbed his wrist. "Don't," she stammered. "Don't open anything. I like it this way."

He turned toward the double window on the wall beside her

bookcase. Tessa used to keep it flung wide open all summer long to let in the cool cross breeze. Even in the wintertime, she rarely closed the blinds. The window overlooked a sprawl of undeveloped scrubland, with a few massive sycamore trees scattered along the dusty gravel lane. The next house down the road looked like a mere speck from her window. It would probably have taken a telescope to catch sight of any neighbors.

Her boyfriend pursed his lips at the ugly horizontal slats, shut tight to block out the late-summer sunshine. They both knew that Tessa hadn't opened the window in weeks. Scott ran a hand across his forehead to wipe away the beading sweat, but he let the subject drop. "Whatever, babe. So what are you up to today? Anything exciting?"

"Not really." Tessa let go of his wrist and drew in her legs, hugging her knees. "Eat. Sleep. Therapy exercises. Maybe listen to some music."

"That's it? All day?"

"I might do some writing later."

His eyebrows lifted a fraction of an inch. "Really? What are you writing?"

Tessa scrunched her nose, mentally smacking herself on the forehead. She hadn't confided in him about her account on the story-sharing website. She couldn't tell her boyfriend how she spent her days dreaming up fanfics about Eric Thorn. "Nothing," she said. "I just meant that I write in my thought journal. You know, therapy stuff."

"Can I read it?"

She shook her head sharply, and Scott pulled away. He got up off the bed and jammed his feet back into his well-worn canvas sneakers.

Was he leaving? Already? "I'm sorry, Scott! It's like asking to read my diary. I only show it to my therapist."

"Is it even helping, Tessa? All this therapy?"

"Of course it is! Dr. Regan is really happy with my progress." Tessa scrambled onto her knees and crawled after him toward the edge of the bed. She cast about for something she could say to undo the damage—any kind of encouraging detail from her therapy session, even if it meant she had to stretch the truth a tad. "She thinks I might be ready to leave the house. Soon."

"Really? That's awesome." Scott sat back down beside her, and Tessa touched his arm to anchor him in place.

"I know. I'm excited." She smiled at him softly. "I can't wait till I can go visit you at your dorm. Then we can be alone. We won't have to worry about my mom walking in on us all the time."

Scott inched a little closer, matching her smile with a playful look of his own. "Your mom's not here right now."

"She'll be home any sec."

Now that was a bald-faced lie. Her mother wasn't due back from work for hours. Why did she just do that? Why did she feel this flicker of anxiety whenever Scott even suggested the *possibility* of physical contact?

Scott must've known she was lying, but he didn't press the issue. Instead, he turned his face away and slipped his phone out of his pocket. "I gotta get going soon anyway," he muttered, distracted by a text message.

"What? Why? You just got here. Scott, please just give me a little more time…"

Tessa's voice trailed off. He didn't seem to be listening in any case. His full attention was directed at his phone. It pinged with another incoming text, and the corners of his mouth quivered as he read it. "Gimme a sec, babe," he said without looking up.

Tessa gazed longingly at her own phone out of the corner of her eye. If he could check his messages, why shouldn't she? Was she missing anything important? Probably another follow spree, knowing her luck.

She didn't dare look. Not in front of Scott. Her time with him was way more important than Twitter anyway. This was real life. Her boyfriend. There had to be some way to salvage this pathetic excuse for a visit. "Scott, don't go yet," she said. "What time is it? Did you eat breakfast yet? We have some leftover sausage in the fridge if you want—"

"Nah, I'm meeting people for brunch." He stuffed his phone back in his pocket and looked over at her hesitantly. "Listen, Tessa. I actually came here today to ask you something. Are you serious about leaving the house soon?"

"Yeah! Really, really soon."

"Perfect." He nodded enthusiastically, and Tessa felt a tightness in her throat. What was he about to ask? Maybe she shouldn't have sounded quite so optimistic…

"Because there's this thing I'm going to in a couple weeks.

It's a freshman rush event for Kappa Sigma. We're supposed to bring a date. So I was kind of hoping, maybe—"

She cut him off with a sharp intake of breath. "Scott, what are you talking about?"

"I told you, I decided to rush a fraternity."

"You want *me* to go?"

"Well, I told all those guys that I have a girlfriend. I don't want them to think I just made you up or something." His eyes left her face and drifted back down to her clingy tank top. "Anyway, I want to impress them. I was kind of hoping I could show you off."

Tessa stared back at him, speechless.

"Come on, Tessa. I really need this. And you just said you're basically ready."

"I said soon! Not two weeks from now!"

"So by *soon* you meant more like two months? Two years?" His face darkened, and Tessa bent her arms protectively across her chest. She knew what she was in for next. Scott's epic tantrums could put most toddlers to shame. He'd be red as an overripe tomato soon.

"Scott, it's not like I'm doing this on purpose," she said, still hoping to nip it in the bud. "I have a disorder. You understand that, right?"

"I know, I know. And I've been *extremely* patient about the whole thing. You can't tell me I haven't been patient, Tessa." He raised his eyebrows meaningfully. They both knew he was talking about more than leaving the house. There'd been nothing between them all summer beyond a few chaste pecks on the lips. "I just need you to put in an appearance, so they see you really exist. That's it. Is that really so much to ask?"

She shook her head. "Scott, I'm sorry. I wish I could."

He glowered, and the mattress bounced beneath him as he stood. "Isn't that what a relationship is supposed to be about? I'm here for you. I'm sitting here sweating my ass off in this slow cooker of a bedroom—and you're supposed to be there for me too! Right? Or is that not how this works?"

"Scott, wait!" she called after him. "Don't be like that. I'm trying. I'm making progress. Dr. Regan says—"

"Whatever, Tessa." He waved a hand to silence her. "Forget it. Forget the whole thing."

"Scott…"

"I'll see you later. I need to get some air." He headed for the door.

She lurched after him, but she stumbled. Her foot had fallen asleep from the hours of inactivity. "You're coming back, right?"

"Of course I'm coming back," he snapped. "I always come back!"

"Wait!" She reached out in his direction, hopping awkwardly. "Come here. Can I have a hug at least?"

Instead, he pulled out his phone to check his messages as he paused in the threshold. Tessa felt a twinge of irritation mingled with relief. She knew he was ignoring her, but she might just prefer his neglect to the usual drawn-out fight.

"Later," he mumbled over his shoulder, typing a new text as he went. "I'll see you later. I gotta go."

BLANK SLATE

ERIC SET DOWN his phone next to the black marble sink and stood to towel off his hair. He could feel the tension gathering at the base of his skull as he thought through the jam-packed day that lay before him. First his workout—and some publicist had the bright idea to schedule him for a radio call-in while he finished up on the treadmill, just to add to the fun. Then he had to rush off to hair and makeup so he could spend the afternoon on location at a poultry farm, shooting an ad for chicken nuggets. Never mind that he was a strict vegetarian… and never mind that he was supposed to be a musician. His reps at the record label seemed perfectly content to set those facts aside. The day that stretched before him wouldn't involve a single finger on a guitar string.

His phone buzzed on the countertop with a new incoming text.

Maury: You're late, cowboy. Where are you?

Eric closed his eyes. He couldn't face it. He'd give anything to escape the nonstop grind that his life had become. Just for a day. Or not even a day. Just a few measly hours when he didn't have to work.

He picked up the phone and wrote back:

Eric: New song idea! Christmas song. You'll love it. I just need an hour to work it out.

He paused, holding his breath as he waited for his manager's reply. "Come on, Maury," he whispered to the phone. "*One* hour. Come on."

The phone buzzed again.

Maury: You got 30 minutes.

Eric pumped his fist. Half an hour of freedom? He'd take it.

Now the only question was how to use it. Songwriting could wait. Should he crawl back under the covers and grab a few more minutes of sleep?

His phone lit up again, and Eric glanced anxiously at the screen. Not another text message, thank God. Just more Twitter notifications rolling in. He wondered if the #EricThornObsessed thing hit number one yet and picked the phone back up to check. Yup. There it was. He made a low growl in the back of his throat when he saw his name at the top of the trending list.

Forget sleep. He needed to take action. He had half an hour to stop this thing in its tracks.

Should he send another tweet? It couldn't be anything too hateful. The goal wasn't to make the fans angry—the goal was to turn them off. Make them all lose interest and find another victim for their drooly-tongue emojis.

He needed #EricThornObsessed to generate some backlash. That was the key. He'd seen it happen to others in the past— guys who blew up too big, too fast. Invariably, they all ended up labeled the same way. Vain. Arrogant. Narcissistic. Self- absorbed. He'd seen guys swing overnight from international sex symbol to universal joke.

Then the girls would unfollow in droves. No one wants to retweet a walking punch line. Honestly, it might be the best thing that could happen to him. Record sales would fall. Maybe his label would drop him.

Eric felt a ray of hope. He could take a more subtle tack. Lay on the self-infatuation a touch too thick, and let them all have a good, long laugh at his expense. Hell, maybe he didn't even need to do that much. The backlash might be brewing right that second for all he knew. Maybe the haters were already out there, tweeting by the thousands about what a douche he really was.

He brought up the search bar and typed in a new hashtag:

#EricThornIsADouche

0 tweets

OK, too complicated. Try again.

#EricThornDouche
0 tweets.

"Dammit!" How could it be this hard?

Eric took a deep breath and closed his eyes. OK. Think. Think like a hater.

#EricThornSucks
24 tweets

"There we go!" A smile lit his face for the first time since he'd gotten out of bed that morning. Twenty-four tweets. Not much compared to the millions under #EricThornObsessed, but it was a start. He ran his eyes down the list.

@EricThorn YOU ARE UGLY AND HAVE NO
TALENT #ERICTHORNSUCKS

OK, then. Not the most compelling argument. Next.

Does anyone actually listen to Eric
Thorn's music? No? That's what I thought
#EricThornSucks

Ouch. That one hit a little close to home.

It wasn't true, of course. Eric knew he had musical talent. He never would have gotten this far on looks alone. He'd pumped out one hit after another on his first two albums, and he knew those songs were good. They deserved to play on the radio.

But lately he'd begun to wonder. Did it even matter? Would anyone notice if he put out a bunch of half-assed suckitude, ghostwritten by other songwriters? Or would he hit the Billboard Hot 100 with any piece of overproduced crap, just as long as he took off his clothes for the music video?

Eric shot his phone a dirty look. It didn't matter anyway, he told himself. Not if his career was over. Back to the task at hand: #EricThornSucks. Next tweet.

@EricThorn I'VE HEARD WALRUS FARTS
THAT SOUND BETTER THAN YOUR
FUGLY ASS #ErICTHoRNSuCKS

Eric couldn't help but laugh out loud at that one. Walrus farts? That actually wasn't half-bad. Maybe he should use it for his next album title—or better yet, his greatest hits. What would happen if he hit Reply and said so? How many thousands of retweets would it get?

It was a tempting thought, but he couldn't do it. The fans might find it amusing, but the record label wouldn't. Anything coming from his Twitter account had to be squeaky clean.

Maybe that was the key, come to think of it. Eric froze as a new idea hit him. Of course! How had he never thought of it before? The label would never even know...

@EricThorn couldn't use Twitter to jettison his own career, but someone else could.

He began typing again with renewed energy.

Create new account.

> Full name: **Taylor**
>
> Username: **@EricThornSucks**
>
> Password: **%5L$Rsw**

His finger hung in the air, poised above the Create Account button, but he paused for a moment. Could any of it possibly be traced back to him? He'd used his middle name, Taylor—common enough not to raise any eyebrows. But what about that password? He'd automatically put in the same series of random characters that he used for his real account. Could that come back to bite him in the ass?

Better safe than sorry. He didn't need to worry about cyber-security anyway. This was one social media account that no one would bother to hack.

He filled out the form again.

> Full name: **Taylor**
>
> Username: **@EricThornSucks**
>
> Password: **password**

His eyes slid down the new profile he'd created.

TWEETS	FOLLOWING	FOLLOWERS
0	**0**	**0**

A blank slate. It felt like three hundred pounds lifted off his shoulders. He could tweet anything from here. Total freedom. He could tell his fans what he really thought of them in no uncertain terms. And he could lead them all to the conclusion that Eric Thorn wasn't worth their wasted time.

He just needed to get their attention first. Zero followers. That needed to change. What could he do to get noticed? He needed to make his debut tweet something good—something even more colorful than walrus farts. Something to illustrate the point that Eric Thorn was a vain, self-absorbed, pretty-boy douche canoe. And most importantly, something juicy enough to get retweeted fourteen million times.

"Come on, Eric," he muttered to himself. "Think."

Think vain. Think narcissistic.

He looked up from his phone and met his own eyes in the bathroom mirror. An idea had sprung to mind, and he turned his head slowly from side to side as he considered how best to pull it off. Could he get away with it? Would it work? Maybe. Just maybe…

With a well-practiced motion, he stripped his shirt over his head and switched his phone to selfie mode.

Oh man, this was going to be fun.

Tessa sat on her bed and contemplated the cover of the spiral-bound notebook in her lap. She should probably open it to a clean page and make her daily entry. God knows she had enough thoughts whirling around her head to fill a page or two.

Where to start? She should write about Scott, probably. Tessa grimaced, recalling the way her boyfriend had brought their visit to a halt. How could he be so dense? Even if she were ready to leave the house, he expected her to go to some overcrowded frat party? He wanted to... How had he put it exactly? He wanted to *show her off.*

So, not just a party—a room full of strangers *watching* her. *Great idea, Scott.* Hey, maybe the week after that, she could go recite poetry in her underwear on *America's Got Talent.*

Tessa sniffed. What was wrong with him? She hadn't told him the exact events that triggered her phobias, but he should've gotten the gist. Honestly, he was the one being selfish and unreasonable, not her. That wasn't the way you should treat someone you care about. Someone you love. How long had it been since he said the words "I love you"? She couldn't even remember. She could only think of someone else who said it just that morning.

Follow spree complete. Don't be upset if I missed you. I love each and every one of you more than you could ever know.

Tessa shut her journal with a snap. To hell with Scott. Why shouldn't she tweet about Eric Thorn all day long if it made her feel better? She picked up her phone and glanced at the screen to see what she had missed. Her eyes landed on a new Twitter notification, but not from Eric Thorn. Not from anyone she knew. Her eyes narrowed as she read the unfamiliar username:

> **Eric** @TheRealEricT
>
> @TessaHeartsEric Follow back please?

The sight of it made Tessa's mouth go dry. It was one of those weird Eric Thorn impersonator accounts that popped up from time to time.

@ErricThorn… @ErickThorne… @EricThornOfficial…

Tessa seemed to be the only one who found them disturbing—fan accounts pretending to belong to Eric Thorn himself. Some of the more gullible fans actually believed in them. "Maybe Eric really has a second account," they'd suggest to one another. "Maybe he secretly tweets with all of us, all the time." They fangirled up a storm whenever @ErickThorne retweeted one of them, and Tessa could never quite tell if they were kidding.

Eric (@TheRealEricT) was proving to be a real pest. He'd just tweeted at her two more times.

> **Eric** @TheRealEricT
>
> @TessaHeartsEric Follow for follow?

> **Eric** @TheRealEricT
>
> @TessaHeartsEric Why don't you follow back?

I'm asking you nicely....

Why did this account keep hassling her? Could it be some-one she knew? It couldn't be Scott spying on her, could it? Or even Dr. Regan? She'd told her therapist about her Twitter account this morning. But Dr. Regan wouldn't... Tessa dis-missed the thought with a shake of her head. She'd obviously been watching too much *Catfish* on MTV. It was probably the second account of some other Twitter friend, some Eric Thorn fan that she already followed. She should keep an open mind. She didn't hit Follow, but she tweeted in reply:

Tessa H @TessaHeartsEric
Do I know you, @TheRealEricT? Who are you?

The answer that came back only unnerved her more:

Eric @TheRealEricT
@TessaHeartsEric Who do you think,
dummy? I'm Eric! And I'm getting really
pissed that you won't follow me back.

Pissed? The word hit Tessa like a slap. This was no friend. Why did Twitter bring out the worst in some people? This was what she got for trying to open herself up to strangers. No wonder she had an anxiety disorder.

Ignore it, Tessa commanded herself, feeling her stomach knot.

She pulled in a long, slow breath and held it deep in her lungs, reciting the usual mantra inside her head.

Eric one…Eric two…Eric three…Eric Thorn…Eric five…

Better. See? Everything was fine. Tessa navigated to the mute option. She wouldn't let one creep-o cyberbully chase her off Twitter. If this account ever tweeted at her again, she wouldn't have to see a single trace of it.

Tessa's finger shook slightly as she input one last tweet.

> **Tessa H** @TessaHeartsEric
> @TheRealEricT I don't appreciate your tone.
> Go bother someone else, please. Bye.

With that, Tessa tossed the phone onto her bedspread. So much for social interaction. She didn't feel like journaling about it either. Right now, she needed something mindless to distract herself from the nervous tension bubbling around in her chest.

Her eyes wandered to the small TV she kept on top of her dresser. Maybe some morning talk shows would do the trick. She reclined against the pillows and reached for the remote control as another notification lit up her cell phone's screen:

> @EricLove333, @ThornAddict98, and 173
> others just retweeted a photo

Tessa sat up straight again. A hundred and seventy-five

retweets? That must be something new. Normally only a tweet from Eric himself would spread so quickly among the users she followed. But it couldn't have come from him. She had her account set up to notify her instantly every time he tweeted. What, then?

She swiped her thumb eagerly. Not another message from Eric, but from his biggest fan:

Mrs. Eric Thorn.

Of course it would be @MrsEricThorn, or MET as everyone in the fandom referred to her. The girl never slept and somehow discovered every Eric Thorn–related tidbit five minutes before the rest of the pack. She'd started following Eric back in his lowly YouTube days, and she'd maintained her status as queen bee of the fandom ever since. These days, her follower count stood just north of 500K. No one knew much about her—not even her real first name—but that didn't stop the whispered rumors from spreading among the other fan accounts: she must have gotten inside information from somewhere. Maybe even from Eric himself. He'd followed her for a while now, and MET sometimes hinted at a secret message exchange, although she always added a wink emoji for punctuation.

Tessa didn't know what to believe. It would certainly explain how the girl knew so much. She'd been tweeting up a storm just last night about trying to meet Eric at his hotel. Had she succeeded? Tweeted a selfie of herself and her Twitter husband, arm in arm?

Tessa let out a startled gasp as her eyes skimmed across the tweet:

MET @MrsEricThorn
WHYYY IS THIS SO HOT????
#EricThornObsessed

And then that picture… Tessa knew she'd never seen it before. She wouldn't have forgotten an image like that.

She hit Retweet as a matter of course and then switched to her timeline to read what all the other fans had to say. Everyone was online right now and buzzing—and no wonder. First the follow spree. Then the second tweet. And now this picture surfacing out of the blue like a gift from above.

But where had it come from? Everyone seemed too busy making new #EricThornObsessed tweets to ask any questions.

Tessa flicked onto MET's account again, her lips curving with satisfaction at the header:

> MET (@MrsEricThorn) FOLLOWS YOU

She still felt a glow of pride at the sight. Five days had passed since MET had followed her, and Tessa's own follower count had skyrocketed as a result. Everyone knew that MET only followed the accounts that really mattered.

But a follow from @MrsEricThorn meant more than just a vote of confidence. It also gave Tessa access to the coveted, little button beside MET's name—the one that allowed her to send a private direct message.

Tessa entered a DM now, and she let out a small sigh of pleasure when a reply popped back within seconds.

> **Tessa H:** Where did that pic come from??
> **MET:** Some new kid tweeted it earlier. This one's going viral. WOOT!

Tessa's forehead furrowed. Why hadn't MET retweeted it, if it came from another fan's account? She sent back a quick reply.

> **Tessa H:** Who? Can you tell me?
> **MET:** Just an egg making trouble. Nice try, troll! LOL
> **Tessa H:** What username?
> **MET:** @EricThornSucks

An egg? Tessa searched for the account and brought it up on her screen: an egg account as the other girl said, with the anonymous eggshell silhouette that Twitter provided as the default profile picture. Whoever owned this account hadn't bothered with a bio either. Just the first name Taylor and that one lonely tweet:

> **Taylor** @EricThornSucks
> What a narcissistic pretty-boy douche

nozzle. Get over yourself @EricThorn
#EricThornSucks

pic.twitter.com/Z4GGn0HZpj

The link brought up the picture once again. MET must have poached it and composed her own tweet with an ever-so-slightly revised caption. Tessa saved the photo to her camera roll, ignoring the other thousand pictures of Eric Thorn she'd already accumulated. There was something extra drool-worthy about this one. She wanted it preserved. A fresh blush of heat crept up her neck as her eyes drank in the image:

Eric Thorn, shirtless, with a white towel around his waist… making out with his own reflection in a steamed-up bathroom mirror.

UNREAL

ERIC SILENTLY MOUTHED the lyrics of the chicken nugget jingle, while his team of stylists sculpted his unruly hair into some semblance of order. He sat perched on a high stool in front of the same hotel mirror that he'd used for his early-morning selfie shoot. *The scene of the crime*, he thought to himself, lightly drumming his palms against his thighs.

It was no use. He couldn't focus. His mind kept turning back to the same topic. How far had that photo traveled in the hour since he posted it? How many memes had it spawned, calling him out for his self-absorption? Did it break the Internet, like that famous picture of Kim K's ginormous naked ass?

He'd hit Tweet without a moment to spare this morning, barely throwing on some gym clothes before Maury came knocking again. Now, with his workout behind him, Eric longed to check the retweet count, but he didn't dare. Not with the prying eyes of the hairdressers all around him.

Eric felt a cold trickle work its way down the back of his neck. Doubt or stray hair gel? He wasn't quite sure. He couldn't remember the last time he'd done something so impulsive. Was it all a huge mistake? If anyone at his label figured out where that picture came from…

A harsh voice rang out behind him, and Eric's hands stopped drumming in midair at the sight of his manager's cell phone, thrust into his face.

"You wanna tell me what the hell this is, kid?"

Eric expected to see the bathroom mirror, but apparently that photo hadn't yet registered as a blip on the PR radar screen. His eyes fell instead on a *Hollywood Life* blog post. He'd forgotten about that one. It was a pap photo from LA a couple weeks ago. The cameraman must have taken his sweet time selling it to the highest bidder.

"That dickwad was asking for it," Eric muttered.

Maury glared. "What did he do? Did he get up in your face?"

"No, he didn't get in my face, Maury. He tailed me for three hours straight!"

"So you had a pap following you? That's it?"

A hairdresser placed her finger at the base of Eric's jaw. He swatted her hand away in annoyance. "It was my first day off in a month! It's kind of hard to relax when some prick has a telephoto lens pointed at your face all day long."

Eric scowled to himself even as he said the words. He knew Maury had a point. He'd lost his cool with that photographer for no good reason. He'd been more than a little on edge after the story broke about the Cromwell murder—especially out in public. He couldn't deny feeling stalked. Maury called it paranoia, but how could Eric help it? He was followed everywhere he went. When he somehow managed to escape the fans for a few blissful moments, then the paps started sniffing around. It never stopped. From the moment he'd first signed his record deal at age fifteen, his entire life had been punctuated by the faint sound of camera shutters clicking in the background.

Maury clapped a heavy hand on Eric's shoulder. His face was grim. "Eric, you can't go around flipping off reporters."

"Reporters." Eric snorted. "That asshole was stalking me, Maury!"

"You *will* get a reputation for bad behavior. These guys can destroy a career faster than you can say 'cheese' if you get on their bad side."

Eric opened his mouth to retort, but he forgot what he was about to say. His ears had perked up at that last remark. "Wait a minute. Do you think it'll cause a backlash?"

Maury gave him a playful cuff on the cheek. "Nah. The publicists are spinning it that you were provoked. But you only get one get-out-of-jail-free card before—"

"I *was* provoked!" Eric stood abruptly from the stool. The makeup people could finish him up on set later. He couldn't take another minute with all those hands pawing at his face.

Maury whirled a finger in the air, signaling the army of stylists to gather their supplies. They trooped out, and Eric stood to follow them, but Maury stepped into his path.

"Get yourself together, kid." Maury poked him in the chest. "I don't know what's eating you lately, but enough's enough. We've got too much work to do."

Maury cast him one last warning look and shuffled out. Eric watched him go, but his foul mood faded after a moment. He was finally alone, and he had more pressing matters to attend. Eric pulled his phone from his pocket and tapped to open Twitter, still set to the new username:

@EricThornSucks

He held his breath as his eyes flicked down to check his notifications. The count normally stood at the maximum, twenty plus, but on this account…

Nothing.

Dead silence.

Really? Not one single retweet? Eric rested his weight against the bathroom countertop. Was it possible that no one had seen the picture yet? Maybe he should try directing it @ some of the fan accounts. He closed his eyes, straining to dredge up some likely usernames. They all ran together in his head:

@EricThornFan… @EricThornLuv… @MrsEricThorn… @EricThornifed… @ErictHorny… @EricThornPorn…

Where to begin? There was that one Maury wanted him to follow. The one who started the whole Obsessed trend. He'd intentionally passed her over during the follow spree, but she might be the ideal person for his purposes. He entered in her username, @TessaHeartsEric, and nearly choked at what he saw.

There it was at the top of her recent tweets. A retweet, but not from his account. Somehow she'd retweeted the same picture from a different fan.

MET @MrsEricThorn

WHYYY IS THIS SO HOT?????
#EricThornObsessed

⟳ 751   ♥ 1327

What the hell?

How could they fangirl over *that* picture? He must have snapped twenty versions before he got the pose just right. He'd caught himself at an angle to keep the reflection of the phone out of the frame. He'd pressed his lips to the mirror and closed his eyes in mock passion, with his free hand clutching one of his well-defined pecs. Honestly, it was perfect—the ultimate caricature of vanity and self-absorption. How could they have possibly missed the point?

"Unreal," he muttered hoarsely, balling his hands into fists. He should have known. He'd seen their smutty fanfics. His fans were nothing if not predictable. They had one thing, and one thing only, on their #EricThornObsessed minds.

Eric's vision clouded with a surge of red-hot anger. Sick, every one of them. Someone needed to call them out. Make them feel ashamed of themselves. Tell them to get a life.

This one, this @TessaHeartsEric, seemed like a good place to start.

He raised his finger above the screen, already composing a blistering rant inside his head. But his finger came down on... nothing. Blank white space.

Where was the DM button?

He stared at the screen for a full thirty seconds before comprehension dawned.

He'd forgotten who he was for a minute there. It had been years since someone he wanted to message didn't follow him as a matter of course. But that only applied to his real account. Now he was @EricThornSucks, with no history and zero followers. He was nobody. He couldn't DM a soul.

He glared down at the profile in front of him.

Tessa H @TessaHeartsEric

FOLLOWING   FOLLOWERS
170   **30.1K**

He could try to put her on blast over public tweets, but she might not even hear him. Not with 30,000 followers. No, if he really wanted to get through to her, he needed to do it over DM. And that meant he needed her to follow him.

This was going to be trickier than he'd thought.

Tessa tore her eyes reluctantly from her new favorite Eric Thorn picture. It had given her the perfect idea for a fanfic: a riff on Dr. Jekyll and Mr. Hyde, featuring a sensitive young songwriter named Eric and his bad-boy rock-star doppelgänger, Thorn. Identical twins? She pondered, tapping her chin. Or maybe one character with a split-personality disorder...

Tessa reached for her journal to jot it down (at least not *all* her story ideas were "projecting"), but the sight of her phone distracted her. It still displayed the account that had first tweeted the photo:

Taylor @EricThornSucks

Tessa squinted at the empty profile. Whoever this Taylor girl was, she clearly intended for that image to hurt Eric. Not a fan. Someone with an ax to grind. Maybe a fan he passed over in the follow spree that morning? Apparently, Tessa wasn't the only one whose curiosity had been piqued. Another new DM popped up from @MrsEricThorn.

MET: Do you know a Taylor? Is there a fan I don't know called Taylor?

Tessa racked her mind, wishing she could come up with a bit of useful gossip to impress the other girl.

Tessa H: Don't know her. There was some

other weird account tweeting me this
morning. @TheRealEricT? That wasn't you,
was it?

MET: Uhhh why would you think that?

Tessa H: Never mind… Hey, maybe this
@EricThornSucks isn't even a fan? Maybe
it's one of his exes or something!

Tessa's eyes widened as she thought of the possibilities. Eric hadn't
been in a confirmed relationship for as long as she'd followed him.
Whenever interviewers asked about his love life, he always insisted
he was way too busy to date. But that didn't stop the rumors from
flying. Anyone that gorgeous had to be getting action somewhere.
Could it be someone famous? Someone named Taylor…

Tessa H: OMG do you think it could be
Taylor Swift?

MET: Hahahah NO WAY! ARE U FOR
REAL??

Tessa H: You never know

MET: LMAO kinda doubt T-Swizzle has the
Photoshop chops

Tessa H: You think it's Photoshop?

MET: Obviously. No way that's real. Fakety
fake fake. Still sexy as hell tho!!

Tessa chuckled as she stood up from her bed and paced the

room. She was about to reply to Mrs. Eric Thorn again when a new notification distracted her.

> Taylor (@EricThornSucks) favorited your retweet

Speak of the devil. Why was this Taylor person stalking her account?

A new mention appeared on her screen, and Tessa sank down heavily into her beanbag chair. "Not again," she whispered. Why was she suddenly the target for every creepy fan account on Twitter?

> **Taylor** @EricThornSucks
> How can you obsess over that pic @TessaHeartsEric? He is LITERALLY in love with himself!

Tessa eyed the tweet suspiciously. She knew she should ignore it. This Taylor could be anyone. Tessa flicked on the account settings menu, and her finger hovered over the first option once again:

> Mute @EricThornSucks

She was about to select it, but something stopped her. She could almost hear Dr. Regan's words from this morning, echoing inside her head:

Any kind of social interaction can potentially hold therapeutic value.

Was it a mistake, all this muting? Maybe it was just a defense mechanism, like hiding here in her room. Wasn't that what Dr. Regan would tell her? To open herself up? Make an effort to interact? "I need to try harder," she whispered to herself.

What had this @EricThornSucks account really done, other than try to strike up a conversation? She and her therapist had spent weeks running through role-play scenarios for every imaginable social encounter, friendly or otherwise. She had the tools. She could do this. She was ready.

In any case, Tessa couldn't deny her curiosity. Who was this girl, Taylor, and where did she get that picture? Had she photoshopped it herself? Maybe she had more where that one came from.

"OK," Tessa said out loud, screwing up her courage. "You want to talk to me, Taylor? Let's talk."

She flicked away from the mute option and composed a tweet instead:

Tessa H @TessaHeartsEric
@EricThornSucks who are you?

The answer popped back immediately, setting off a series of rapid-fire tweets back and forth:

Taylor @EricThornSucks

@TessaHeartsEric no one special

Tessa H @TessaHeartsEric

@EricThornSucks are you a fan or a hater?

Taylor @EricThornSucks

@TessaHeartsEric just calling it like I see it.
You can't tell me that pic isn't douchey

Tessa H @TessaHeartsEric

@EricThornSucks it's fake duh

Taylor @EricThornSucks

@TessaHeartsEric says who?

Tessa H @TessaHeartsEric

@EricThornSucks says my magic
Photoshop detector

Taylor @EricThornSucks

@TessaHeartsEric BULLSHIT. Trust me it's
real

Tessa H @TessaHeartsEric

@EricThornSucks and you have it…why
exactly?

Another notification flashed onto Tessa's screen just before the next reply:

Taylor (@EricThornSucks) followed you

Taylor @EricThornSucks
@TessaHeartsEric I'll tell you over DM.
Follow me back.

THE INTERROGATION (FRAGMENT 2)

December 31, 2016, 9:17 p.m.

Case #: 124.678.21–001

OFFICIAL TRANSCRIPTION OF POLICE INTERVIEW

—START PAGE 1—

INVESTIGATOR: Ms. Hart, I'm Lieutenant Charles Foster. This is Detective Terence Newman. For the record, today is December 31 at 9:17 p.m. This interview is being recorded.

HART: I need my therapist. Dr. Laura Regan. Is she here yet? She was supposed to meet me here at the police station.

INVESTIGATOR: Terry, can you look into that? [pause] OK, Ms. Hart. Can I call you Tessa?

HART: I really need my therapist. This is the first day I left my house in, like, forever.

INVESTIGATOR: I understand. We're working on locating Dr. Regan. In the meantime, Tessa, can you please state your full name, birth date, and occupation for the record?

HART: Tessa Lynn Hart. April 3, 1998. I'm eighteen.

INVESTIGATOR: Occupation?

HART: Um, I don't know. Not applicable? I was supposed to start college this past fall, but I-I couldn't. I had to defer.

INVESTIGATOR: Can we say unemployed?

HART: Right. Unemployed.

INVESTIGATOR: Good. Now, can you please identify what this is right here?

HART: That's my cell phone. Oh my God, I thought I lost it! Where did you get that?

INVESTIGATOR: How did you lose it, Tessa? Was it taken from you?

HART: Maybe. I don't...I don't want to talk about that. I should probably go to the hospital or something—

INVESTIGATOR: Tessa, please stay in your seat. We're looking for your therapist right now.

HART: Can I have my phone? Maybe I can text her.

INVESTIGATOR: I need you to walk me through a few things first. I'm looking here at your Twitter account. Could you please tell me when you first set up this account?

HART: Back in high school. Junior year. But then I changed the username this summer, around the end of June.

INVESTIGATOR: June 2016?

HART:	Right. Because…because of what happened. I deleted a lot of my old tweets then too.
INVESTIGATOR:	We'd like to take a look at your direct messages with the account in question, if you don't mind. Do I have your permission to read through this?
HART:	Go ahead. It doesn't matter.
INVESTIGATOR:	The first message is dated August 12, 2016. Does that sound about right?
HART:	I guess so. August. I remember Scott came to see me that morning. He was just about to head off for freshman orientation. So yeah. August.
INVESTIGATOR:	Scott?
HART:	My ex-boyfriend.
INVESTIGATOR:	I see. Let's finish discussing your Twitter activity, and then we'll come back to Scott. Do you recall if you had any other correspondence with this individual before the first direct message on August 12?
HART:	Just a few tweets back and forth. He followed me first. I followed him back. I was trying to be social. For therapy. I have agoraphobia. I was supposed to work on interacting with different people. But I didn't realize who…who it was. I should have blocked him. I should have deactivated the account. I should have deactivated back when I left New Orleans. I'm so stupid [unintelligible].

INVESTIGATOR: Tessa?

HART: Eric. Eric Thorn—

INVESTIGATOR: Are you OK, Tessa?

HART: You don't understand. I need my therapist. I need
to go home.

BATTLE

ERIC GRIPPED THE phone in both hands as he exited the hotel bathroom. This Tessa person had better follow him fast. He only had a few minutes before Maury expected him downstairs, and then he'd have to endure his manager's company for the hour-long ride to the poultry farm. Eric didn't know if he could face it. Not without venting his overwhelming sense of frustration—fourteen million followers worth of pent-up rage.

He silently willed the Twitter notification to appear, and he let out a grunt of satisfaction when he saw it.

> Tessa H (@TessaHeartsEric) followed you.

Eric tapped the DM button so hard he nearly cracked the screen.

Taylor: Hey, Tessa. Thanks for the follow.

> **Tessa H:** Hi
> **Taylor:** Hey can I ask you a question?
> **Tessa H:** Um OK

Eric's mouth twisted dangerously as he entered his next message. He knew exactly how to play it. He'd been around enough fangirls to know how they all talked.

> **Taylor:** Personality quiz! If you were an
> animal, what kind of animal would you be?
> **Tessa H:** I dunno. A gazelle maybe? Why?
> **Taylor:** Cuz you know what kind of animal
> Eric Thorn would see, if he ever noticed you
> existed?
> **Tessa H:** Ummm. I dunno. Not a gazelle?
> Maybe a chicken? :P

Eric didn't even read her answer. He plowed on, texting like a man possessed, entering new messages as swiftly as he could move his fingers—not even thinking about the words.

> **Taylor:** A leech.
> **Tessa H:** Excuse me?
> **Taylor:** That's right. A nasty, bloodthirsty
> leech. With no purpose to your miserable,
> meaningless existence except to suck.
> **Taylor:** And when he saw you there,

sucking, he would shudder with disgust.

Taylor: And he would flick you off with his fingernail.

Taylor: And then you know what he'd do, Tessa? Then he'd forget you ever existed and go about his day.

Tessa's jaw dropped open at the words that flashed across her screen. She'd been sitting in her beanbag chair, but she stood now and paced back and forth across the narrow bedroom. Her stomach churned. This couldn't be happening. Her first foray into social interaction with a stranger, and she'd picked some nasty troll. She should have known better. She'd totally misread the signs. Personality quiz…

A leech?

It wasn't true, of course. As if this Taylor person could see inside Eric Thorn's head any more than Tessa could. Ridiculous.

Still, the DMs hit her like a gut punch. They knocked the wind right out of her, and Taylor managed to fire off a whole string of messages before Tessa finally gathered herself to reply.

Tessa H: Wow. Thanks for the insight. And this is from…who exactly? Oh that's right. An egg.

Taylor: Yeah, I'm an egg. You know why I'm

an egg? Cuz I actually have a life. In the real
world. You might want to try it.

Tessa H: You don't know anything about
me!

Taylor: Why don't you find a real person
to obsess over instead of some pathetic
celebrity?

Tessa H: For your information I have a
boyfriend.

Taylor: Oh really? And what does your
"boyfriend" think about your Twitter
account?

Tessa winced. She'd already been feeling guilty about
Scott—as if she somehow betrayed her boyfriend every time
she tweeted about Eric Thorn. But that was all just paranoid
nonsense. Lots of people had fan accounts. Celebrity crushes.
It wasn't like Scott even cared what she did on Twitter.

She'd only traveled a few feet across her room, but her legs
felt like she'd just completed a marathon. She sank down heavily onto the edge of her bed.

Dr. Regan had it wrong, Tessa thought, as her breath rushed
in and out in shallow gasps. Not every interaction had therapeutic value. This one would probably set back her progress
for months.

Taylor: And…silence. Isn't that interesting?

Tessa H: I'm done with this conversation.
Bye.
Taylor: I'm guessing this "boyfriend"
probably doesn't exist.

Tessa moved to the settings menu. Her finger skimmed past Mute this time. She eyed the other options. Block, perhaps? Or should she hit Report and call out this Taylor person for abusive language?

Taylor: But if he does exist, I feel sorry
for him because you're kind of a shitty
girlfriend.

Tessa's eyes flew back to the message thread, and the last remnants of oxygen left her lungs. Her mind could barely put together a coherent thought. *Really? Like…really though? OK, no. No way.* The Report button wasn't good enough for this creep. With a burst of adrenaline, Tessa leaped to her feet and texted back.

Tessa H: You have no idea who I am or
what I'm dealing with!
Taylor: Oh let me guess. Are the cool kids
mean to you at school? Boohoo.
Tessa H: For your information, I'm on Twitter
a lot because I have a condition called

She stopped herself in midsentence. It was none of this loser's business. Tessa quickly deleted the words from her message bar and wrote something else instead.

> **Tessa H:** You know what? I don't owe you an explanation. You're the one with the problem. Maybe you should go take a good long look in the mirror.
> **Taylor:** Hmmm like Eric? He loooooves taking good long looks in the mirror LOL

Tessa's chest heaved as she sucked in the air, in full fight-or-flight mode now, texting too fast for Taylor to get a word in edgewise.

> **Tessa H:** So according to you, Eric sucks. And I suck. And basically everyone sucks except for you. Do I have that right?
> **Tessa H:** You know there's a word for that. It's called projection.
> **Tessa H:** You should look it up sometime.
> **Tessa H:** Or are you too "super busy" attacking random strangers?

She paused after the last message, clutching her chest with outspread fingers as she struggled to catch her breath. The whole exchange had brought to mind a Tumblr quote that she saw once. Tessa liked to save them to her camera roll sometimes—little quotes and sayings she could go back to and recite to herself whenever her anxiety level started to rise. She knew the one she wanted, and she scrolled through the endless sea of Eric Thorn pics to bring it up:

Tessa added the image to her message bar, with her finger poised to fire it back the moment Taylor responded. She stood stock-still, ready to spring, like a sniper waiting for her prey to wander between the crosshairs. The seconds ticked by as she held back.

Silence.

Was it over? Had she won? She had the distinct impression that Taylor had left the conversation. Off to find a new victim, perhaps.

The Tumblr quote still remained, and Tessa hit Send before shutting down her phone: a punctuation mark on the end of her victory.

8

BE KIND. ALWAYS

TESSA LAY IN her darkened bedroom, staring up at the ceiling. It was almost midnight, but she knew she wouldn't get much sleep tonight. Her sleep schedule was completely out of whack—one of the lovely side effects of staying cooped up inside twenty-four hours a day. She hadn't seen the sun in weeks.

Circadian rhythms were the least of her problems though. She'd taken a dose of her anxiety meds, but she still felt the grip of barely suppressed panic weighing on her. She could see the ugly messages every time she closed her eyes, like they were imprinted on the inside of her eyelids.

> **Taylor:** You know what kind of animal Eric Thorn would see, if he ever noticed you existed?

Eric. Eric Thorn. Eric one…Eric two…Eric three…

It was no use. Breathing exercises had their limits. Tessa rolled over in bed and reached for her phone. She knew she shouldn't look at that DM thread again but, honestly, what difference did it make? She couldn't stop thinking about it. She'd probably spend the next month dissecting every word.

She should be proud of herself, right? She handled herself well. Someone had come after her, and she'd stood her ground. She'd fought off her attacker. She didn't turn and flee. Not like she had in June…

Tessa brushed a hand in front of her face to shoo away the memory. She didn't want to face it. Not yet. Probably not ever. Better to obsess over this Twitter conversation, as awful as it was.

She lowered her eyes to the Tumblr quote that marked the end of the thread. Something about it kept bugging her. Maybe it was those three words at the end:

Be Kind. Always.

Not: *Be Kind. Sometimes.*

Not: *Be kind. Unless the other person is mean to you first.*

That was what bothered her most, she realized. Not that she'd been attacked, but that she'd struck back. She'd been so busy defending herself that she hadn't even stopped to think *why* the other girl might be coming after her. *Everyone you meet is fighting a battle…* What kind of battle was Taylor fighting to make her act that way? She might be dealing with mental health issues of her own. Maybe undiagnosed, untreated. Maybe she just needed to talk to someone.

Tessa closed her eyes for a moment, and the panicky tension in her chest loosened its grip. She'd gotten to the bottom of it. She knew what she needed to do.

The DM thread stood open on her phone. With a resolute nod, Tessa entered one more message.

⇄

Eric slouched down in the backseat of the limo and rubbed his bleary eyes. The car ride from the poultry farm back to the hotel would take a little over an hour. He should probably grab some extra shut-eye, but he had a feeling that sleep wouldn't come easy. Not after the hellish day he'd had.

He'd been on edge all day, waiting for his publicists to find out about his morning Twitter escapade. By some miracle, his selfie slipped by them unnoticed. They must have written it off as a fan's twisted Photoshop edit—no different from the usual crude filth they tweeted about him all day long.

Eric tried to summon some righteous indignation, but he knew it was pointless. He couldn't blame the sick feeling in his stomach on anyone but himself.

He gazed through the limo window at the darkened land-scape passing by, but his mind remained fixed on the topic that had occupied his thoughts all day. Bits and pieces of that DM conversation kept coming back to him. He couldn't shake the memory or the ever-deepening sense that he'd done wrong.

Eric scrubbed a palm down the length of his face, trying

to force his mind onto some less depressing train of thought. Maybe he should call someone, he thought. Maybe his parents? He hadn't talked to them all week. Maybe it would help, just to hear familiar voices.

Not that he could tell them how he really felt deep down. They always changed the subject whenever the conversation turned to darker thoughts. They only saw the concert lights— the dazzling glitz and glamour—and the money rolling into the bank. He knew what he would hear if he tried talking to them now: his father's voice, full of laughter. "Champagne problems." And then his mother would remind him how a solid eight hours of sleep always made everything better in the morning.

Eric sighed. His parents didn't get it. Maury didn't get it. No one got it. Eric could talk until he was blue in the face, but no one ever listened to a single word he said.

Angry tears pricked his eyes, and Eric rubbed them away harshly with the backs of his hands. He met eyes for a fleeting moment with the limo driver, who was watching him in the rearview mirror. Something about the man's unblinking stare creeped Eric out. He pressed the button to close the privacy barrier as he reached into his pocket for his phone.

Eric scanned the list of contacts, but he didn't place a call. His finger moved to open Twitter instead, and he sucked in his breath with a hiss when he saw the username:

@EricThornSucks

He hadn't bothered to switch back to his real account when he abruptly closed the app this morning. He'd missed that fangirl's final words to him: one of those tidbits of holier-than-thou Tumblr wisdom.

Eric groaned as he read it. Not because it was preachy—although it was. Preachy as hell. But because he couldn't imagine any words better designed to make him hate himself. *Fighting a battle...* This girl could have some battle of her own going on for all he knew. She hadn't spelled it out. It could be anything, really. She could have terminal cancer.

And he'd attacked her.

What was wrong with him? Here he was, consumed with fear that some random stranger might come after him—and he'd turned around and done the same thing to someone else. He'd slipped into attack mode so easily. It was just Twitter after all. Just words. Not real.

But that was a real person on the other end, wasn't it? A real person who obviously wasn't as mindless as he'd painted her to be. She seemed like she might have half a brain, actually. "Projection," she'd said. "You should look it up sometime."

Maybe he should, he thought. Maybe that was his penance. Go look up *projection* like she said, and maybe then he'd feel less horrible about himself.

He entered the word into his phone and pulled up a Wikipedia page.

Projection

A psychological phenomenon first described by Sigmund Freud, in which the individual denies his or her own negative qualities while ascribing them to others.

Eric could already feel his eyes glazing over after the first sentence. He'd never had much patience for homework. He hadn't even bothered finishing high school. Once he had his record deal, there hadn't seemed much point.

He skimmed farther down the page.

Examples include:

Blaming the victim…

Justifying infidelity…

Bullying…

Something caught in his chest when his eyes fell on that last word: *bullying*. He forced himself to click on the detailed explanation.

Bullying: The classic bully engages in activities that target the weakness of others as a projection of his or her own sense of personal insecurity or vulnerability.

Eric winced. There it was on Wikipedia—exactly what he'd

done. He'd been feeling vulnerable for weeks, ever since the details started to emerge about the Cromwell case. And the label's reaction, or lack thereof, had only added to his growing sense of powerlessness. He had absolutely no control over his life. That was what had made him so angry that morning. And he'd taken it out on that girl. *The classic bully.* He couldn't deny how well the label fit. Apparently, he was a textbook case.

Eric squeezed his eyes shut for a long moment. He knew what he had to do.

No more angry hate-tweeting, for one thing. He needed to deactivate this fake account and find a healthier way of dealing with his demons. Like maybe talking to someone. Someone who would actually listen and try to understand. Not Maury. Not his parents. Not his personal trainer or his hairdresser or his limo driver, who were all on the record-label payroll. Not his old friends from back home either, whose interactions with him now were always tinged with jealousy. There had to be someone somewhere on this planet without a hidden agenda. Someone who would listen.

But first he owed @TessaHeartsEric an apology. Plain and simple.

Eric began to type a DM into the message bar when something else flashed onto his screen. A new message had been added at the end of the thread.

He blinked, confused. Had he hit Send by accident?

No, it wasn't from him.

She must have DM'ed him something else just now. He ran his eyes across the words:

> **Tessa H:** I don't know what kind of battle you're dealing with, but if you ever want to talk for real, just let me know.

Eric felt a fresh wave of shame buffet him. She wasn't what he'd expected, was she? To reach out like that after the way he attacked her? To a total stranger on Twitter?

He finished his message and hit Send.

> **Taylor:** I'm sorry for what I said. I've been having a rough time, and I took it out on you. I feel horrible. You didn't deserve it. I'm so sorry.

Her reply popped back a moment later.

> **Tessa H:** It's OK. I get it.
> **Tessa H:** Do you want to talk about it?

Eric looked away from the phone. He fiddled idly with the limo's seat temperature buttons as he considered his next move. He'd made his apology. Now he should end the conversation. Close the account. Destroy the evidence. The consequences could be devastating if the wrong person ever found it.

But it was just so tempting...

It was perfect, really—the answer to a prayer he didn't even know he'd made. She didn't know anything about him. An egg:

that's all he was to her. And she was offering to talk, one human being to another, with no other motive than pure kindness.

Just one little conversation, he thought. *One innocent little heart-to-heart.* He could deactivate in the morning.

Tessa H: Are you there?

"What harm could it do?" he whispered to himself as he entered his reply.

Taylor: Yeah, I'm here. Let's talk.

THE INTERROGATION
(FRAGMENT 3)

December 31, 2016, 8:42 p.m.
Case #: 124.678.21–001
OFFICIAL TRANSCRIPTION OF POLICE INTERVIEW

—START PAGE 4—

INVESTIGATOR:	Mr. Thorn, do you deny setting up a social media account under a false name on August 12, 2016?
THORN:	Is that a crime? Am I being charged with something?
INVESTIGATOR:	At this point in time, you're being interviewed as a witness.
THORN:	I should probably call a lawyer.
INVESTIGATOR:	You're free to do that. I can only tell you that it will delay our investigation.
THORN:	What about Tessa? Will you please just tell me if she's OK?
INVESTIGATOR:	I'm not at liberty to say anything further until we have your complete statement.
THORN:	I don't know what to do. Shit. I didn't mean any harm. I know it seems sketchy, but I never meant it to go that far. It was just a spur-of-the-moment thing. People set up fake accounts all the time. I

was just going to tweet one thing and then deactivate. It was just a prank, really. I mean, that can't be a crime. MTV had a whole show called *Punk'd*, for God's sake! Ashton Kutcher faked all kinds of shit. He, like, faked people's deaths! Didn't he? Way worse than some Twitter account. That was before that *Catfish* show though. Is that illegal now?

INVESTIGATOR: So you did in fact create the Twitter account with username @EricThornSucks on August 12, 2016?

THORN: Huh? Oh right. Yes.

INVESTIGATOR: And you did not deactivate it or transfer it to another account owner at any point?

THORN: No, but I only used it to talk to her.

INVESTIGATOR: To talk to Tessa Hart?

THORN: Right. We stayed up all night that first night, DM'ing each other. We just connected really fast. I know it sounds strange. I can get lonely sometimes. I'm on the road all the time, and it's hard to know who to trust. I don't have a lot of friends. And the Dorian Cromwell thing had me all twisted in a knot. It was just a safe way for me to confide in someone.

INVESTIGATOR: You confided specific details of your personal life to Ms. Hart using this Twitter account?

THORN: Yeah. I mean, I-I kind of...distorted it a little.

INVESTIGATOR: Can you be more specific?

THORN: Well, you saw the messages. She thought my name was Taylor. I told her I was stuck in a contract for a job I hated, but I didn't tell her what kind of job. I kind of made it sound like I was a traveling salesman or something. I might have let her believe I was a little older. That's what she assumed anyway, and I didn't correct her. And I told her someone else in the same job had been stalked and killed recently, but I didn't say... You know. I didn't say it was Dorian.

INVESTIGATOR: Anything else?

THORN: Probably. It was just the details though. I had to change certain things to protect myself, but the feelings were true. I know it was just texting over Twitter, but we kind of...took care of each other. We always made each other feel better—even when it seemed like everything else in our lives was going straight to hell.

9
HE SAID, SHE SAID

September 15, 2016

"WELCOME ABOARD, MR. Thorn."

Eric shot a limp salute to the flight attendant who stood before him in a formfitting, blue uniform. He had to admit, fame sometimes had its perks. He didn't miss the indignities of commercial air travel. Far more civilized to make the trip from LA to Seattle on his label's private jet.

"Call me Eric," he said with a self-deprecating shrug.

The flight attendant smiled back warmly and leaned closer over the armrest of his chair. "Is there anything I can get you from the galley to start you off?" The top two buttons of her blouse had come undone, and her arm brushed lightly against his shoulder.

In a different mood, he might have ordered a bowl of mixed nuts and asked her to join him for a snack. But he had other plans today...

"No, thanks. I'm going to grab a nap, if you don't mind." Eric pushed the lever to recline his seat. He already had one hand in his pocket, reaching for his phone. He hoped this flight attendant wouldn't be the type who insisted on checking in with him every five minutes. As an afterthought, he jerked a thumb at the man who sat on the other side of the aisle. "Maury over there will take a Jack and Coke."

His manager had taken out his cell phone the moment they stepped on board, and Eric was grateful for the excuse not to talk. He didn't know how much time he had before Maury interrupted, but perhaps he could manage to scrape together a few minutes. He might not get another chance all afternoon— and he knew he would be otherwise occupied that night.

The flight attendant teetered away on her high-heeled pumps, and Eric rolled onto his side, presenting her with a view of his turned back. He pulled out his phone and rested it on the seat beside him, shielded from view by his body.

As he fired up Twitter, he couldn't help thinking how far he'd come in the past month. Back in August when he first created the fake account, he would've been way too paranoid to open it anywhere in his manager's vicinity. He'd been feeling less anxious in general lately. Less quick tempered. More relaxed. His secret message exchange with Tessa had more than a little to do with the transformation.

It just felt good to have a simple friendship: a pressure valve where he could release all the stresses of the day. He could vent to her about his irritating "manager" at work. She could complain about her crappy boyfriend back at home. Just normal conversations that most people took for granted, but Eric hadn't had a friend like that in years.

The Twitter home screen came up, and he smiled. A new message.

> **Tessa H:** Are you online?

Eric darted a glance over his shoulder. Maury was still yakking on his phone, with a cocktail glass balanced in one hand. The flight attendant had disappeared into the galley.

He hastily texted back.

> **Taylor:** For now. I'm on a plane. Might have to log off quickly…
>
> **Tessa H:** Traveling again? That sounds fun.

Eric snorted. Fun? Not exactly. More like stressful and exhausting.

> **Taylor:** Nah. Work trip. I'd pretty much rather blow my brains out, but what else is new.
>
> **Tessa H:** You shouldn't joke about that, Taylor.
>
> **Taylor:** Sorry. Just an expression. So what's up? Did you hear from Scott?
>
> **Tessa H:** Nope. Not a peep. He's kind of being a jerk at the moment.

Taylor: You should talk to him, Tessa. Stop messaging me and go call your boyfriend.

Tessa H: Maybe later. I have therapy in a sec. I'm just waiting for Dr. Regan to show up.

Taylor: Uh-oh. Have you been projecting again, young lady?

Eric bit down on the back of his thumb to stifle a laugh. He got such a kick from throwing all her Freudian mumbo jumbo back in her face. The two of them could go back and forth for hours, calling each other out on their various psychological shortcomings.

Tessa H: Of course. Projecting all day long. Except when I'm too busy catastrophizing…

Taylor: Catastrophizing? Pretty sure that's not a word.

Tessa H: Pretty sure it is, and you do it all the time.

Eric tittered. This ought to be good.

Taylor: Such as?

Tessa H: You'd rather blow your brains out?

Taylor: OK, Dr. Tessa. That might have been a slight exaggeration.

> **Tessa H:** Where are you headed anyway?
> **Taylor:** Seattle.

He hit Send on the message and immediately winced. Crap. He hadn't meant to let his guard down quite that much. He normally fudged the truth when it came to geographical locations. He bit his lip, hoping that she wouldn't put two and two together.

> **Tessa H:** OMG!!! SEATTLE? SERIOUSLY????

"Shit," he muttered under his breath.

> **Taylor:** Whoa. Didn't realize you were such a Seattle fan.
> **Tessa H:** Don't you know who else is in Seattle??????

Of course she'd caught it. This was what he got for befriending an Eric Thorn superfan of all people. He squeezed his eyes shut for a moment, considering how best to cover his tracks.

> **Taylor:** Oh no. Don't tell me.
> **Tessa H:** ERIC THORN!!!!
> **Taylor:** Huh, that's weird. I didn't pick up a signal yet on my douchebag detector.

> **Tessa H:** He's playing a stadium show tonight! I wonder if there are still tickets?
>
> **Taylor:** Nope. Pretty sure I got the last one.
>
> **Tessa H:** Wait. Wait. YOU HAVE TICKETS????
>
> **Taylor:** Well, not exactly. More of a corporate VIP type situation.
>
> **Tessa H:** OMG WHAT??? I thought you said it was a work trip!
>
> **Taylor:** Mostly work, and I'm sure the concert will suck monkey balls...
>
> **Tessa H:** Whatever. Do you have any idea how jealous I am right now? You know I've never even seen him live, right?

Eric paused, his finger hanging in the air. Really? He knew Tessa was confined to her home, but her condition had only started in June. How was it possible that she'd never come to see him play in all the years before?

> **Taylor:** Never? I thought you were such a fangirl!
>
> **Tessa H:** He never tours within five hours of my house.
>
> **Taylor:** Where? What part of the country?
>
> **Tessa H:** Let's just say it's a rural area... I can't believe you're seeing ERIC THORN. Will you please try to enjoy it? For my sake?

Taylor: OK. For your sake.

Tessa H: Promise? Will you sing along?

Eric broke into a playful grin. Sing along… Yes, Tessa. That much he could definitely promise.

Taylor: Every word of every song.

Tessa H: Good. And maybe try to smile at least once. Do you think you can manage that?

Taylor: Smiling right now, sweet pea. You tend to have that effect on me :)

Tessa H: Sweet pea?

Taylor: Well, you won't even give me a hint what you look like, so I choose to envision you as small, green, and spherical.

Tessa H: LOL. Pretty close. I gotta go though. Dr. R is here.

Taylor: OK, talk to you tomorrow. Have a good session.

Tessa lay on the bedroom floor, doing leg lifts. She slowly counted the reps inside her head. She had to do something to combat the atrophy from all the endless hours spent indoors. Dr. Regan had suggested a free fitness app at their last session, and she didn't seem to mind if Tessa followed along with the exercise routine while they spoke.

The therapist sat as usual in the beanbag chair, jotting notes on her yellow pad. Tessa thought she looked a little less uncomfortable than usual. It had to be the first time Tessa had ever seen Dr. Regan wear a pair of slacks.

"OK, Tessa. Let's take a look at what you wrote in your thought journal this week. Can you walk me through this?"

Tessa shifted to her other side as her therapist thumbed through the spiral-bound notebook. *More of the same*, she thought to herself. Sometimes she wondered why she bothered writing anything at all.

"Tessa?" Dr. Regan prompted.

"I guess it's mostly about Scott again," Tessa replied, lifting her leg in the air and holding it for a ten count. "He didn't come to see me at all last week. It kind of sucked."

She could sense Dr. Regan's thoughtful nod in response. "And how did that make you feel?"

It made me feel like shit, Tessa thought. What did her therapist expect her to say? Warm and fuzzy? With an effort, Tessa bit back a sarcastic reply. She'd save that for later. For Taylor. That was the nice thing about talking to her new friend. She didn't have to dissect every passing emotion that flitted through her head like a butcher carving up a side of beef.

"I don't know," she said to Dr. Regan, playing for time. "It's not Scott's fault. He started his fall semester, so he's busier now with school. I understand that."

"OK, Tessa. Try to dig a little deeper for me if you can."

"I don't know!" Tessa snapped back. "How do you think I feel? I feel lonely and hurt and angry. And scared. I feel scared. OK? Is that deep enough?"

Dr. Regan's blank expression didn't change. She nodded calmly. "That's good, Tessa. I hear you saying that Scott's behavior frightens you. Could you tell me more about that?"

Tessa swallowed a groan. Honestly, couldn't Dr. Regan ask a straightforward question for once in her life?

Tessa flipped onto her back and started doing crunches. She didn't know why she found therapy so annoying lately. She should probably write about *that* in her thought journal. What would Dr. Regan say to that? *Tessa, I hear you saying that I annoy the crap out of you. Could you tell me more about that?*

"Tessa?" Dr. Regan interrupted. "Did you hear me?"

"Sorry." With a final grunt of exertion, Tessa sat up all the way and clicked the fitness app closed. She knew she had to focus. She was never going to get better if she didn't take therapy seriously. "I guess I'm worried that Scott might be drifting away from me. Like I'm a chore on his to-do list. And I'd be really isolated if I didn't have him. I'd be completely alone. That scares me."

Dr. Regan made a note. "I see. Have you expressed these feelings to Scott?"

Tessa shook her head. Her pulse rate had slowed back down after the exercise, but she felt it quicken again in response to Dr. Regan's question. How exactly would that conversation go?

She could just picture Scott's eyes glazing over at the first hint of criticism. Then he'd either change the subject—or worse, cut the visit short. "I don't want to seem clingy. Taylor says—"

"Taylor? This is your new online friend?"

"From Twitter," Tessa confirmed. "We've been chatting a lot lately."

Dr. Regan flipped to a clean page. "That's good, Tessa. How frequently do you and Taylor chat?"

"Every night for about a month now." Tessa broke into a shy smile. "Sometimes Taylor messages me during the day too, but she has to work a lot."

Dr. Regan kept her eyes fixed on her notepad, scribbling again. Tessa couldn't help but wonder what her therapist did with all those notes. She didn't really save them, did she? Maybe she used them for origami paper. Or no, even better: papier-mâché. Maybe she made them into a gigantic piñata and beat it with a stick in her backyard. Probably, right? Anyone that robotic had to have some serious pent-up frustration…

"And you feel comfortable sharing your feelings about Scott with your friend Taylor?"

Tessa coughed to cover her giggle. Right. Taylor. Back to Taylor. "Sure," she said. "We're friends. We talk about all kinds of things."

"Keep going, Tessa. Tell me more about your friendship."

"We just understand each other," Tessa said. "Taylor has a lot of anxiety too. She's not in therapy or anything, but she probably should be. I try to tell her things you told me, to help her a little. And then we just have common interests. We talk about Eric a lot."

"Eric Thorn?"

"Yeah. She's funny. Her username is @EricThornSucks. She pretends like she hates his guts, and she makes fun of me for obsessing about him, but she's obviously a huge fan too. She follows everything he does almost as closely as I do."

Tessa cracked a grin. Her friend constantly surprised her with just how much she knew about Eric. Taylor always caught the song references whenever Tessa quoted lyrics. It was no exaggeration when her friend promised to sing along with every song tonight.

"It's deeper than just fangirling together," Tessa continued, musing out loud. "We kind of analyze Eric together. I keep telling her my theories about him—about how he's secretly unhappy. She's the first person I've met in the whole fandom who doesn't think I'm hallucinating."

Dr. Regan cocked her head to the side, studying her client's face. "OK, Tessa. I hear you saying that you talk a lot about Taylor's personal life, and you talk about Eric Thorn's personal life. But do you ever talk with Taylor about your own personal life?"

"Yeah. We talk about that too. All the time."

"Do you feel comfortable sharing things with Taylor that you wouldn't share with me?"

Tessa's eyebrows rose slightly at the question. Maybe Dr. Regan wasn't quite so clueless after all. "Probably," she said.

"There's less pressure, I guess. It's not so formal. And it's just texting. Sometimes that's easier than talking face-to-face."

Dr. Regan paused a beat. Tessa watched her curiously as the therapist gathered her thoughts. When Dr. Regan spoke at last, her voice had fallen a notch lower. "Tessa, do you think you might feel comfortable enough to tell Taylor what happened in New Orleans?"

Tessa froze—a deer, but not in the headlights. More like a deer staring down the barrel of a gun. Every muscle of her body went rigid as the question rang in the air.

New Orleans.

She slammed her eyes shut and squeezed them tight, waiting for the wave of nausea to pass.

"Did you hear me?" Dr. Regan prompted softly.

"No," Tessa whispered. "No. I'm not ready. I'm not there yet."

10

TURN AROUND

"MAKE SOME NOISE, Seattle!"

Eric spoke into the mic and listened to the echo booming through the packed stadium. His words were rewarded by a deafening roar, and he plastered a grin on his face, wide enough that even the girls in the cheap seats might stand a chance of seeing it.

Not much of a chance though. Tonight's sellout crowd topped 50,000 fans. It still blew his mind that anyone would throw away a hundred bucks on concert tickets, just to sit up there in the stratosphere and gaze at his image on a Jumbotron scoreboard.

"What's going on up there?" He extended a lazy arm in the direction of the highest row. "You guys still awake?"

Eric could sense the buzz of anticipation running through the crowd. He stepped casually off the main stage, and the fans rewarded him with another round of screaming as he strutted down the fifty-foot-long runway that lay before him. They all knew where he was heading: out to the round second stage, planted dead center in the middle of the stadium floor. "Aloe Vera" was up next, and he would sing it on his own out there, with no band members or backup dancers gyrating around him. Just Eric Thorn alone with a microphone, surrounded on all sides by the mass of squirming fans who pushed and shoved for position.

Those were the pit girls encircling the stage—the most fanatical worshippers of all, who'd lined up outside in the misty, gray Seattle rain since the wee hours of the morning. Anything to get a coveted spot along the railing, where they could hold out their hands in supplication and pray that he might reach down and graze their fingertips.

Most of them would leave here disappointed. He tried to keep all physical contact to a minimum these days, as much as the girls loved it. He'd gotten spooked at a show last year in Melbourne, after some Aussie managed to grab him by the wrist and yank him off his feet. Only the quick reflexes of a nearby stadium security guard had kept him from being engulfed by the waiting mob. Eric shuddered just thinking what they might have done to him. He'd seen the way they treated his discarded sweat towels, ripping and clawing like vultures over a carcass.

Safer not to touch the fans or even look at them too closely. For the most part, Eric tried to ignore their existence altogether when he played a venue this size. The key, he found, was to keep moving. Let them all blur together into one amorphous mass—one living, breathing organism with 50,000 gaping mouths, 100,000 upraised arms, and a seemingly infinite number of smartphone camera flashes, twinkling all around him.

Tonight though, he couldn't deny the temptation to sneak a glimpse at their eager faces. He felt oddly curious, and he knew the reason why. There was one face in particular that he kept trying to envision lately.

He hadn't seen her picture yet. Tessa didn't seem like the type to tweet selfies, and he didn't dare ask for one. But that didn't stop his imagination from running rampant. The fact was, he knew what she must look like, more or less. He only had to look out into the crowd. He had 50,000 female faces surrounding him. No doubt Tessa would blend right in.

Eric fingered the hem of his T-shirt, preparing to lift it over his head. He turned in a slow circle and ran his eyes across the faces of the girls in the front row—all completely interchangeable, aside from a few variations in hair color and skin tone. His gaze locked with a pair of pretty, brown eyes, peeking back at him from behind her upraised phone. He took a step closer to get a better look, all the while pulling his shirt up over his head in a single fluid motion. He watched as her phone dropped and the brown eyes widened. Then her face contorted into a mask of senseless hysteria as she opened her mouth to scream.

Eric looked away. Better not to make eye contact. Leave Tessa's face where it belonged—safely tucked away, somewhere on the fringes of his imagination. With one final jerk, he quickly tossed his shirt in the opposite direction.

Pandemonium.

Eric did his best to ignore the brewing scuffle where the shirt had landed. The opening chords of the song pounded through the stadium, drowning out the crowd. He held the mic in both hands and let his eyes drift closed as he sang the lyrics that he could've repeated in his sleep.

Come on and soothe this sunburn.
Baby, take away my pain…

He slipped in his earpiece to hear the music, but his ears weren't greeted by the sound of his own singing. Some other voice, half-concealed by static, buzzed instead. Security? What were they squawking about? How was he supposed to stay on key?

Eric turned his head in annoyance, ready to flick the earpiece back out again, but something in the cross talk caught his attention.

"Code Delta. I repeat. Code Delta."

He stutter-stepped, nearly tripping. Did he just hear that right? Code Delta?

He knew what it meant. His security detail thought he didn't understand their secret lingo, but he'd been through enough drills to figure most of it out by now. Alpha, Bravo, Charlie, Delta…

At least they hadn't said Code Alpha—not that he'd be around to hear that one. Code Alpha meant he'd been killed. Delta, as he recalled, referred to a breach of the perimeter.

The stream of chatter continued in his ear. Eric's own voice faltered, distracted by the growing urgency he heard in their clipped phrases.

"Unit 32, report to your station. Come in, Unit 32. Code Delta. Unit 32, please come in. Code Del—correction. Code Charlie. Code Beta."

Beta? Which one was that?

"Code Beta. I repeat. Code Beta. Unit 32, do you copy? Unit 32—Shit. Eric! ERIC! ERIC, TURN AROUND!"

And coming up at the top of the hour: It's normally home to the NFL's Seattle Seahawks, but this was no defensive lineman who jumped offside last night. Scary moments at Seattle's CenturyLink Field…

Tessa's head swiveled at the newscaster's words. She had her back to the TV, and she'd missed whatever image they'd broadcast to go along with their cryptic teaser. But the Seattle football stadium? It had to be the Eric Thorn concert.

The *Today Show* went to commercial without explaining further. Tessa dropped to her knees in front of the screen and clapped a hand over her thudding heart as she waited for the segment to continue.

She'd only switched on the TV a few moments earlier—a mindless distraction to occupy her time as she prepared for the day's activities. She'd awoken this morning relaxed and refreshed, with a sliver of bright sunlight penetrating through a crack in the horizontal blinds, and the sight of it had filled her with an irrational sense of optimism.

She'd felt so certain that today would go without a hitch. She'd forced herself to turn in early last night, and she'd set her phone to silent mode to ensure a peaceful night's sleep. Today was a big day. Probably the most important therapy exercise Tessa had yet attempted under Dr. Regan's careful guidance. Today, with her mother at her side, Tessa would set foot outside the house for the first time since she moved back home.

At least, that was the plan until a few moments ago. She was supposed to be relaxed for this. She'd purposely avoided Twitter this morning, just to be on the safe side. Calm. She was supposed to be calm! Not sitting in front of the TV at 8:59 a.m. with her heart in her throat.

The show resumed, but Tessa could barely follow what the news anchors were saying—not over the sound of her own pulse rushing in her ears. At last, a blurry image splashed across the screen. A concert. A circular stage, surrounded by fans. And there was Eric. Shirtless. Standing in the center, all alone.

Tessa hastily read the caption at the bottom of the screen:

Eric Thorn attacked onstage by fan.

"Oh my God," she breathed. "Oh no! No, no, no, no, no…"

The image began to move. A video clip but not professional quality. It had the jerky, pixelated look of a cell phone video, taken by someone in the crowd. Tessa watched in horror as a second figure appeared at the edge of the screen, running full speed in Eric's direction.

The fan looked tall for a girl, only a few inches shorter than Eric himself, with long, brown hair that streamed behind her as she sprinted up the lighted runway. Eric stood with his back to her. He sang into his microphone, completely unaware of her presence.

There was no sound from the clip—only the drone of a female reporter's voice in the background. "A fan from the general admission section climbed over the railing and evaded security long enough to—"

"Eric, look out!" Tessa whispered at the TV screen. "Someone stop her!"

The picture wasn't clear enough to get a good look at the girl's face, but Tessa could see something clutched in one of her hands. What was that? Something long and metallic, glinting beneath the concert spotlights as she came up behind Eric's back.

"What's that in her hand?" a TV cohost interrupted. "Is that what I think it is?"

The fan took a flying leap at Eric's back and managed to wrap both arms around his neck. His face was out of focus—too fuzzy to make out his expression, but Tessa could see his whole body jerk backward in surprise. He dropped his microphone and side-stepped, grabbing at the girl's wrists. The shiny object went tumbling to the ground.

"What exactly was that thing in her hand?" the host's voice asked again. "Do we have any word on that?"

"In the official statement from Thorn's spokespeople, they say there was no weapon. It was apparently a metallic glitter pen. The whole incident appears to be nothing more than a fan trying to get an autograph…"

The video paused for a moment and then skipped forward. Eric had broken the girl's grip around his neck. He managed to turn to face her. He had one arm wrapped around her waist as the girl clawed wildly at his bare chest. Tessa saw him cock back his free arm and clench a fist. For a moment, it looked like he might hit her. Instead, he dipped one shoulder and grabbed the girl's right hand, scooping her gracefully into a ballroom dance position.

"Wow." The newscaster chuckled in admiration. "Smooth move. I can see why the ladies go for this guy."

The image froze and then switched angles—this time to a video taken from closer range. Eric's face appeared more clearly now: calm and serious, looking deep into the fangirl's eyes. She'd stopped thrashing around. Eric's lips were moving, but only a lip reader could have interpreted what he said.

"Just look what he does now," the reporter's voice buzzed from the TV. "This part is so adorable!"

The video zoomed out as Eric whisked the girl into motion, whirling her round and round in a fast waltz. The girl broke into a beaming smile as the pair of them made a full circuit around the circumference of the stage. Then, at last, a pair of burly men with walkie-talkies stepped into the frame, and Eric danced the girl straight into the waiting arms of his security guards.

"Such a class act. That could have turned ugly so easily."

"A genuinely nice guy," the cohost agreed. "You can tell he's had his fair share of run-ins with overeager fans."

"And he's funny too!" the reporter added. "Look how he had the whole crowd laughing afterward."

A new clip began to roll: Eric, alone again onstage. He held a white towel in his hands and dabbed with it at his chest. The girl must have scratched him deeply enough to draw blood. He knelt to pick up his microphone, and Tessa pressed a clammy palm over her mouth as she watched him address the crowd.

"What the hell? I think I just crapped my pants!" He craned his head around and pretended to look down at his backside. "Uhhh, anyone have a spare pair of underwear they could lend me?"

Tessa could hear the laughter in his voice, but it sounded false to her ears. Her own hands were shaking. She could swear she heard a matching tremor in his voice. Was she imagining it? Just projecting?

A piece of pink fabric appeared at his feet, and he picked it up delicately, dangling it before him with one finger: a pair of women's panties.

"Men's underwear," he said with a wry smile. "I probably should have specified." He tossed the panties back into the crowd and wiped a weary hand across his eyes.

Tessa hit Pause on the TV remote to freeze the image. She knew she wasn't imagining things. She could see the expression on his face now, clear as day. He might have put up a good front, but that look in his eyes had nothing to do with laughter. He looked like a cornered animal, watching its predator approach. Terrified and utterly exhausted.

Tessa couldn't bear to look. She forced her eyes away. The clock icon at the corner of the screen showed the time: 9:02 a.m. She shouldn't be watching this anyway. Her mother would be home any minute. Tessa was about to click the TV off again when her eyes landed on something else at the bottom of the screen.

Credit: Videos posted on Instagram by MET (@MrsEricThorn)

At the sight of it, Tessa's panicky tension gave way, replaced by a tingle of excitement. MET!

Tessa took a step closer to the screen to make sure she'd read correctly. Was the *Today Show* really crediting MET like an actual media source? A fan account? Someone Tessa knew... even counted as a friend?

Tessa automatically reached for her phone to send off a quick DM. Not that she expected an answer. MET obviously had bigger fish to fry. But to Tessa's surprise, the other girl wrote back straightaway.

Tessa H: Your IG is on Today! Are you watching this?

MET: Yep. It's all over the place. E News, MTV... Gained 10K followers since I got up this morning.

Tessa H: That's ridiculous! How did it

happen? Do you know people who work on
TV?
MET: Who me? Nahhhh. Right place, right
time ;)

Tessa's eyes narrowed at the other girl's choice of emoji. Why
the winky face? Did she mean…

Tessa H: Were you in Seattle? Some of
those videos looked like they were from the
first row!
MET: Yeah, people sent those to me. I just
posted them.
Tessa H: Were you there though? Do you
know that girl who jumped onstage?

Long seconds ticked by with no reply. For a moment, Tessa
thought that MET might not answer. Probably distracted by
one of the countless other DM conversations she must have
going on…

Or was she purposely dodging the question?

MET: Was I there? Tessa, I'm
EVERYWHERE!
MET: LOLOLOLOL

Tessa's head drew back in surprise at the tone the other girl had taken. LOL? What was there to LOL about? Something truly terrifying had happened to the person they both professed to love. How could MET find it funny?

With a shaky finger, Tessa clicked the Twitter app closed. *Forget it*, she told herself. MET could LOL about it with one of her other half million followers.

But it wasn't just MET's laughter that disturbed her. A vague suspicion had entered Tessa's mind during the lull in the conversation. Now she couldn't erase the thought that made the hair rise on the back of her neck.

What if the fan who'd jumped onstage was Mrs. Eric Thorn herself?

11

THINK FAST

ERIC SAT IN his trailer, perched on a narrow stool, trying his best not to scratch. There'd be hell to pay if he gave in to the maddening itch that burned across his chest. Wardrobe and grooming had just completed prepping him for his music video shoot, and they'd used some especially foul concoction to cover all the scratches—a thick, Crisco-like glop that smelled like motor oil and stung like iodine. Eric had to give them credit though. It left his chest looking smooth as a plastic Ken doll's.

He had to find a distraction. Anything to keep his hands busy…and keep his mind off what had happened last night in Seattle.

He'd taken his private jet back to LA after the concert. Most nights, he slept like a rock after the physical exhaustion of a big show, but not yesterday. Not even in his Italian leather, fully reclining, heated airplane seat. Every time he tried to close his eyes, he felt those wiry fingers closing around his gullet once again.

"*Code Del—correction. Code Charlie. Code Beta...*"

He'd only remembered what the codes all meant after the fact. Code Beta: suspect armed and dangerous.

He hadn't turned fast enough. The fan jumped him from behind and put her hands around his neck. He managed to shake her off, and he heard the faint sound of something metallic clattering to the floor as they met eyes beneath the blaze of the concert lighting. Green eyes. Brown hair. Tall... From the look on her face, he knew in an instant that she'd completely lost touch with reality.

The words she kept screaming didn't help much either.

I LOVE YOU! I LOVE YOU! I LOVE YOU!

He'd somehow kept his wits about him. His mind remained clear and focused, almost like an onlooker watching the whole scene unfold from out in the audience. Only after the guards led his attacker away had he felt his knees start to buckle.

The whole incident was over in a matter of seconds, but it felt like an eternity at the time. He could still hear the girl's shrill yowls of protest as the guards removed her. "No, no! Let go of me. Stop it! Eric! Wait! He knows me! I'm telling you— he follows me on Twitter! He's followed me for years..."

A shiver coursed through him. He should have asked the wardrobe girl for a robe earlier. Eric flicked his eyes toward the trailer door, considering whether to stick his head outside and call for one.

Not now, he thought. He'd rather enjoy a few more minutes of precious solitude. He didn't need a robe anyway. What he needed was to get that shrieking voice out of his head. Eric picked up his phone, pressing his lips together in a grim line as he typed out a direct message.

Taylor: Hey sweet pea. You there?

A shadow fell over his shoulder, just as he hit Send.

"Think fast!"

Eric's back went ramrod straight. He swiveled on his stool, but his reflexes weren't quick enough. An all-too-familiar hand darted out and ripped the cell phone from his grasp. Eric looked up to see his manager eyeballing the screen.

"What the hell?" Eric lunged to grab it back, but not before he was blinded by the phone's camera flash. "Goddammit, Maury!" Eric blinked, shielding his eyes. "Don't sneak up on me like that! Try to have an ounce of sensitivity, would you?"

"Sensitivity to what?"

"I'm a little jumpy today, OK?"

"Oh, give me a break. Are you still hung up on the concert last night?" Maury cracked a broad grin. "Nice moves, kid. By the way, *Dancing with the Stars* called—"

"No!" Eric stood up from his stool with a lurch. He couldn't believe that his manager would joke about this. The incident the night before was a wake-up call. The current security procedures had utterly failed to protect him. Anything might have happened if he hadn't been so quick on his feet. "Maury, this is serious," he said. "I want a twenty-foot perimeter between me and the fans. No more touching people's hands. No more general admission either. Reserved seating only. Everyone in the first five rows has to provide a photo ID—"

Maury interrupted with a dry cackle. "Eric, you know that's not feasible."

"Somebody tried to assault me!"

"Assault you? She tried to hug you."

Eric gave his head a violent shake. "She had her fingers around my neck. What if she had a knife? She could've slit my throat before—"

"You handled it just right, Fred Astaire." Maury waved away Eric's worries, gesturing with the cell phone in his hand. "That was a gift from the heavens last night. The videos are going viral. We couldn't have staged a better PR stunt if we tried."

Eric took a step back and leaned heavily against the dressing table. He cast a suspicious glance at Maury's face. A PR stunt... That was just another of his manager's bad jokes, right? The publicists would never go quite that far.

Eric couldn't help but wonder, though, about the press release this morning. Not a knife in the girl's hand? Some kind of metallic pen? He remembered the sound as it fell from her grasp and clattered to the stage. It hadn't sounded like any pen he ever encountered before...

Eric fisted both his hands. Paranoia. That's all it was. Maury would have told him if she'd really had a knife. The publicists might lie to the press, but not to him. They had his back. He looked at his manager again. "We're pressing charges, right? Why haven't the police come by to take my statement?"

Maury rested a hand on Eric's shoulder, wrinkling his nose at the sticky makeup residue. "Listen to me, kid. Relax. Your fans love you. They don't want to hurt you. That one just got a little overexcited."

"You didn't see the look in her eyes!" Eric brushed his manager's hand away, frustration welling in his chest. "What if she tries to do it again? Maury, I danced with her. I put my arms around her."

"You did what you had to do to get her off the stage."

"I know, but I totally played into all her sick fantasies. It'll only encourage her more!" Eric's voice rose with emotion, but his manager wasn't even paying attention. Maury had his eyes cast down instead at Eric's cell phone.

The sight of it struck Eric with a new wave of dread. Crap. He just remembered which Twitter account he'd been using when Maury grabbed it.

"Not half-bad," his manager said. "A little washed out, but you kinda got the Greek god marble statue thing going on. It'll work."

"What'll work?" Eric snatched the phone and looked at the screen, sending up a silent prayer of thanks that he didn't see Twitter. Maury must have closed it when he opened the camera app. No way his manager could've noticed the username on the account.

Still, Eric chastised himself for his carelessness. He needed to keep his wits about him. Talk about a near miss.

"Social media wants you to tweet a selfie," Maury said.

Eric eyed the photo that his manager had snapped. Maury had caught him in profile, with one eyebrow raised in surprise, and the muscles of his bare chest and shoulders rippling as he turned. The tacky layer of grease on his skin reflected the light from the flashbulb like a sheen of sweat after a hard workout. Not an unflattering look, Eric had to admit. The makeup people knew what they were doing.

"This? They want me to tweet this?"

Maury nodded. "Sure. Show you survived unscathed, and keep the buzz going for the music video."

"Oh great." Eric rolled his eyes. "Hey, I have an idea! Run this by the label, why don't you? Maybe we could get some buzz going for the video by—I don't know—releasing the song? There's going to be a *song* involved, right? Or is this video just silent footage of me getting molested by evil fangirls?"

Maury glowered back, all trace of humor fading from his face. He glanced at his watch impatiently. "You know what, Eric? Don't worry about it. I'll tweet it for you."

The manager reached for the phone again, but Eric saw him coming this time. He jerked the phone away, out of Maury's reach, perhaps a bit more violently than necessary. "Don't touch my phone, OK? This is my personal cell."

"Whoa!" Maury put up his hands in defense. "Just trying to help, big guy. You got something on there that I should know about?"

Eric ignored the question. He prayed that the pancake

makeup would cover the guilty flush of color prickling his cheeks. "I'll send the tweet," he said, turning his face away. "Just give me a little space, please. Like three inches of personal space. That's all I'm asking."

"Sure," Maury replied. He waved an arm expansively around the six-foot-wide trailer. "You got the whole place to yourself, kid. Just send the tweet and get yourself ready to start shooting. The director's going to call for you in five."

DESENSITIZING

BREATHE IN.

Hold.

Eric one…Eric two…Eric three…Eric Thorn…Eric five…

Tessa let her breath out with a slow sigh, visualizing the ball of tension in her chest rising up through her throat and out of her mouth like a puff of smoke. The breathing exercises that Dr. Regan taught her usually had some effect, but not today. Not after that scene she'd just witnessed on TV and the creepy DM conversation afterward.

She never should have gone on Twitter. She'd vowed to herself that she wouldn't—not until today's desensitization exercise was complete. Now Tessa only had a few more moments to undo the damage. She could already hear her mother's heavy footsteps on the stairs.

"Tessa? Are you ready?"

Tessa buried her face in her hands. She sat cross-legged on

the floor in front of her TV, with the image of Eric's face still freeze-framed on the screen. Tessa grabbed for the remote. The picture faded to black just as her mother entered.

"Watching TV?" Her mother had a work bag slung over her shoulder and a white cardboard box in one hand. She set them both down heavily on Tessa's dresser and strode over to the window to open the horizontal blinds. Then she pulled up the window sash with a jerk.

"Mom, don't!" Tessa raised her arm to shield herself from the sudden burst of sunlight and the gust of crisp fall air. "Close the window!"

"It smells like dirty sweat socks in here."

"Just close the blinds at least!" Tessa said, turning her back. "Please, Mom. Someone could see."

Her mother answered with a heavy sigh, but she complied with the request. Tessa felt the jagged edge of panic ease at the sound of the blinds clattering closed.

Not that she felt relaxed now. Not even close. They would have to reschedule the desensitization exercise for another day.

Tessa opened her mouth to say so, but she hesitated at the sight of her mom's outfit: hospital scrubs, rumpled and stained after a long overnight shift. Her mother had rearranged her whole work schedule to make time for this today. Tessa could just imagine the explosion when her mom found out that she had worked a night shift for nothing.

"Why aren't you dressed, Tessa?" Her mother eyed her with hands on hips. "You're going outside like that?"

Tessa looked down guiltily. She'd started to put on clothes when she first got up that morning, but the *Today Show* had stopped her in her tracks. Now, she still wore her cotton pj's from last night, with a pair of fuzzy, hot-pink bunny slippers.

"Bright eyed and bushy tailed," Tessa mumbled.

"Fine." Her mother stifled a yawn. "Whatever. Come on. I'm tired. Let's get this over with. Are you coming?"

Tessa gulped, working up the courage to break the news. "Can we do it later, Mom?" she asked in small voice.

"No, we can't do it later. I need to sleep!"

Tessa chewed on her lower lip. Should she try to go through with it after all? Maybe she could do her breathing exercises on the way downstairs…

Her mother picked up the white cardboard box again, and her tone softened as she opened the lid to reveal the contents: a half dozen freshly glazed donuts. "Krispy Kreme," she said, waggling her eyebrows. "Come on, I swiped these from the nurses' station. We can sit out on the front stoop and eat."

Tessa pulled in a deep breath and held it for a five count. Then she nodded resolutely and took a step toward the bedroom door.

Small steps, she reminded herself. *One foot in front of the other.* She could do this. No big deal.

She made it to the top of the stairs before her confidence started to waver. Her ears registered the sound of a low rumble from outside. Was that a passing car?

"Mom, maybe we should go on the back deck instead," Tessa said. Why hadn't she thought of that before? Still outside, but at least it was protected from view of the road. The rickety, old deck jutted out over a ten-foot drop-off. Tessa always used to love it back there: her own private hideaway, suspended in the air, peaceful and secluded.

Her mother didn't break stride as she replied over her shoulder. "No way."

"Why not?" Tessa trailed her mother quickly down the stairs.

"No one's used that deck for years. The railing's rotted through. Only a matter of time before someone falls and breaks their neck."

Tessa scowled, wishing her mother would stop for one second to discuss. She hit the bottom landing and rushed onward. "I thought you were getting that fixed," she said.

"With what, Tessa? All that money went to a certain someone's college fund."

Tessa didn't miss the bite in her mother's tone. She knew a guilt trip when she heard one. Her mother had been livid when Tessa had deferred freshman year of college, months after the nonrefundable tuition deposit had already been paid. Tessa had promised that it was only a temporary setback. She'd head off to college once her recovery was far enough along.

Now here they were, a week into the fall semester, and Tessa had yet to trade her bunny slippers for an actual pair of shoes.

"OK then." Tessa drew in a shaky breath. "Front stoop it is."

She could do the front stoop. She must have run down those steps a million times over the course of her childhood. She just needed to shut her mind off. Focus on the task at hand.

Her mother reached for the door, but she stopped and stepped aside. She knew the drill. The two of them had been doing these desensitization exercises for weeks now. It was Tessa's job to open the door herself.

"Sometime this century, perhaps?"

"Mom, I'm trying," Tessa said. "I'm almost there."

The door loomed before her, and Tessa closed her eyes.

Breathe in.

Eric one…Eric two…Eric three—

"For goodness sake, Tessa. It's just a doorknob!"

But Tessa didn't hear her mother's voice. Not anymore. When her eyes reopened, she didn't see her own front door at all.

Tessa's head swiveled wildly as she tried to orient herself, but the edges of her vision had gone black. Tunnel vision. The area that remained visible slowly constricted. Soon she would be blind. And where she couldn't see, she could sense the lurking menace all around her.

The rational corner of her mind gave way as the mindless fear overtook her. Tessa staggered against a side table as the memory crashed down. She was somewhere else now. Not her childhood home. A darkened hallway…a different door…fiddling with an unfamiliar lock, with the sound of those shuffling footsteps coming up behind her… Her head swam as her clumsy fingers fumbled, and for a moment she thought she would fall. Only the fear kept her upright. The terror that she wouldn't get the door open before…before…

Her vision clouded over completely, and the blood in her

veins turned to ice. She felt the gentle pressure of a hand on her upper arm. "No!" she cried, wrenching free.

"OK, sweetheart. Take it easy." Her mother kneeled beside her, pulling the hair out of Tessa's face. "You're OK. Let's go back upstairs and get your pills. Are you dizzy? Are you going to faint?"

Tessa barely heard, her thoughts still fragmented with all-consuming terror. She never should have left her room. Not today. She knew how it would go. Now she stood unsteadily and allowed her mom to lead her toward the narrow stairwell, all the while trying desperately to block out the images from her mind.

Think about something else.

Anything.

Anything else.

Like the click of a deadbolt, her mind switched over to a different scene. Two figures danced before her. A waltz around a stage. Then he stood alone in the center, dabbing at his chest with a bloodied towel.

"Eric," Tessa whispered. She knew she was projecting, but she didn't care. Defense mechanisms had their purpose. She let her words tumble out, unchecked. "How can they laugh about it? He was bleeding! What if she had a knife? It's not funny! How can they all think it was funny?"

They reached her bedroom door now. Tessa lunged across the room for the bottle of anxiety pills by her bed as her mother tried to make sense of the jumbled words. "Who had a knife? Tessa, did someone at your summer program have a knife?"

"What? No. I'm not talking about that." Tessa quickly palmed two pills and let them dissolve under her tongue.

"What are you talking about?"

"Nothing. It's nothing." She sprawled across her bed, overwhelmed with the urge to be alone. She felt the heavy blanket of anxiety still smothering the breath out of her. It would lift soon, she told herself. Any minute now, the drug would take effect. "I'm OK," she said. "Just leave me alone, please."

Her mother lingered in the doorway, a crease of concern between her eyes. "Sweetheart, if someone came at you with a knife, you need to—"

"No," Tessa moaned. "Forget it. It wasn't even about me. I was talking about Eric."

"Who?"

"Eric Thorn! A fan attacked him. It was on the *Today Show* just now." She waved a hand vaguely in the direction of the TV.

"Eric Tho—this is a celebrity you're talking about?"

Tessa saw her mother's face change, the mask of worry replaced by irritable impatience.

"It was scary," Tessa said.

"Unbelievable. A singer. Something happened to some singer, and that's it? We're done? You know I changed my whole schedule—"

"I know!" Tessa cut her off. "I'm sorry! You don't understand. I tried to tell you. I'm not in the right place mentally today—"

She broke off as her mother knelt to pick something up by the foot of the bed. She tossed the object in Tessa's direction, and it bounced beside her on the mattress: the TV remote control.

"Here. Go ahead. Watch your *Today Show*."

"Mom," Tessa said miserably. "Don't. I'm sorry."

The bedroom door slammed as her mother left the room, but Tessa could still hear her grumbling all the way down the hall. "That's fine, Tessa. Take your time. I'm going to bed. When you're in the right place mentally, let me know."

13

EXPOSED

"OK, THANKS, EVERYONE. Take ten."

Eric gingerly disentangled his limbs from one of his delightful new love interests. Olga or Oksana? He couldn't say for sure. Day four of shooting, and he still couldn't keep their names straight. Neither could the film crew, from what Eric could tell. Maybe the director should have thought of that before he cast a pair of Latvian identical twins to star in the latest music video.

Music video, Eric thought with a grim smile. What a joke. Ever since the Billboard charts started counting YouTube views, the whole video business had taken an ugly turn. They should dispense with the pretense and call it what it was: softcore porn. A footrace to see who could expose the most flesh without getting banned by the FCC.

Eric slipped a robe around his shoulders and ran a towel across his face to rub away the lipstick stains. Makeup would have to touch him up before he undressed again for the next scene, but that could wait. Right now, he needed privacy. He'd passed the last several hours shooting the threesome scene with his lovely costars, and he'd spent the entire time with his mind on someone else.

Eric glanced over his shoulder to make sure no one followed him back to his trailer. Then he eagerly whipped out his phone. He'd sent out the selfie before shooting began, but he hadn't found a spare moment to check for a response.

> **Eric Thorn** @EricThorn
> Selfie day! Tweet me a selfie wherever you are at this exact moment, and maybe we'll use it in the new #MusicVideo

He had to hand it to himself: one of his more ingenious Twitter ploys. He needed something to look forward to today—anything to take his mind off yesterday's ugliness at the concert. The answer had come to him this morning as he sat staring at his selfie, struggling to compose a caption. He'd been wondering for weeks now what Tessa looked like. He didn't dare ask her for a pic. But this was perfect. She was sure to send one. After all, it wasn't just some random stranger off the Internet asking to see her. It was her idol. Her obsession. Her true love, Eric Thorn.

Had she seen it? He scrolled eagerly through the replies.

The response was overwhelming, of course. His notifications

overflowed with pictures of teenage girls making faces at their phones. Kissy faces. Duck faces. Oh look! One of them made a GIF of herself twerking. He scrolled past all of them, scanning for the only username he cared about. Where was it? Hadn't she sent one?

He didn't have time to wade through all the noise. He entered her name into the search bar to pull up her profile. There it was at the top of her recent tweets:

Tessa H @TessaHeartsEric
@EricThorn Here's a kiss from someone cute. Glad you're OK!

pic.twitter.com/1cdl6DZmTe

Eric bit his lip as he clicked to expand the picture. He couldn't help but laugh at what he saw. She'd arrayed a mountain of Eric Thorn fan paraphernalia at the head of her bed: poster, T-shirt, coffee mugs, CD cases... Was that a pillowcase with his face on it? The only sign of her own presence in the photo were her feet, decked out in a pair of fuzzy pink bunny slippers. She had one bunny positioned next to the poster, kissing his image on the cheek.

Eric shook his head. So frustrating! He couldn't see *anything*. Hell, he couldn't even tell how big her feet were!

Still, he couldn't erase the grin plastered across his face. *Here's a kiss from someone cute.* She was awfully cute, wasn't she? Even if he couldn't see what she looked like, at least she made him smile. Probably the first real smile that had crossed his face all day.

Eric wondered if she'd replied to him on his fake account as well. She hadn't answered his DM earlier, but that was hours ago. She must have seen it by now.

He clicked the privacy latch on the inside of the trailer door, and then he leaned his weight against the edge of the makeup counter as he quickly switched accounts.

No more @EricThorn. Back to @EricThornSucks.

Time Stamp 9/16/16, 1:29 p.m.
Tessa H: Hey, sorry I was off-line before.
Not having the greatest morning.

Eric's initial pleasure gave way to a sliver of concern. Something must have shaken her. He had a feeling he knew what it was.

Taylor: What happened? Was it because of
the concert last night? Did that freak you
out?
Tessa H: Yeah, among other things…
Taylor: Are you OK? That kind of scared the
crap out of me too.
Tessa H: Thank you! Everyone else seems
to think it was funny. I don't understand
how people can make jokes about it!

Taylor: Trust me, I'm right there with you. I
didn't sleep a wink last night.
Tessa H: I didn't hear till this morning. I was
supposed to go sit on the front stoop with
my mom today, and I totally bailed. She's
so mad at me now.

"Crap," Eric said under his breath. Tessa had mentioned her therapy exercises before, and he knew this one was a big deal for her. She hadn't set foot outside in months. He hated to think that he might have set back her progress.

Taylor: Do you want to tell me about it? I
don't have a ton of time right now, but I can
talk for a couple minutes.
Tessa H: It's OK. At least Eric's OK, right?
He must be fine if he went on with the show
afterward.
Taylor: I guess. He seemed kind of shaken
up. He did the rest of the concert from the
main stage.
Tessa H: Poor Eric. I just hope he has
someone there to give him a big hug :(

"Yeah," Eric muttered. "That makes two of us."

But he was less concerned about his own state of mind. He could count on one hand the number of times he'd ever seen

Tessa use a frown emoji. She always had such an air of optimism about her, even in the face of all her problems. It was one
of the reasons he felt compelled to chat with her so often. It
helped him keep his own issues in perspective.

He longed to lift her spirits now. If only he could talk to her
for real. Hear the sound of her voice. Or better yet, FaceTime.
But of course that was impossible.

He settled for another DM instead:

> **Taylor:** Hey, so that selfie you tweeted was
> pretty smokin' hot ;)
> **Tessa H:** OMG did you see it?
> **Taylor:** Not bad. I'm not sure that's exactly
> what Eric Thorn was looking for. Maybe you
> should tweet him a real one…
> **Tessa H:** Ummm, did you miss the part
> of the conversation where I have SEVERE
> anxiety?
> **Taylor:** So tweet and delete. You can do it.
> Face your fears.
> **Tessa H:** But I'm supposed to face them in
> small steps! Like today I was just supposed
> to spend five minutes on my front porch.
> It's called desensitization.
> **Taylor:** OK, small steps. So maybe tweet a
> picture of your feet without the slippers.
> **Tessa H:** Can I wear socks?

> **Taylor:** Nope. Take it all off, baby.
>
> **Tessa H:** That is SO not happening today.
> Seriously, you didn't see me this morning :(

There she went with the frowny face again. Eric had never heard her sound so negative before. There had to be something he could do to cheer her up. He glanced down at his own feet, crossed at the ankles. They were bare for the video shoot. He only donned a pair of black plastic flip-flops to protect his soles from the sunbaked asphalt of the studio backlot.

He wiggled his toes, one corner of his mouth quirking mischievously. Maybe he couldn't show her his face, but at least he could try to make her laugh.

> **Taylor:** C'mon. Tweet a nude. I'll do it if you
> do ;)

Eric snickered to himself as he toggled back to Tessa's bunny slipper tweet. He composed his own tweet in reply and quickly snapped a picture for illustration. He held the camera low to crop out the hem of his robe, just showing his hairy calves on downward. He had one foot lifted off the ground, with his flip-flop dangling from his big toe.

> **Taylor** @EricThornSucks
> I'm more of a thong kind of guy…*wink
> wink* @TessaHeartsEric @EricThorn

pic.twitter.com/z9H81X9hPi

He held his breath, awaiting her response. He hadn't gone too far, had he? She had to know he was just joking around—not actually flirting. She had a boyfriend after all.

Eric felt a twinge of some unpleasant emotion he couldn't quite identify. Guilt, perhaps? A pang of conscience for talking to another guy's girlfriend? He didn't think so. His conversations with Tessa were innocent enough.

So maybe it wasn't guilt, then. Maybe it was more like… jealousy?

Ridiculous. How could it be jealousy? Jealous of what? Of some loser guy named Scott who barely visited his girlfriend?

Eric shook the thought out of his head, waiting for her to reward his clever line with laughter. At least a smile. Something must have distracted her on the other end. He DM'ed her again, still teasing.

> **Taylor:** Are you blushing? Too revealing?
> **Tessa H:** Is that supposed to be a joke?
> **Taylor:** Ummm, no? Not funny?
> **Tessa H:** Why would you tweet a pic of men's feet?

Men's feet? Eric's smile slowly faded. He added another message to the thread.

Taylor: Tessa, you do know I'm a guy,
right?

She didn't answer. Silence. No reply. He tried to keep his next message light, but his heart had started beating like a drum.

Taylor: Ugh. So annoying! Everyone
assumes Taylor is a girl's name now.
Thanks a lot, Taylor Swift.

"Say something," he whispered to the phone. "Shit, Tessa. Say something."

Taylor: Hello? Tessa?
Taylor: Crap. I thought you knew. Are you
there?

Her answer came back at last, and he let out a gasp of relief when he saw it. For a moment there, he'd thought he might never hear another word.

Tessa H: Please tell me you're gay.
Taylor: No… What difference does that
make?
Tessa H: Why is a straight guy tweeting
about Eric Thorn?

Eric paused again, considering his reply. Was she upset? She'd taken so long to write back just now, but maybe it didn't mean anything. Still, some instinct told him to tread lightly. Should he apologize? Try to make another joke out of it? In the end, he simply played for time.

> **Taylor:** Tessa, you know I was just kidding around, right?

He hit Send, and then he sat staring at his phone in utter baf-flement. An error message had popped up—words he'd never seen before in all his years on Twitter.

> Message Not Sent

> You can no longer send Direct Messages to this person. Learn More

Eric gave the phone a shake, as if to clear away some speck of dust. A glitch, he thought. Some hiccup in the software. It took him a moment to comprehend the truth.

No mistake. It meant just what it said:

@TessaHeartsEric had just unfollowed @EricThornSucks.

THE INTERROGATION (FRAGMENT 4)

December 31, 2016 9:17 p.m.
Case #: 124.678.21–001
OFFICIAL TRANSCRIPT OF POLICE INTERROGATION

HART:	Did you talk to Dr. Regan? Is she coming?
INVESTIGATOR:	We left several voice mails. Is there anyone else we can call for you in the meantime? A family member, perhaps?
HART:	No, just my therapist.
INVESTIGATOR:	What about your mother, Tessa? You said that you live with her, correct?
HART:	Yes, but she's working. I can't... You don't know how she gets. She'll kill me. She just started at the new hospital in Midland. She's on a double shift. You don't have to call her, do you?
INVESTIGATOR:	Only if you want us to. It's up to you.
HART:	No. No. Just get Dr. Regan.
INVESTIGATOR:	We're doing our best to get hold of her. You said your mother works at a hospital? She's a doctor?
HART:	No, a phlebotomist. She just takes blood from

people. You know, when they need blood tests and stuff.

INVESTIGATOR: I see.

HART: She doesn't know about tonight. I didn't want to tell her.

INVESTIGATOR: Why was that?

HART: She wouldn't approve. She thinks anyone who so much as watches MTV is a Satan worshipper. She's going to find out now, isn't she? Oh God, she's going to kill me. I really, really need my therapist.

INVESTIGATOR: OK, Tessa. We're working on it. In the meantime, can we go back to the Twitter activity we've been discussing? In particular the direct messages you exchanged on September 16. Now, it looks like there's a gap starting that afternoon. Do you happen to recollect that date?

HART: Yes.

INVESTIGATOR: Can you explain to me what happened?

HART: I blocked him. I was weirded out.

INVESTIGATOR: I see. And why exactly were you "weirded out," as you put it?

HART: You saw. You just read it.

INVESTIGATOR: I'd like to have you explain in your own words, if you don't mind. Let me remind you that this interview is being recorded.

HART: Well, I freaked because I thought he was a girl. I had a mental picture of the person I was talking to, and it was definitely not a...not a "him." I felt like he misled me. Like he'd been flirting with me all that time, and I didn't even realize. It was very unsettling.

INVESTIGATOR: But you resumed communication with him a few days later? On the night of September 20?

HART: I know. I should've followed my instincts.

INVESTIGATOR: Tessa, what led you to resume communication?

HART: Um, stupidity? Is that not a good enough reason?

INVESTIGATOR: Were you aware that he'd been tweeting at you? We have record of a number of public tweets originating from the account @EricThornSucks, dated from September 16 to September 20. There were a total of thirteen tweets by my count, all tagging the username @TessaHeartsEric. Does that sound about right, Tessa?

HART: I don't know. He was blocked.

INVESTIGATOR: You had him blocked over that entire period?

HART: Yes.

INVESTIGATOR: And yet on September 20 at approximately 11:31 p.m., you replied to one of his tweets?

HART: I can't believe I did that.

INVESTIGATOR: Tessa, can you confirm for me that you tweeted on September 20 at 11:31 p.m., and I quote: "@EricThornSucks thanks for ruining my life."

HART: I never should've unblocked him.

INVESTIGATOR: Can you confirm it for the record, Tessa?

HART: What? Yes. I tweeted that.

INVESTIGATOR: And what exactly did you mean?

HART: That's hilarious actually, come to think of it: "Thanks for ruining my life."

INVESTIGATOR: Tessa? You mean you were joking when you said that?

HART: No, I wasn't joking. I just mean I didn't even know the half of it. I had no idea how true that would turn out to be.

14

TRIGGER

A CLAMMY HAND *clapped her on the shoulder, and Tessa turned her head. The room was hot, the air heavy with the sweat of undulating bodies pressing in on her from all sides. She twisted around, scanning for any sign of her friends. She must have lost them in the crowd.*

"Hey, what's your name? I'm—"

"Sorry, what? It's really loud in here!"

She spun around again, searching for the nearest door. Fingers grazed against the bare skin of her arm. They left a trail of goose bumps, despite the heat.

She shrugged her shoulder to shake the hand away, and she went up on her tiptoes, searching. There! She saw the neon red of the Exit sign. A group of familiar faces stood beneath. Tessa held her arms in front of her chest as she pushed her way through the crowd. She didn't stop to look for the source of the unseen voice that called after her.

"Wait! Are you here for the program? You're creative writing, right? I'm—"

🔁

Tessa jolted awake. She blinked rapidly to chase away the half-remembered fragments of her dream. In an instant, she felt the familiar choke hold of anxiety squeezing around her neck. She reached toward her bedside table. She needed to swallow two of the little pills before the full-blown panic attack overtook her.

Her fingers closed around the pill bottle, but she froze with her arm suspended in midair. Some instinct had alerted her to another person's presence in the room.

She darted a glance in the direction of the doorway and saw the shadow of a human form. Male or female? She couldn't tell. She didn't dare turn to look. Instead, she let her arm drop lifelessly beside her, praying it would look like she had reached out in her sleep.

"Get up," a voice commanded. "I know you're awake."

The crushing panic evaporated then. Gone. Or not exactly gone, but replaced by something even stronger: searing anger.

It was him, she realized. Here, in her room. Watching her sleep. How many times did she have to tell him? Tessa sat up with a jerk and turned to face her boyfriend. "What are you doing here, Scott?"

He glared back at her from the foot of the bed. "Nice to see you too."

"You asshole! You just scared the crap out of me! Do you understand that? Do you see these pills?" She waved the bottle of anxiety meds in his direction. "I'm not kidding around. I have a phobia. A diagnosed medical condition. You can't just come into my room. It's not OK!"

"Oh, I'm sorry," he shot back. "I forgot. You don't like waking up and realizing someone's creeping around behind your back. Is that it?"

"Yes!"

"That's interesting, Tess. I know the feeling."

It was only then that she noticed what he was holding in his hand. Her cell phone. He held it up and turned the screen around for her to see. She recognized the photo she'd chosen for her lock screen: Eric Thorn, making out with himself in a mirror.

"Classy, Tessa."

Had Scott been looking at her phone? Her camera roll? How much had he seen?

"Give it to me." She reached out to grab it from his hands, but he backpedaled.

"No, I think I might hang on to this a little longer."

"You have no right!"

"What? To snoop around your cell phone? You're right. I probably don't. But then again, I didn't actually expect to find anything."

He stood rigid as a statue, but the silent venom in his stare made Tessa shrink away. She inched backward toward the far corner of her bed. "Scott, it's nothing. It's a celebrity crush. Lots of people have them."

"You think I care about this loser?" He swiped to clear the picture from her screen. "Honestly, if you think I'm pissed because you like to diddle yourself to Zac Efron here—"

"That's not... That's Eric Thorn!"

"Wow, Tessa. Way to miss the point." He let out a harsh laugh. "Here, you want your precious phone back?" He hurled it in her direction, not quite close enough to hit her, but with enough force to make her flinch. It smacked against the wall behind her head, and she scampered off the bed to pick it up.

"Did you break it? I need that!"

"Yeah, I know exactly what you need it for." His eyes narrowed into slits. "Little miss innocent over here. Won't go past third base after two whole years of dating."

She didn't answer, too concerned with checking if her screen had cracked.

"I saw everything, Tessa."

"What are you talking about?" She looked up at him, bewildered. "My camera roll? My iTunes?"

Scott shook his head, his lip curling in an ugly smirk. His face had turned beet red. She expected him to yell, but his voice came out in a rumble, low and menacing. "I can't believe I'm killing myself playing the dutiful boyfriend over here, and the whole time you're on Twitter, sexting it up with some dickhole—"

"Sexting?"

"Don't play ignorant with me. I read your message thread. I heard that selfie you tweeted was pretty smokin' hot."

Tessa took a hasty step in his direction, holding out her hands. "Scott, that wasn't... Did you even look at the picture?"

"Do I need to?"

"Scott, it was a joke. And anyway, I blocked him. I didn't even realize Taylor was a guy!"

He cocked his head. "You thought a girl was tweeting you to take your clothes off?"

"Yes!" Tessa's mind raced, her heart pounding like a jackhammer, as she recalled the incriminating details of that final conversation.

Take it all off, baby... C'mon. Tweet a nude...

All this time, she'd been worried that Scott would discover her Eric Thorn obsession, but this was so much worse. This was a real guy that she'd been chatting with. She'd flirted with Taylor, however unwittingly. She saw how it must look.

"Scott—"

"Save it. Don't insult my intelligence."

He turned to leave the room, and Tessa trailed after him. Her anger had lost its edge, and a new wave of panic swept over her. She had to undo the damage somehow—make Scott understand. She followed him as far as she dared, halting just across the threshold of her bedroom door. For a moment, he paused at the top of the steps with one foot hovering over the edge.

"Scott," she called after him. "I'm sorry. Please come back. I can explain everything."

He didn't even look at her. "I'm out," he said.

"Wait! Don't go yet. You know I can't follow you down there!"

"Good," his voice called back as he descended. "Don't follow me, Tessa. Don't call. Don't text. Don't talk to me at all. I hope you and your phone have a nice time together. I got the message loud and clear."

CATASTROPHIZING

15

I'm never going to get better. I feel like I spent the last three months climbing my way out of a deep, dark hole, and I just lost my grip and fell all the way back down to the bottom again. I don't know if I even want to try anymore.

Tessa's vision swam as she tried to focus on the handwritten words in her thought journal. She sat listlessly in her beanbag chair, dressed in a pair of rumpled pajamas.

Since the argument with Scott three days ago, she could barely summon the energy to leave her bed. She hadn't moved a muscle, except to dial Scott's phone number. He'd finally texted back this evening, but her relief had evaporated the moment she read the message.

Scott: Stop calling. It's over. Don't make me change my number.

Tessa felt her eyes welling up again, and she swiped an angry hand across her lids. To hell with Scott. As if she were some kind of pathetic stalker who couldn't take a hint…

At least his message had shaken her out of her lethargy enough to pick up her journal. She had to keep writing, she told herself. Keep going. It didn't even matter what it said. Just fill up one page so she had something to show for herself at the next therapy session.

She hunched forward in the beanbag, shoulders slumped, as she put her pen back to the paper.

> I could've dealt with losing Taylor, or even losing Scott. But both of them? In the space of a day? How do I bounce back from that? There's nothing left. It's hopeless.

Tessa closed her eyes, trying to channel her inner therapist's voice. She knew what Dr. Regan would say when she read this entry back. *Tessa, do you think it's possible that you're catastrophizing?*

She remembered when Dr. Regan first explained the concept. Catastrophizing: a form of distorted thinking that made problems seem more insurmountable than they truly were. Was that what she was doing?

Tessa shook her head, and her pen flashed across the page.

It's not catastrophizing if it's actually a catastrophe!
A real catastrophe. Sometimes horrible things actually
happen. I can't just pretend like they didn't!

With a shaky breath, Tessa flipped the journal closed. It wasn't helping. All she felt right now was an overwhelming bitterness. She didn't know whom she hated most. Scott, for his blithe dismissal? Dr. Regan, for her emotionless reserve? Or Taylor... Taylor, the liar, who brought her whole world crashing down with his oh-so-clever jokes and innuendoes.

She needed a distraction—anything to soothe away the painful ache inside her chest. Her eyes landed on her phone, and Tessa crossed the room to pick it up. Even if she didn't have a single person in the world who actually cared about her, she still had Eric Thorn.

Tessa plugged in her earphones and pulled up her favorite song. "Talk to me, Eric," she whispered. "Tell me a secret. Tell me what's going on with you."

As if in answer to her request, his soft, smooth tenor voice sang the opening verse of "Aloe Vera."

> *We lingered on your terrace.*
> *I drank up all your wine.*
> *You said, "Baby, take your clothes off.*
> *Get rid of those tan lines."*

With a low moan, Tessa pressed her thumb down against

the volume button until the music hurt her ears. Eric's voice pounded inside her skull, too loud to bear for long. But not quite loud enough to drown out the burning anger.

> *I fell asleep to the sound of your voice*
> *Whispering to me.*
> *But you left me there to blister.*
> *Ran off with the only key.*

Taylor @EricThornSucks

@TessaHeartsEric I swear I'm not a bad guy. Talk to me? Please?

Eric sat up in his hotel bed, looking over his recent tweets. He'd been tweeting at Tessa for days with no reply. His account looked utterly dead now.

He banged the back of his head against the headboard.

He knew it was probably hopeless at this point. He should cut his losses. Deactivate the account. Forget she ever existed. And yet he couldn't quite bring himself to pull the trigger. He'd grown accustomed to their nightly chats—downright dependent on them, apparently. He'd finally found a safe place to vent his worries and frustrations, and she offered more than just a sympathetic ear. She had this sixth sense for telling him whenever he was exaggerating.

No, he thought. Not exaggerating. What was that word she used the other day?

Catastrophizing.

Pretty sure that's not a word, he'd replied. But it was a word—another psychobabble term he'd looked up afterward on Wikipedia—and she was damned good at catching him whenever he was guilty of the crime.

Now she wanted nothing more to do with him, and he couldn't shake the sense of loss. Life had felt less bleak these past few weeks. He'd even started smiling again.

Maybe that was why he couldn't sleep these days. Maybe it was the sinking realization that, without her in his life, he had nothing left to smile about.

Or was he just catastrophizing?

"Come on, Tessa," he whispered to his phone. "Come back. You can't really be that mad."

He started entering another useless tweet:

Taylor @EricThornSucks
@TessaHeartsEric I can't sleep. I miss talking to you.

He rubbed his eyes wearily, his finger hovering over the Tweet button. What difference did it make, really, whether he sent it or not? He had zero followers. No one would hear him either way.

Eric set the phone back on his nightstand and switched off the lamp.

Sleep. He needed sleep. The dark circles under his eyes were growing deeper by the day. He'd heard the makeup artists whispering about it behind his back. They could only cover it up for so long before the record label got on his case.

He rolled over in bed again and reached to plump his pillow, but a flash of color from his nightstand caught the corner of his eye.

His phone?

A notification?

He grabbed it and let out a yelp of triumph. At last. She'd answered. A new tweet:

> **Tessa H** @TessaHeartsEric
> @EricThornSucks thanks for ruining my life.

The message probably should have discouraged him, but he couldn't prevent the crooked grin that popped onto his face. She was still out there somewhere. He hastily sent back a reply, before she could ghost on him again.

> **Taylor** @EricThornSucks
> @TessaHeartsEric ok now who's
> catastrophizing?

Eric waited to see if she would tweet back, but the minutes ticked by. At least she'd unblocked him. Her profile was visible to him again, no longer hidden away behind an error message.

He longed to DM her, but Twitter wouldn't let him go that far. She hadn't refollowed him. He could only reply by tweeting at her again.

> **Taylor** @EricThornSucks
> @TessaHeartsEric what happened???
> follow me back so we can DM

Eric had gotten out of bed now. He paced back and forth across the spacious room with his phone gripped in his hand, and he bounced on the balls of his feet when the next notification hit his screen.

> Tessa H (@TessaHeartsEric) followed you.

"Yes," he murmured, as he flipped back to the message tab again. She had already added another new DM, but he barely paused to read it.

> **Tessa H:** Don't think this means I'm talking to you again.
> **Taylor:** Tessa, I'm sorry you thought I was a girl. It was an innocent mistake. I swear.
> **Tessa H:** Right…sure…and you just happen to be the ONLY male Eric Thorn fan on the face of the earth. Is that it?
> **Taylor:** I never said I was a fan! I believe

I called him a narcissistic douche nozzle.
Does that ring any bells?
Tessa H: And you know all his songs by
heart because...why exactly?
Taylor: It's complicated.
Tessa H: In other words, you're full of shit.
Taylor: No. In other words, it's gonna take
me more than 140 characters to explain.
Take a breath, please.

Eric sat down on the edge of the bed. The truth was, she had a point. He'd seen the demographics from his recent album sales, and males didn't even make up one percent. Not that he needed a pie chart to tell him that. All he had to do was look out over the crowds of screaming girls at his concerts.

Eric scrunched his mouth to the side as he cast about for some kind of believable explanation.

Taylor: OK, here's the deal.
Taylor: I used to be a fan back before he
got signed. He used to be good.
Taylor: I mean, he still is. I listen to all his
new stuff too.
Taylor: I just think he shouldn't need to do
the Magic Mike routine to sell it. That's why
I get so pissed off at him sometimes.
Taylor: And with the fangirls too. Maybe

> he wouldn't parade around half-naked if he
> didn't have girls screaming at him to take
> his shirt off every five seconds.

There. He hadn't technically lied, had he? He really was his own biggest fan, back before he got his record deal. He'd started out as nothing more than a kid with a guitar and an unshakable belief in his own talent. He'd refused to listen whenever his friends laughed or his parents told him he was wasting his time. He'd spent two long years posting video after video on YouTube before he finally got his big break.

It was a half-baked version of the facts, but technically not untrue. Eric held his breath, waiting to see how Tessa would respond.

> **Tessa H:** So why did you start talking to me
> if you hate fangirls so much?
> **Taylor:** I didn't start talking to you. I
> attacked you. Remember? You're the one
> who started talking to me.
> **Tessa H:** Reverse psychology
> **Taylor:** I'm not that smart.
> **Tessa H:** How do I know that?
> **Taylor:** I'm stupid, OK? You caught me.
> Guilty. I'm very, very stupid. But I'm not
> some kind of predator. C'mon, you know
> I'm not.

Tessa H: Why should I believe a single
word you say?
Taylor: I don't know, Tessa. What reason
would I possibly have to lie?

Eric covered his face with his hand, reading the words
between his fingers. Why did he feel like a total creeper right
now? It wasn't like he could tell Tessa the whole truth anyway.
How would that conversation go? *Surprise! I'm actually Eric
Thorn, and this is my secret second profile!* She'd write him off as
a compulsive liar and unfollow him once and for all.

He hadn't done anything wrong, he told himself. It was a little
white lie at most. If it ever seemed like any harm might come
of it, all he had to do was end things. Say good-bye. Deactivate
the account. And Taylor the phantom fanboy would disappear
into Twitter oblivion.

Somewhere in the back of his mind, Eric knew that he probably
should have deactivated already. He'd been on the receiving end
of his share of little white lies. He knew they had a nasty way of
changing color when viewed from someone else's vantage point.

But he couldn't deactivate now. Not when he finally had her
talking again.

Taylor: So are you going to tell me how I
ruined your life or what?
Tessa H: Scott
Taylor: What about Scott?

Tessa H: I fell asleep to the sound of your voice whispering to me...

Taylor: What does that mean?

Tessa H: Hmmmm. I thought you were such a huuuuge fan

Taylor: I know it's a line from "Aloe Vera." What does it have to do with Scott?

Tessa H: We lingered on your terrace. I drank up all your wine.

Taylor: Is this a test?

Tessa H: You tell me. What's the next line?

Eric let out a growl of irritation. *Honestly, Tessa.* If she'd had the faintest clue who she was talking to...

Taylor: You said, "Baby, take your clothes off. Get rid of those tan lines."

Tessa H: No. YOU said, "Baby, take your clothes off."

Taylor: Isn't that what I just wrote?

Tessa H: I believe your exact words were: "Take it all off, baby." Scroll up. Our last conversation.

Taylor: What? That thing? I was talking about feet!

Tessa H: Scott didn't find that very amusing for some reason.

Taylor: What happened?

Tessa H: I fell asleep to the sound of your voice whispering to me. What's the next line?

Taylor: But you left me there to blister. Ran off with the only key.

Tessa H: Exactly. I got burned. I was depressed, I fell asleep, and Scott found my phone.

Taylor: He broke up with you?

Tessa H: Let's just say he wasn't very pleased that I'd been flirting for the past month with some guy I met on Twitter.

Taylor: Shit, Tessa.

Tessa H: Yup. I believe his exact words were, "I'm killing myself playing the dutiful boyfriend over here, and you're off sexting some loser."

Taylor: Sexting? How were we sexting?

Tessa H: "C'mon. Tweet a nude. I'll do it if you do..."

Taylor: It was a picture of your bunny slippers! He's never heard of sarcasm?

Tessa H: I don't think he actually looked at the picture.

Taylor: Well, it sounds like you two just need to talk. I'm sure if you explain...

Tessa H: He won't return my calls, Taylor.
Taylor: He just said that thing about sexting and left?
Tessa H: No, I think he threw my phone at me and called me a cheating ho-bag first.

Eric squinted at his phone, trying to picture the scene. Something about it stirred a memory, and he let out a muffled gasp when he realized what it was.

Taylor: Wait a minute. I know what happened.
Tessa H: I just told you what happened.
Taylor: No, no. Hold on a sec.

He'd read it a month ago now—almost an exact description of Scott's behavior. Of course... It was the first night he and Tessa started talking. He navigated over to Wikipedia and pulled up the entry for projection.

There it was, in the section on practical examples.

Bullying...

Blaming the victim...

Justifying infidelity...

Bingo.

Eric took a screenshot and added the image to the DM conversation.

Justifying infidelity: The cheating partner may project his own unfaithful thoughts or actions onto the innocent partner in order to justify his infidelity and assuage his own sense of guilt.

> **Tessa H:** What is this?
>
> **Taylor:** It's projection! Maybe Scott jumped to "sexting" cuz he's been doing a little "sexting" of his own?
>
> **Tessa H:** No. No way.
>
> **Taylor:** Tessa, he's been distant with you for a while now.
>
> **Tessa H:** He's busy with school...
>
> **Taylor:** Busy, my ass. I'm busy too. I still find time to talk to you.

Eric's fingers clamped down hard on his phone. It boggled his mind how anyone could treat a girlfriend that way. Especially under the circumstances. Tessa needed someone desperately right now. She'd obviously been through some kind of trauma. Her boyfriend should've been first in line to offer her support.

> **Tessa H:** He was always texting someone... God, I can't believe I didn't think of that.
>
> **Taylor:** Well, we can't all be as sensitive and insightful as I am.
>
> **Tessa H:** Spare me. You never even heard of projection before you started talking to me.

> **Taylor:** This is true. This is why I need you
> to keep talking.

The conversation paused then, and Eric leaned his head against the headboard of the bed. He could sense her indecision, despite the sharpness of her tone. She needed someone, and they both knew it.

And the thing was, Eric needed her too. The past few sleepless nights had made that all too clear. He'd been coming apart at the seams without her calming influence.

> **Tessa H:** I don't know.
> **Taylor:** I just want to talk. I swear, there's
> nothing sinister. You help me deal with my
> shit. I help you deal with your shit.
> **Tessa H:** I have to think about it.
> **Taylor:** Tessa, please. Who else do you
> have to talk to now?
> **Tessa H:** My therapist.
> **Taylor:** But she can't keep up with all your
> Eric Thorn references.
> **Tessa H:** Are you sure you can?
> **Taylor:** "Come on and ease this sunburn.
> Baby, take away my pain…"
> **Tessa H:** Such a fanboy.
> **Taylor:** See? We speak the same language.
> **Tessa H:** I dunno. If I do decide to talk

to you again, I need you to promise me
something.

Taylor: Anything.

Tessa H: No more surprises, OK? I don't do
well with surprises. Promise me right now
there's nothing else I need to know.

Eric sucked in his breath between his teeth. *No more surprises.* Of all the things she could've asked.

But what could he say? He couldn't refuse. She'd just get spooked and unfollow him again. And he could help her. It couldn't be wrong if he only meant to help her.

Anyway, she didn't need to know because she would never find out the truth. Never. Over his dead body.

With a resolute nod, he sent back his reply.

Taylor: Nothing else you need to know. I
promise.

THE INTERROGATION (FRAGMENT 5)

December 31, 2016, 8:42 p.m.
Case #: 124.678.21–001
OFFICIAL TRANSCRIPTION OF POLICE INTERVIEW

INVESTIGATOR:	Mr. Thorn, are you familiar with the term "catfish"?
THORN:	Oh, come on.
INVESTIGATOR:	It's a yes-or-no question.
THORN:	Yes. I'm obviously familiar with the term.
INVESTIGATOR:	Would you care to define it for us, for the record?
THORN:	No.
INVESTIGATOR:	No?
THORN:	It was a yes-or-no question, right?
INVESTIGATOR:	That's cute, Eric. What do you think, Terry? You think he's getting cute with us?
THORN:	I'm not... I wasn't trying to be cute. I'm just not in the mood for stupid questions.
INVESTIGATOR:	You know, Terry and I could do this all night.

So if you just want to sit around and insult our intelligence—

THORN: No, no, no. I'm sorry. I didn't mean it like that. I'm just a little thrown right now. There are other things I would prefer to be doing. I'm sure you understand. So could we please just cut to the chase?

INVESTIGATOR: And what other things would you prefer to be doing, Eric?

THORN: Well, I'd like to speak to Tessa, for one thing.

INVESTIGATOR: You care about her.

THORN: Of course.

INVESTIGATOR: And she cares about you?

THORN: Yes.

INVESTIGATOR: That's sweet. Isn't that sweet, Terry? Really heart-warming. You ever write a song about her, Eric?

THORN: What does that have to do with anything?

INVESTIGATOR: Oh, I'm just curious. I've got a niece. She's about fifteen years old. Huge fan of yours.

THORN: I'd be happy to sign an autograph for her.

INVESTIGATOR: Now that's not necessary. Just answer the question, if you don't mind.

THORN: What was the question?

INVESTIGATOR: Did you ever write a song about Tessa Hart?

THORN: Really? I have to answer that?

INVESTIGATOR: You just put out a new single, right? What was
                    that one called?

THORN: "Snowflake."

INVESTIGATOR: That's it. "Snowflake." Pretty song. Did you write
                    that song about Tessa?

THORN: I really don't talk about the meanings behind my
                    song lyrics.

INVESTIGATOR: Don't you? I got the sense that you and Tessa
                    talked quite a bit about the meanings behind your
                    song lyrics.

THORN: That's different.

INVESTIGATOR: How so?

THORN: I talked to her about things that I can't tell other
                    people. Personal things. She's the only person I
                    could talk to about a lot of stuff.

INVESTIGATOR: Because those conversations took place within
                    the context of a private correspondence. A private
                    relationship, you might say?

THORN: Right.

INVESTIGATOR:	And there was one other way it was different too. Wasn't there?
THORN:	What do you mean?
INVESTIGATOR:	I mean, she didn't know it was you, right? She thought she was talking about your song lyrics with somebody named Taylor.
THORN:	Right. Exactly.
INVESTIGATOR:	"To lure someone into a relationship by means of a fictional online persona."
THORN:	Sorry, what?
INVESTIGATOR:	That was a quote, actually. Let the record show that my previous statement was a quote from the *Oxford English Dictionary*, third edition. That was the second definition of the verb "catfish." Did you know they put it in the dictionary?
THORN:	It wasn't like that.
INVESTIGATOR:	OK, Eric. You want to cut to the chase? Let's cut to the chase. Did you, or have you ever, lured someone into a relationship by means of a fictional online persona?
THORN:	That's a crappy definition.
INVESTIGATOR:	The *Oxford English Dictionary*?
THORN:	It wasn't catfishing. It wasn't like on the MTV show.

INVESTIGATOR:	That's the defense you want to go with? It wasn't like on the MTV show?
THORN:	Come on. You know what I mean.
INVESTIGATOR:	I'll admit, I'm not totally up-to-date with MTV's programming.
THORN:	Well, maybe you should ask your niece.
INVESTIGATOR:	Maybe. But then again, my niece isn't involved in a criminal investigation into false impersonation, fraud, unlawful surveillance, and stalking.
THORN:	Whoa, whoa, whoa, whoa, whoa—
INVESTIGATOR:	So why don't you just go ahead and spell it out for us, Eric? How would you define *catfishing*?
THORN:	I didn't do anything illegal.
INVESTIGATOR:	But you did, in fact, lure Tessa Hart into a relationship by means of a fictional online persona, correct?
THORN:	You have to understand the position I was in.
INVESTIGATOR:	What position was that?
THORN:	She was my fan. She practically worshipped me. Catfishing is when you set up a fake profile to make yourself into someone more attractive. That's the opposite of what I did.
INVESTIGATOR:	So you set up a fake profile to make yourself less attractive?

THORN: No. It wasn't about being attractive. It was about being anonymous. It was the only way I could be myself.

INVESTIGATOR: By pretending to be someone else? By willfully misleading someone about your true identity?

THORN: Look, I'm not the villain here. I know how it must seem, but you have to understand that I started talking to Tessa in...What? August? It didn't change all at once. It snuck up on me...on both of us. I didn't even realize where it was heading until about a month ago. Almost Christmastime.

INVESTIGATOR: And what exactly changed for you a month ago?

THORN: I never meant for it to go the way it did. I swear. I just wanted to talk to someone. I didn't mean to fall in love.

16

WHITE CHRISTMAS

December 3, 2016

"OK, TESSA. LAST week you planned to accompany your mother on a brief outing to pick out a Christmas tree. How did that go?"

Tessa idly traced the pattern on her bedspread with her thumb as she paused to gather her thoughts. Her therapist sat across from her in a folding metal chair. Dr. Regan had given up on the beanbag somewhere around month four of therapy, after it burst beneath her weight in a cascade of flying beads.

Tessa could feel Dr. Regan studying her as Tessa's own eyes wandered around the room. She'd strung a strand of Christmas lights across the footboard of her bed, and they cast her therapist's face in a glow of pale green and red. Tessa's mother had taken the lights out of storage to decorate the tree, but it looked like the Christmas tree might not happen this year after all.

Tessa hadn't even made it past the driveway when they went to pick it out. Her mom had left the car idling outside, and everything went smoothly until Tessa slid into the passenger seat. She'd turned toward her mother with a triumphant smile—only to be blinded by a camera flash.

"Tessa?" Dr. Regan prompted.

"Yeah, I kind of bailed." Tessa fiddled with a loose button on her cardigan.

"What happened?"

Tessa couldn't even explain it to herself, much less to her therapist. Maybe if her mom had warned her, instead of trying for a candid shot…

At least she managed not to vomit in the car before she abandoned the passenger seat and went scurrying back into the house.

Dr. Regan asked her something else—something about her mother. Tessa didn't quite hear the question. She jiggled her foot impatiently, counting the minutes until the session came to an end. She'd agreed to switch her weekly hour with Dr. Regan to an evening time slot, but she regretted it now. She forgot that she had a date with her TV tonight. Eric Thorn was slated to give a live performance at 8:00 p.m. Tessa had her DVR set to record it, but she couldn't bear the thought that she might not get to watch him in real time.

"Tessa?" Dr. Regan spoke a bit more sharply. "Did you hear me?"

"Sorry. What did you say?"

Dr. Regan had her head bent forward, leafing through the pages of Tessa's thought journal. "In your entry this week, I see you saying that you feel judged by your mother. Could you tell me more about that?"

Tessa heaved a sigh. She hardly saw the point of hashing it all out again. Her mother had stomped all over the house after the incident in the driveway. She didn't even try to understand what Tessa might be going through.

"Honestly, what's the point?" Tessa said in a dull voice. "As far as my mom's concerned, I'm the worst thing that ever happened to her. I ruined her life from the moment I was conceived."

Dr. Regan's face remained expressionless, but she made a careful notation on her pad. "Have you told your mother any details about last June?"

Tessa shook her head. "She would only blame me. She'd say I must have done something to bring it on myself. I must have led him—" She broke off and clapped a hand across her mouth.

Dr. Regan raised an eyebrow. "Go on, Tessa. What exactly would your mother say you brought on yourself?"

"What?" Tessa's hand lingered at her throat. "No. Nothing. I just meant that she blames me for everything. That's all." She held her breath, hoping that Dr. Regan wouldn't press her further. It would only trigger a flashback, and Tessa didn't have time for a panic episode. Not tonight.

Dr. Regan removed her reading glasses and left them dangling on the chain around her neck. "And how does that make you feel?"

Tessa didn't answer. Some questions were safer to ignore. She darted a surreptitious glance at the phone that sat beside her on the bed, and she scowled to herself as the screen lit up. Already seven forty-five.

"Tessa?"

"Huh?" Tessa's head snapped up. "Sorry."

Her therapist smiled tightly. She moved to put her notepad back in her briefcase. "You seem a bit distracted. Perhaps we should pick up here next week."

Tessa nodded. With a tiny sliver of guilt, she stood to walk her therapist to the door. She knew she'd wasted Dr. Regan's time tonight, but she couldn't help it. She'd spent the whole day preoccupied with the same thoughts circling around and around inside her head: Would Taylor be online tonight? Would he get off work in time to watch the broadcast with her? Maybe she could convince him to live chat…

Eric fished in his pocket, groping for his phone. He only had a few minutes to hide out in his dressing room before he headed back on set—just long enough to respond to Tessa's latest DM.

He flicked to open Twitter, and he frowned. The damn thing kept signing out of his account lately. It started acting up after the latest software update, although the glitch only seemed to affect his second username. Every time he shut down, he had to reenter his password to log back in.

He didn't have time to worry about it now. He quickly filled out the information:

Username: @EricThornSucks

Password: **password**

Then he navigated over to the message thread.

> **Tessa H:** Taylor, are you there?
> **Taylor:** Yeah, I thought you had therapy.
> **Tessa H:** Just finished. The show starts in
> fifteen minutes! Are you watching?
> **Taylor:** Can't do it, sweet pea. Gotta work.

Eric knew he needed to wrap the conversation up. He was performing tonight on live network TV: one of those star-studded December Christmas specials, complete with Santa hats and mistletoe. Eric was supposed to spend the final moments before airtime running through the lyrics of his solo, "White Christmas," but his attention kept getting sucked back in to Twitter.

> **Tessa H:** Seriously, you can't take a break
> for ONE hour? Not even for Eric Thorn?
> **Taylor:** I wish I could, Tessa...but it has
> nothing to do with Eric Thorn.
> **Tessa H:** Who? Ariana Grande?
> **Taylor:** Since when was I an Arianator?
> **Tessa H:** I'm just guessing. You're a guy.
> She's probably your type.

Eric snickered. Where did Tessa come up with this stuff? His type? The truth was, he and Ariana were slated to perform back-to-back that night. He'd been passing by her dressing room all afternoon, but he hadn't even bothered to poke his head in. What made Tessa think that he had any interest... Wait a minute. One corner of his mouth hitched upward as he texted back.

> **Taylor:** Is that a hint, Tessa? Are you secretly an Ariana Grande look-alike?
>
> **Tessa H:** Yep. Currently lounging in my thigh-high stiletto boots. I can send you another foot selfie if you like.
>
> **Taylor:** Feel free, but I might need to see an entire leg this time.

Eric had yet to see a picture of her. He didn't want to push his luck after the fiasco with the feet. But they'd been dancing around the topic more and more lately. He could tell he was slowly gaining her trust. It was only a matter of time before she sent him a selfie, and he couldn't pretend he wasn't dying to see.

> **Tessa H:** Legs? What legs? I thought I was green and spherical?
>
> **Taylor:** Then where do you put the boots?
>
> **Tessa H:** OK fine. You got me. I have legs. Two of them.

> **Taylor:** Interesting. Anything else you care
> to tell me about these legs?
> **Tessa H:** Nice legs. Not gonna lie.
> **Taylor:** Yeah. I had a feeling.
> **Tessa H:** You should really stay online,
> Taylor. Who knows what other body parts I
> might mention in the next hour…

Eric covered his mouth with the back of his hand to wipe away the sly grin. She had no idea how much he wanted to stay and chat. That had to be the most flirtatious thing she'd ever said to him. Dammit, why did tonight's show have to be a live broadcast?

> **Taylor:** Oh man, you're killing me.
> **Tessa H:** Stay!
> **Taylor:** I can't. I'm late. I gotta run. I'll catch
> you later, OK?

With that, Eric glanced up at the lighted mirror to check if he'd smudged his makeup. He nearly fell over at what he saw reflected in the glass. His manager leaned against the half-open dressing room door, with his feet crossed at the ankles and his hands stuffed in his trouser pockets.

Maury cleared his throat as their eyes met in the mirror. "Sometime today, perhaps?"

"Sorry." Eric swiveled to avert his face. He slipped his phone into his back pocket and turned to leave the room, but Maury stood squarely in the doorway.

"No problem, buckaroo. You wanna let me in on who the lucky lady is?" Maury tilted his head in the direction of the phone, and Eric stopped in his tracks. How long had his manager been standing there?

"What lady?" Eric replied, striving to keep his voice light. "What are you talking about?"

"Eric, you spent the past ten minutes giggling like a schoolgirl at your phone." Maury pulled down a sprig of mistletoe from above the doorframe and tossed it in Eric's direction. "You know you're supposed to disclose if you have a new girlfriend, right? The publicists appreciate a heads-up."

The mistletoe landed at Eric's feet, but he ignored it. Apparently, his manager was spying on him now. Good to know exactly where he stood.

At least Maury hadn't discovered the fake Twitter account, as far as Eric could tell. He tried again to step past his manager into the hallway, but Maury didn't budge. "Yeah right," Eric said at last. "Like I have time for a relationship."

"Maybe not a girlfriend, then. But definitely a girl." Maury nudged him with an elbow between the ribs. "It's fine, Eric. About time, if you ask me. Just tell me who she is, and I'll pass it along—"

"It's no one."

"No one, huh?" Maury scratched his chin, studying Eric's face. Eric stared back with wide, unblinking eyes, the picture of choirboy innocence. "That's a little more serious," Maury said. "Don't tell me you're in love."

Eric rolled his eyes upward and planted them to the ceiling. He could feel his manager's gaze on him, and he couldn't suppress the guilty flush of color that rose above his shirt collar and worked its way up his neck.

"You know you're the color of a pomegranate right now?" Maury's voice shook with laughter, and Eric turned his face away, bracing himself for the coming onslaught. He knew how Maury operated. His manager would be peppering him for weeks with obnoxious jokes.

But to Eric's surprise, Maury stopped chuckling after a moment. When Eric met his eyes again, he almost thought he saw a trace of sadness in his manager's expression. With a sigh, Maury stooped to pick up the mistletoe and tossed it in the trash. "What happened to you, Eric?" he said softly. "You used to tell me everything. I used to be your guy."

"Maury—"

Maury just shook his head. Eric watched him spin around and head down the long corridor toward the stage. His manager's final words floated back to him from the far end of the hall. "It's no one, huh? You're a crappy liar, kid. Always have been. Only this time, I can't quite tell if you're lying to me…or lying to yourself."

17

BOUND AND GAGGED

ERIC STEERED HIS baby-blue Ferrari around the hairpin turns of Mulholland Drive, reveling in the purr of the engine as he pushed down on the accelerator. It felt great to be behind the wheel again. He'd spent too many nights in the back of a limo lately, and he missed the feeling of control that came from driving.

He'd bought himself a Ferrari 458 Spider a little over a year ago to celebrate his latest album reaching multiplatinum status. But so far, the odometer only registered a few thousand miles. Maybe he should bring his car along on the tour kicking off soon. Leave the tour bus to the roadies. Eric made a mental note to float the idea by Maury in the morning.

Maury…

Eric drummed his fingers on the steering wheel. He couldn't get that awkward conversation with his manager out of his head. Maury didn't know what he was talking about, obviously. All that nonsense about *love*… His manager had only leaped to that conclusion because he didn't have all the facts. He didn't know about the fake Twitter account—or that the girl on the other end of the conversation was a fan. How could Eric Thorn be in love with a fan? A random fangirl who wouldn't even tell him her last name or where she lived? A girl whose picture he'd never even seen?

"Ridiculous," Eric muttered as he pulled his car into the long, gated driveway of his house in the Hollywood Hills.

He rolled to a stop and popped the car door open, bracing against the chill of the night air. His hand reached automatically for the phone in his pocket as he made his way inside, but he stopped himself. Maybe he needed to give it a rest—spend one night without pouring out his every passing thought to Tessa. It would be the first night in months that he hadn't fallen asleep reading her messages and imagining her voice whispering him good night.

But he was perfectly capable of setting it aside, right?

Eric kicked off his sneakers and sprawled on the couch. Maybe this was what he needed, he told himself. Some solitude. Put on some music and crack open a pint of cookie dough ice cream. No phone. No Twitter.

Where was the stereo again? His eyes wandered restlessly about the oversize room. Vaulted ceilings. Hardwood floors. Black leather furniture. White baby grand piano in the corner. Someone had arranged his collection of Grammys, AMAs, and MTV moonmen on top. Home, sweet home. All very tasteful...and very unfamiliar.

This place felt no more like home than any of the swanky hotel suites where he laid his head most nights. Between his tour schedule and his acting and modeling duties, he barely cobbled together six weeks a year in LA. He wasn't exaggerating when he told Maury that he didn't have time for a girlfriend. Not unless he found one that he could cart along wherever he went—a handy-dandy girlfriend the size of a cell phone, who fit conveniently in the back pocket of his jeans.

He couldn't help but wonder what Tessa thought of the Christmas song tonight. Had she caught the hatchet job he'd done on the second verse? He'd covered it at the time with a cocky grin straight into the camera, and Maury had slapped him on the back afterward for a job well done. But did Tessa see through it? Was she satisfied? Or did she know that smile was fake?

"Who am I kidding?" Eric said to himself as he reached again for his back pocket. He'd die of boredom if he spent the evening all alone, eating ice cream straight from the carton.

Eric pulled out his phone and opened Twitter, but he saw in an instant that it was set to the wrong account:

Eric Thorn @EricThorn

FOLLOWERS
14.8M

He rarely bothered to open his real account nowadays,

but he'd been commanded from on high to tweet about the Christmas special. His eyes skimmed down to the message he sent out just before airtime.

> **Eric Thorn** @EricThorn
>
> Wishing an early #HappyHolidays to my amazing fans! What do you want for Christmas? All I want is for you to watch me LIVE tonight at 8 PM!
>
> ♺ 70.4K   ♥ 257.2K

He hadn't crafted that particular gem himself. Some social media expert from the TV network had stood over Eric's shoulder and dictated the words. The replies had started pouring in the moment he hit Tweet. Now Eric couldn't quite peel his eyes away fast enough to avoid reading the first few responses.

> **Anna Thorn** @EricAddict3
>
> @EricThorn ILY

> **Eric Thorn Lover** @EricLuv982
>
> @EricThorn FOLLOW ME!

> **MET** @MrsEricThorn
>
> @EricThorn I'll give you ANYTHING you want for Christmas, baby

Eat Me Eric @EricThornPorn
@EricThorn I WANT U TO HIT THE
FOLLOW BUTTON WITH UR ROCK
HARD—

Eric choked. His thumb slammed down on the home button, clicking the app closed before his eyes could register another word. He really should have known better than to look at the replies. Nothing like a dose of holiday cheer from his *amazing* fans to ruin his mood. He was more than a little tempted to chuck his phone across the room just to obliterate that last one from his memory. It wouldn't have been the first time he cracked his screen that way.

But he didn't throw his phone. He didn't need to resort to violence—not anymore. He merely slumped back against the couch cushions and pulled up Tessa's profile. He felt his anger ebb the moment he read her reply.

Tessa H @TessaHeartsEric
@EricThorn All I want for Christmas is to
see a smile on your face. Love you! Merry
Christmas!

Eric let out a long breath, releasing the tension from his shoulders. He knew her reply was genuine. That was what made it so sweet. He'd always assumed that the fans who tweeted shirtless pictures of him only viewed him as a piece of meat, but Tessa had proven him wrong. Honestly, she must be the only fan left who saw him as a human being. It was unbelievable, the effect she had on him. She must have had some kind of supernatural power, the way she could slice through his mood with a few simple words. He knew she'd have him laughing again in no time if he DM'ed her. With a few flicks of his thumb, he switched accounts and fired off a message.

Taylor: This fandom is so f'ed up.

Tessa obliged him with an instantaneous response. Eric kicked up his feet on his living room couch and settled in for a chat.

Tessa H: What happened?
Taylor: The fangirls! Can't they just wish him a Merry Christmas? It's disgusting, some of the shit they tweet at him.
Tessa H: Well, I wished him a Merry Christmas.
Taylor: You're a sweetheart. The rest of them can rot.
Tessa H: I know, it goes too far sometimes. Did you see the picture MET tweeted after he messed up the Christmas carol?

Eric's brow furrowed. MET? He didn't recognize the acronym. Was that another TMZ?

> **Taylor:** What's MET? A gossip blog?
> **Tessa H:** No, you dork! @MrsEricThorn. It's the most important account in the whole fandom! How are you so clueless?

Perfect. Eric couldn't help but laugh. He'd been vaguely aware of that account, of course. He knew it had a lot of followers. But the most important person in the fandom? Really?

> **Taylor:** Silly me. And here I thought the most important person in the fandom was that other douche rocket. What's his name, again? Oh yeah…Eric Thorn.
> **Tessa H:** You know what I mean. The most important fan account :P
> **Taylor:** Got it. And does Eric's wife have an actual name?
> **Tessa H:** Everyone just calls her MET. She likes to maintain an air of mystery. Kind of creeps me out, to be honest. Go look at her recent tweets.

Eric entered the handle and pulled up the tweet that Tessa meant.

MET @MrsEricThorn

Haha way to go @EricThorn. Retweet if you think he should've performed the song like this ;) #EricThornObsessed

MET had illustrated her point with a doctored photo, and he drew in a sharp breath when he saw what it depicted: Eric Thorn, shirtless, splayed across a bed, bound and gagged with duct tape.

A shudder passed through Eric's frame as he glanced at the retweet count, hovering just north of 1K. How could there be a thousand people out there who didn't find that image utterly repugnant? It was all fun and games until someone decided to act it out in real life. If anyone made an edit like that of Ariana Grande, they'd probably get arrested. But he was a guy, so that somehow made the sexploitation funny…and retweetable.

In the past, that picture would have sent him through the roof, but Eric felt surprisingly calm about it now. He merely rolled his eyes and tucked one arm behind his head as he slouched down farther on the couch.

Taylor: Ugh! He's a human being! How is that pic supposed to make him feel?

Tessa H: I know. It's gross. But he's kind of asking for it in a way.

Taylor: Why? Because he messed up the song? That justifies sexual harassment?

> **Tessa H:** No, but he's the one who keeps
> flashing everybody. And why does he put
> his sex life into his song lyrics, if he doesn't
> want to be objectified?

One of Eric's eyebrows quirked up at that. His sex life? What was she talking about? He knew the tabloids liked to pair him off with a different female celebrity every week, but Tessa knew better than to believe that crap.

> **Taylor:** What sex life??
> **Tessa H:** Um, have you heard "Aloe Vera"?
> That song's obviously about some girl he
> was sleeping with.
> **Taylor:** C'mon, Tessa. You're smarter than
> that.
> **Tessa H:** What? You think it was about a
> man?

Eric hesitated. He'd never told another living soul the true meaning of "Aloe Vera." Not even Maury. The record label probably wouldn't have released the song if they'd known. It made his heart rate quicken to think about telling Tessa—unnerving but strangely exhilarating at the same time.

> **Taylor:** Not a man...maybe THE man.
> **Tessa H:** ????

Taylor: There's more than one way to get screwed. That's all I'm saying.

Tessa H: OK. So…now he got screwed by THE man?

Taylor: Listen to the words. "You said, 'Baby, take your clothes off. Get rid of those tan lines.'"

Tessa H: So?

Taylor: Who told him to take his clothes off?

Tessa H: Ummm…Ariana Grande? :P

Taylor: All I know is, he was just this shy kid with an acoustic, and then he got signed by a major label, and the next thing you know, he's prancing around half-naked all the time.

Tessa H: So you think his record label told him to take his clothes off?

Taylor: Think about it. "I fell asleep to the sound of your voice whispering to me." Maybe he feels like they kinda seduced him with a bunch of sweet talk.

Tessa H: But the rest of it? "You left me there to blister. Ran off with the only key"?

Taylor: Right. They locked him in. To his RECORD DEAL.

Eric held his breath, waiting for her reaction. Would she get it? He had a feeling it would probably blow her mind. It was her favorite song, after all. She knew the lyrics almost as well as he did.

> **Tessa H:** OMG, Taylor. Are you kidding me
> right now?
> **Taylor:** I know, right? It totally fits!
> **Tessa H:** Talk about projecting.
> **Taylor:** How is this projecting?
> **Tessa H:** Because YOU feel trapped by
> YOUR job. You're talking about YOU. Eric
> Thorn is not YOU. Get it through your head!

Eric bowed his head in disappointment. Projecting. Tessa's favorite word. She had the truth staring her in the face, but she didn't see it. She *couldn't* see it, he knew, because it was only a tiny sliver of the truth. Not the real secret that would blow her mind…

He shifted uncomfortably, unable to avoid the stab of guilt. Maybe he should tell her everything, right then and there. How amazing would that feel? He had the perfect opening right now. He knew exactly how to do it.

Eric switched back over to his real account, @EricThorn, and began to compose a new DM from there:

> **Eric:** Not projecting if you're actually talking
> about yourself, Tessa…

Eric stared at the words in his message bar, but he didn't quite have the nerve to hit Send. Not yet. He wasn't ready. Who knew how she might react? He hastily deleted the message, sucking in a shaky breath.

Still, he had to give her something—something more than ridiculous theories from Taylor the snarky fanboy. Tessa had become one of the most important people in his life, and he didn't even follow her from his real account. He should've done it back when the #EricThornObsessed thing was trending. For the life of him, he couldn't remember why he hadn't. If any fan deserved a follow from @EricThorn, it was @TessaHeartsEric.

What would happen, he wondered, if he hit the Follow button now? A cautious smile crept onto his face as he imagined her reaction.

He couldn't resist. His thumb made swift contact with the button.

Tessa lay on her stomach in front of the TV, bopping her feet in time to the music. She'd recorded tonight's Christmas special, and she hit Rewind to play Eric's performance of "White Christmas" once again, while she waited for Taylor's next reply.

It was strange, she thought, the way Eric had forgotten the words tonight. It wasn't like him. Hadn't he rehearsed before-hand? Something must have happened to distract him. She studied the familiar face on the TV screen for clues. He started out the song slow and serious, with those hypnotic, ice-blue eyes staring straight into the camera—but then he faltered at the bridge, and he butchered the second verse.

Dum dum dum of a white Christmas.

The Christmas snowflakes all look...white...

Tessa couldn't help but giggle as his expression gave way to a self-deprecating smile. What was going through his head, she wondered. Had he panicked on the inside? Or was that crooked grin of his for real?

She longed to ask Taylor for his take on the whole thing. He usually had a pet theory for everything Eric Thorn did. Pure fiction of course, but Tessa couldn't deny that she found his ideas entertaining. Just look at the story he'd concocted about "Aloe Vera." Tessa chuckled again at the thought. As if that song could be about anything other than a hot and heavy one-night stand.

Where was Taylor, anyway? He'd gone silent for the past five minutes. She hit Pause on the TV and returned her full attention to her phone. She felt the urge to message him again, but she resisted.

Her thoughts revolved around Taylor more and more these days. Even in her sessions with Dr. Regan, Tessa couldn't seem to keep him out of her head. She and Taylor chatted every night, and their conversations lately had begun to cross the line from friendship to outright flirtation. She knew her feelings for him had deepened, and she found it vaguely unsettling. As

much as she liked Taylor, and as much as she got the feeling
that he might like her back, Tessa couldn't shake the lingering sense that he was holding something back—some secret he
didn't quite have the nerve to tell her.

Tessa twisted a strand of hair around her finger as she contemplated her phone. Maybe she should cut the conversation
short tonight. Wish him good night and go to sleep. She was
just about to input the message when a notification flashed
onto her screen. Not a new message from Taylor. Her eyes
landed on a different username instead:

Eric Thorn (@EricThorn) followed you

Her finger went slack. The lock of hair fell limply against
her shoulder. A whole lifetime seemed to pass before she could
comprehend the words.

Eric.

Eric Thorn.

Eric Thorn followed…

"Oh my God," she whispered. "OH. MY. GOD!"

CHANGE OF KEY

ERIC PACED HIS living room, eyes glued to his screen as he refreshed his Twitter feed again. "Come on, Tessa." Hadn't she seen the notification yet? What was taking her so long? "Come on! You must have seen it!"

As if in answer to his words, a new message popped up at the top of her recent tweets.

> **Tessa H** @TessaHeartsEric
> OMGGGGGGGGGGGGGGGGGGGGGGGGGGG
> GGGGGGGGGGGGGGGGGGGGGGGGGGG!!!!!!!!!

A broad smile creased his face. "There we go." The standard fangirl response. Only a slight step up from when they tweeted random strings of capital letters. He could just imagine the way she must have been bouncing around her room right then, screaming her head off.

Something about that mental image made Eric pull up short. A new thought had entered his head. Would she DM him something now? The fans usually did after he followed them. Selfies, more often than not. After all these months, would he finally catch a glimpse of Tessa's face?

He sank down heavily on the piano stool in front of the white baby grand, and his fingers picked out a minor chord progression as he waited. He eyed his message tab impatiently, watching for a new DM, but he gave up after a moment.

To hell with it. He couldn't take the suspense. He needed to hear more from her than "*OMGGGGGGGGGGGGGG GGGGGGGGGGGGGGGGGG!!!!!!!*" He switched accounts back to @EricThornSucks and fired off a new message from there.

> **Taylor:** Tessa? Are you there? What
> happened?

Eric tapped a single note in a rapid staccato as he waited for her reply.

> **Tessa H:** ERIC FOLLOWED ME!!!!!
> **Taylor:** Whoa!
> **Tessa H:** OMG OMG OMG OMG OMG
> **Taylor:** Are you freaking out?
> **Tessa H:** OMG MY HANS AR SHAKING
> SPO BAD

Taylor: Deep breaths. Deep breaths. Don't hyperventilate on me now.

Tessa H: I can't stop smiling. OMG, why did he follow me? It doesn't even make any sense!

Taylor: Well, you did wish him a Merry Christmas.

Tessa H: OMGGGGG HE MUST HAVE SEEN IT! HE SAW MY TWEET! ERIC THORN SAW MY TWEET!!!!!!!

Eric laughed out loud. His left hand remained on the piano keys, and he picked out a simple melody, switching to a major key. He couldn't remember the last time he'd felt this way: so happy he couldn't wipe away the goofy grin.

Happy because he'd made her happy.

"Oh, Tessa," he said, chuckling at the phone. "Tessa, Tessa, Tessa. I love you."

The music stopped abruptly as his words hung in the air. Just a figure of speech, of course. He didn't really mean that. Obviously not.

Eric blinked away the thought. He swiveled on the piano stool and brought the DM conversation back around to the topic he had in mind.

Taylor: So? Did you send him a selfie?

Tessa H: Stop. Don't even say it.

Taylor: He probably wants to see a reaction shot.

Tessa H: Ummm, hello? I don't like strangers looking at me. That's one of my triggers.

Taylor: No strangers. Just Eric. No one else would ever see.

Tessa H: NO WAY

Taylor: Trust me, Tessa. He's a guy. He'll like it.

Tessa H: How would you know? You have no idea what I even look like!

Eric bit his lip. "Not for long," he murmured. The corners of his mouth quivered with anticipation. He could sense her resolve starting to crumble. She just needed one more little push...

Taylor: Maybe not exactly, but I know you're beautiful.

Tessa H: You don't know that.

Taylor: Yes I do. Maybe YOU don't know that.

Tessa H: I don't know I'm beautiful?

Taylor: Maybe.

Tessa H: OK, Taylor. And let me guess... That's what makes me beautiful?

Eric paused. He smacked himself lightly on the forehead when he realized what he'd done.

> **Taylor:** Shit. I just plagiarized a song, didn't
> I?
> **Tessa H:** Don't tell me you're a One
> Direction fanboy now?
> **Taylor:** Hey, that was a brilliant song.
> Teenage girls love to hear how they're all
> secretly beautiful :P

Eric's mouth twisted, his giddy smile transforming into a smirk. He knew why his mind had gone to that song, of course. He'd been listening to it the other day. He had a new single in the works along the same lines. "Snowflakes" was slated for release in time for the holidays—a surprise Christmas gift to all his lovely fans.

> *I watch the snowflakes falling,*
> *Too many for me to see,*
> *But I know each one is beautiful,*
> *Special and unique.*

Eric turned back to the piano and played the chorus. He had a hunch that it would be a hit. Maybe not a smash of the same magnitude as "What Makes You Beautiful," but somewhere in the ballpark. The thirteen-to-eighteen demo would go wild for it, assuming they understood the meta-phor: the snowflakes were the fans. And assuming he could convince his record label not to mess around too much with the lyrics. Apparently, they were threatening to bring in an outside songwriter. Maury had broken the news to him this evening after the show.

"Don't take it personally, kid. They just think some of the lyrics come across a little insincere."

Eric frowned, remembering. Insincere? What did the label expect? If he ever wrote a song about how he really saw his fans, they'd ban it in every country for explicit language.

"So go rewrite it yourself," Maury had said to him. "Maybe write a song about your mystery girl on the other end of all the text messages."

"Maury, I told you—"

"Write them a love song about something real, Eric. That's all they're asking."

Eric had been livid at the time, but maybe it wasn't the worst advice after all. The faintest spark of an idea had just popped into his head…

He'd called the song "Snowflakes," but maybe that was the problem. Maybe it should be "Snowflake." Singular. Not a song about all his fans. Just one. A song about feeling cold and alone, and finding that one perfect snowflake in the middle of a raging blizzard.

A love song?

Was it possible?

Eric shook his head, uncertain. How could it be love? Real love? And more importantly, if it was real love, then what on earth was he going to do about it?

He knew Tessa was still waiting for his answer on the other end of the line.

> **Tessa H:** Taylor, do you know how many selfies Eric Thorn must get? He wouldn't even notice it.

Eric's shoulders slumped. For now, he changed his tune. Maybe he didn't want to see her picture after all. Not yet. He suddenly realized where that might lead, and the thought of it made him tremble. If he fell for Tessa, he knew he couldn't hide behind a fake profile any longer. Not if he wanted it to go anywhere. He would have to tell her the truth. And that meant showing her his own face in return.

> **Taylor:** Nah, you're right. Too many fans. Too many faces for him to see just one.
> **Tessa H:** He probably didn't even follow me himself. I bet some publicist was using his account just now, and her finger slipped.

But Eric knew the truth. He'd already noticed her in the crowd. Now he couldn't look away. He hadn't even meant to talk to her tonight, and yet somehow there he was.

He stood up from the piano and padded toward the bedroom, typing out another message as he went.

Taylor: You're right. Probably wasn't even him. Because if Eric ever noticed your existence, Tessa, I think he'd be the one DM'ing you.

THE INTERROGATION
(FRAGMENT 6)

December 31, 2016 9:17 p.m.
Case #: 124.678.21–001
OFFICIAL TRANSCRIPT OF POLICE INTERROGATION

—START PAGE 6—

HART: You have to understand, I never thought it would turn into something real. Something face-to-face. The two of us talked on Twitter, and I figured that was the start and end of it.

INVESTIGATOR: Did you suspect at any time that @EricThornSucks might be someone other than he purported to be?

HART: Of course. I'm not completely naive. I had some concerns. There were a lot of details that seemed sketchy.

INVESTIGATOR: So your suspicions were of a general nature?

HART: Yeah. Just general paranoia. I don't know. I thought it would be like it always is on *Catfish*.

INVESTIGATOR: On the television program, you mean?

HART: Right. Like, it would turn out Taylor was actually a married mother of eight in the witness protection program. Something random like that. Dr. Regan kept encouraging me to move the relationship over to the phone. She wanted me to keep pushing myself for therapy. I was too scared though. Twitter's so nice and anonymous. It felt safer that way.

INVESTIGATOR: Did @EricThornSucks ever suggest communicating more directly?

HART: No, but I was pretty open about my phobias.

INVESTIGATOR: OK, Tessa. Can you walk us through how this plan for the two of you to meet in person first came about?

HART: I can't believe I fell for it.

INVESTIGATOR: Tessa? Do you recall which one of you first suggested meeting in person?

HART: He did. It was all because of the contest.

INVESTIGATOR: Contest?

HART: It was his idea for me to enter. I never thought in a million years that I would win.

INVESTIGATOR: When did this exchange take place? Can you show me on your Twitter account?

HART: Not too long ago. It might have been Christmas Eve… [pause] Here. Here it is.

INVESTIGATOR: Yes, I see. Let the record show that Ms. Hart is indicating a message exchange that took place on December 24. Tessa, was there a message from the other account directly requesting a meeting?

HART: No. I mean, not directly. It was more like…
                 [pause] Here. This. And this one. See?

INVESTIGATOR: I see. That's very helpful. For the record, Ms. Hart
                 is indicating a direct message sent from the Twitter
                 account @EricThornSucks. The time stamp is
                 December 24, 2016 at 2:12 p.m. The message
                 states, and I quote: "I don't know, Tessa. Maybe
                 you just need the proper motivation. Wouldn't
                 you leave your house if Eric Thorn came to your
                 town to play?"

19

SMALL STEPS

December 24, 2016

TESSA STOOD AT her bedroom window. She tilted the blinds half-open, rolling the plastic wand between her fingers. She'd felt more comfortable looking out lately, ever since the fall had come and gone. The cluster of tall sycamore trees had long since lost their leaves. Now, she could see through the empty branches all the way to the road.

See? she told herself. *No one out there.* There was no place in that barren, windswept landscape for some lurking threat to hide. It was all in her head. Pure paranoia. So why couldn't she rid herself of this irrational sense of dread?

Hot tears pricked her eyes, and Tessa quickly blinked them away. She shouldn't dwell on her shortcomings. Better to celebrate her progress and strive to keep moving forward. She should probably work on her thought journal. She had a lot to chew over since her last session with Dr. Regan. Her therapist had zeroed in on the one topic that occupied most of Tessa's waking thoughts these days—even more than Eric Thorn.

Taylor.

"I hear you saying that you care about him, Tessa. Can you tell me more about that?"

Tessa had lost her cool for a moment at the question—the sheer repetitiveness. Her laughter had sounded a bit unhinged, even to her own ears.

"Did I say something to amuse you?"

"I know what you're trying to ask. You want to know if I have feelings for him, right?"

Dr. Regan's answer had surprised her. "No, Tessa. We both know you have feelings for Taylor. The question is how deep those feelings go."

"You mean, am I in love with him?"

Dr. Regan had merely cocked her head, waiting for Tessa to answer for herself.

"I don't know," Tessa had whispered. "Love? That's a scary word."

But it was more than just the word that frightened her. When it came to Taylor, no matter how close they became, she could never quite shake the thought that he was hiding something.

Was it all in her head?

Tessa sprawled across her bed, reaching for her phone. Forget the journal. She needed to go back over their last conversation and search for clues.

Time Stamp 12/22/2016, 1:49 a.m.

Tessa H: I can trust you, right?

Taylor: Sure. What's not to trust?

Tessa H: Maybe I've just seen Catfish too many times...You're not catfishing me, are you?

Taylor: Ummm, I don't think so. Define catfishing.

Tessa H: Don't you ever watch MTV?

Taylor: It's been a while...

Tessa H: Pretty much the same plot twist every time. Are you secretly a girl?

Taylor: You can't seriously think I'm a girl, Tessa. Not after all the shit you gave me when you found out I WASN'T a girl!

Tessa chewed on her thumbnail as she reread it. She assumed he found it funny, but it was so hard to read someone's tone over text. Was he laughing at her total lack of logic? Or was he annoyed by the cross-examination?

He had to know it was just the phobia talking. That was the definition of phobia after all—not just a fear, but an *irrational* fear. Her suspicions about Taylor made no more sense than this lingering sensation that she was being watched.

Did he understand that, or was she slowly driving him away? That conversation had taken place two days ago, and he hadn't come online again since. He said he had some big work project going on, but Tessa wasn't sure she bought it. Family obligations, maybe. But work? On Christmas Eve?

Tessa frowned. Maybe it was true. Some people had to work today. Tessa's own mother always took extra holiday shifts to rack up the overtime pay. Her mother would stay at the hospital overnight tonight and then spend Christmas Day catching up on sleep. Same schedule next week for New Year's Eve.

But Taylor's job didn't seem like the kind that involved extra shifts and overtime. Maybe it was just a flimsy excuse. When it came right down to it, could she believe anything Taylor told her? Or was their entire relationship built on half truths and outright lies?

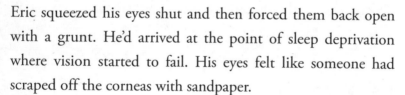

Eric squeezed his eyes shut and then forced them back open with a grunt. He'd arrived at the point of sleep deprivation where vision started to fail. His eyes felt like someone had scraped off the corneas with sandpaper.

He'd just returned home after a marathon recording session. The producer had called it a wrap an hour ago, and not a moment too soon. His label was planning to leak the new single tomorrow morning—a surprise Christmas present to the fans. He'd spent all night in the studio to get the final version perfect. Now, at least the crew would get to spend the holiday with their families.

No such luck for Eric. His latest tour kicked off on December 27, and he still had new song arrangements to rehearse. He didn't have time for holidays. He supposed he'd call home tomorrow morning, and then he'd try to meet up with his parents at some point on the road.

The thought might have upset him if he hadn't felt so tired. At the moment, he counted himself lucky to have a few hours for a nap. He made his way to the large picture window with its panoramic view over the Hollywood Hills and the downtown LA skyline in the distance. He yanked the heavy curtains closed to block out the midafternoon sunlight.

In spite of his fatigue, Eric couldn't help but feel a glow of satisfaction with the new track. He knew a hit when he heard one. That song was sure to smash. He'd rewritten most of the lyrics and played around with the arrangement. In the end, he'd changed the title from "Snowflakes" to "Snowflake," and he'd gotten rid of the former chorus, full of fake flattery and barely concealed contempt.

Maybe he owed the stuffed suits at the record label a thank-you. As much as Eric hated to admit it, they'd forced him to look at the song with fresh eyes. They'd led him to see the truth that had been staring him in the face.

The truth. The reason he'd felt so lost in those dark days after Tessa blocked him. The reason he kept tweeting at her, over and over, begging her to follow him back. And the reason he'd scraped together every spare moment in the months since and spent all of it talking to @TessaHeartsEric.

Because Tessa was the special one. Not the rest of them. Just her.

The rewrite was a piece of cake after that. He'd handed off a brand-new version to Maury the very next day.

> *I watched the snowflakes falling.*
> *Too many for me to see.*
> *Each one just like the others,*
> *Not special or unique.*
>
> *Then I opened up my window.*
> *One snowflake fell inside.*
> *I saw that it was beautiful.*
> *It melted and I cried.*
>
> *Just one snowflake.*
> *Come on and melt with me.*
> *Perfect snowflake,*
> *My love will set you free.*
>
> *Just one snowflake.*
> *You thought that no one cared.*
> *Perfect snowflake,*
> *I'll catch you. Don't be scared…*

Eric couldn't deny his feelings any longer. Even now, exhausted, with a warm bed beckoning, he felt the overwhelming urge to message her. They hadn't chatted at all last night.

He'd been too busy working. He couldn't give in to sleep until he at least wished her a Merry Christmas.

There was only one little problem remaining—one lingering issue that he could no longer push to the back of his mind. He'd kept a secret from her all this time. Not a bad secret, but he knew he had to come clean. Their relationship could never move forward until she knew the truth.

But Eric had a plan to handle that.

He'd pitched the idea himself, and the marketing gurus at the record label were more than happy to comply. They always ran Twitter contests around the holidays: Retweet to win free tickets… Retweet for an autographed poster… This time, he merely upped the ante: "Retweet for a chance to win a private show on New Year's Eve."

They'd set the deadline to enter for today, and the retweet count already stood at half a million. Eric felt a tingle of antic-ipation as he opened Twitter and pulled up Tessa's profile—but his face fell at what he saw.

She still hadn't retweeted it? What was she waiting for? She usually retweeted everything from @EricThorn as a matter of course, but not this one. She was going to need a little more encouragement.

Eric stripped off his jeans and slipped into bed, as he com-posed a new DM to Tessa.

Taylor: You there?

Tessa H: Of course. Are you still working?

Taylor: No, just got home. Had to pull an all-nighter. About to catch a nap now.

Tessa H: Poor baby. You should sleep.

Taylor: I'm lying in bed with my phone tucked under the covers with me... pretending something else is tucked under the covers with me...

Tessa H: Are you getting impatient?

Taylor: Not impatient. Lonely, maybe. It might be nice to spend Christmas with someone special for a change.

Tessa H: Someone special?

Taylor: Tessa, I want to see your face. I want to hear your voice...

Tessa H: Don't.

Taylor: And smell your hair...

Tessa H: Taylor, don't.

Taylor: And touch your skin...

Tessa H: Stop it.

Taylor: It's the truth.

Tessa H: I want those things too, but it's scary for me. Everything is scary for me.

Taylor: If you feel scared, then I want to wrap you in my arms and hold you tight until you feel safe again. I want all of that.

Tessa H: Please stop. I'm not ready. I don't want to lose you, but I'm not ready.

Eric let out his breath with a long sigh. That was the problem, wasn't it? Time. He didn't have time. He'd already let this charade drag on for months. Each day that passed without telling her only compounded the lie further.

He had to come clean.

He had to do it in person.

He had to do it soon.

And that meant he had to speed up the time line just a little. As much as he hated pressuring her, he saw no other choice.

> **Taylor:** OK, let's make a deal.
>
> **Tessa H:** What kind of deal?
>
> **Taylor:** You enter the New Year's Eve contest that Eric Thorn is running. If you win, you tell me where and when, and I'll come meet you at the show. In person.
>
> **Tessa H:** I just told you I'm not ready. Why would some Twitter contest change anything?
>
> **Taylor:** I don't know, Tessa. Maybe you just need the proper motivation. Wouldn't you leave your house if Eric Thorn came to your town to play?
>
> **Tessa H:** Taylor, have you seen how many retweets that thing has? The odds are a zillion to one.
>
> **Taylor:** Exactly! Small steps. Teeny, tiny, little steps.

Tessa H: And if I agree to this right now, do you promise to drop the subject?

Taylor: Yes. Consider it dropped.

Eric couldn't help but smile as he added one last message.

Taylor: That is, unless you win...

THE INTERROGATION (FRAGMENT 7)

December 31, 2016, 8:42 p.m.

Case #: 124.678.21–001

OFFICIAL TRANSCRIPTION OF POLICE INTERVIEW

—START PAGE 8—

INVESTIGATOR: How long have you been in Texas, Mr. Thorn?

THORN: Just today. I came in for the show.

INVESTIGATOR: You were scheduled to perform a private concert here in Midland, Texas, as the grand prize of a contest. Is that correct?

THORN: Well, basically. Except that the contest was a crock of shit. You know that, right?

INVESTIGATOR: By all means, enlighten us.

THORN: My label's always up my ass to do social media. I agreed to do it as long as they let me pick the winner myself this time.

INVESTIGATOR: So you set up a spurious contest as a ruse to meet Tessa Hart?

THORN: Come on, man. A ruse? It was supposed to be a grand romantic gesture.

INVESTIGATOR: And was Tessa aware of this romantic gesture?

THORN:	Not exactly. She thought she won a private New Year's Eve concert for herself and her fifty closest friends. But of course she doesn't have fifty friends. Or if she did, she wouldn't want them all in a room with her. So she just invited two.
INVESTIGATOR:	Two?
THORN:	Her therapist and Taylor.
INVESTIGATOR:	Wait a minute. Are you saying now that there is an actual person named Taylor? The person running the @EricThornSucks Twitter account was not, in fact, you?
THORN:	No, no, no. It was me. Seriously, it's not that complicated. You can't follow this?
INVESTIGATOR:	You'll have to excuse me. It can get a little murky when people start referring to their own multiple aliases in the third person.
THORN:	You really don't like me very much, do you?
INVESTIGATOR:	Let me ask you this, Eric. Now, this might sound like a silly question, but I have to ask. Why all the subterfuge? Why didn't you simply tell Tessa that the person she'd been talking to was you?
THORN:	I was going to. That's why I staged this whole thing. I wanted to tell her in person.
INVESTIGATOR:	Why?

THORN:	It's complicated. You don't understand what it's like to be famous.
INVESTIGATOR:	Go ahead. Help me understand.
THORN:	It's terrifying, OK? It's scary as shit. It means looking over your shoulder everywhere you go, every step you take, forever. For the rest of my life, probably. It means every single person I meet, online or off-line, I have to look at them and wonder if they're some kind of stalker who's going to murder me in my sleep.
INVESTIGATOR:	Murder you?
THORN:	See, that sounds kind of paranoid, right? And I know that, rationally. I know my fans aren't out to get me. I know people with mental illnesses are no more prone to violence than anyone else... But I also know the danger isn't completely in my head. There's an actual psychological syndrome. It has a name and everything: erotomanic celebrity worship syndrome. Celebrity stalkers who genuinely believe their victims are in love with them. They used it at Dorian's murder trial. Some expert witness diagnosed her.
INVESTIGATOR:	You lost me again. Who are we talking about right now? A fan who accosted you?
THORN:	No, no. I'm talking about the fangirl who killed Dorian Cromwell. Did you follow the trial coverage at all? She was totally delusional. He followed her on Twitter, and she somehow talked herself into believing that Dorian was her boyfriend. Like

they were in a secret relationship that no one else knew about. She truly believed it. She thought he loved her. And when it became clear that it wasn't true, she couldn't handle it, and she hunted him down and killed him.

INVESTIGATOR: I'm sorry, Eric. How exactly does this relate to the crime we're investigating here?

THORN: You wanted to know why I didn't just tell Tessa who I was from the beginning. But I couldn't. I have to be incredibly careful about giving my fans any kind of personal attention.

INVESTIGATOR: You considered her a threat to your personal safety?

THORN: Not Tessa specifically. All my fans in general.

INVESTIGATOR: But now you no longer consider Tessa a threat?

THORN: No, not at all. Now I actually am in a secret relationship with her. That's why I came here to meet her.

INVESTIGATOR: And you never revealed your identity to her over Twitter because…

THORN: Because I've been lying to her for months, and I thought it would be better to come clean in person.

INVESTIGATOR: Hence the contest.

THORN: Exactly. And it would have worked just fine…if not for Blair.

DETOUR

December 31, 2016

"EXCUSE ME. I don't mean to interrupt."

Blair made no response. An infinitesimal rise and fall of one shoulder served as the only indication that another voice had spoken. The tall, lanky figure, dressed in jeans and a dark-gray sweatshirt, merely slumped down further in the seat of the Greyhound bus.

The middle-aged woman standing in the aisle cleared her throat again. "Is the window seat taken?"

Blair glanced up, eyes darting around the bus's dim interior. The seats were filling in. They must have picked up twenty new passengers at the bus depot in Dallas. So much for privacy. No choice but to move the bulky canvas duffel bag that currently occupied the next seat.

"It's all yours," Blair grumbled, as the woman shuffled past and sank down heavily.

"Thank you kindly," she replied. "I do appreciate it. I'm Delilah, by the way. How far are you headed?"

A chatterbox, Blair thought. *Perfect. Just perfect.* Every other seat had been occupied by the usual crew of bus riders—silent types, safeguarding their anonymity behind drawn-down baseball caps and hooded sweatshirts—but this lady had to be a chatterbox.

Blair ignored the woman's question and inserted a pair of beaten-up earphones instead. Just a prop, of course. They didn't work. Cheap drugstore earbuds, doomed from the start. The left ear blew out somewhere around Baton Rouge, and the right ear died an untimely death a few hours later, just outside Houston. But that didn't matter. The earphones served their purpose well enough—universal sign language for "I don't want to talk."

"Suit yourself," the woman muttered.

Blair ignored her, flicking on a phone instead. Twitter had signed itself back out again. It kept doing that, ever since the latest software update—a new glitch in the system that wouldn't allow two different phones to remain signed in to the same account.

Some misguided attempt at cybersecurity, no doubt. A minor nuisance. Nothing more. Blair found it easy enough to sign back in to Twitter every time.

Username: @EricThornSucks
Password: **password**

Who used "password," anyway? No one. That's who. No one

who actually *wanted* privacy. This couldn't even be considered hacking, really. That password wasn't a password at all. It was a red carpet, rolled out. An invitation.

Blair directed a fleeting glance at the woman in the window seat. She'd leaned back and closed her eyes.

Good, Blair thought, bending forward over the phone. No time for idle chitchat. Not tonight. Not when there were Twitter feeds to check. Private messages to read.

And reread.

And reread.

And reread…

Time Stamp 12/29/16, 9:03 a.m.

Tessa H: I can't believe this is happening.

Taylor: I know. I'm so psyched. I'm all packed and ready to go. Just tell me where and when.

Tessa H: I don't know… I'm not even sure I'm going.

Taylor: Tessa, you have to! It's Eric Thorn. You've never seen him live before. When are you going to get a better chance than this?

Tessa H: Just give me a sec. I need to do my deep breathing.

Taylor: What does your therapist say?

Tessa H: She thinks I should go. Make it like a New Year's resolution.

Taylor: Exactly! Tessa, you can do this.

Tessa H: I just have this horrible feeling.
Promise me nothing bad is going to
happen.

Taylor: Nothing bad. Only good. Very, very
good.

Tessa H: You promise?

Taylor: I promise. Now promise me you'll
come.

Tessa H: OK, OK. It's a club in Midland,
Texas. The Trail Dust Honky-Tonk Saloon.
Meet me there on New Year's Eve at exactly
6:00 p.m.

Those messages had passed back and forth two days ago, and already Blair had read the exchange a hundred times. It always felt the same. The same ripple of elation bubbling up—the high that came back stronger every time, with every glimpse inside.

The giddiness would only last for a moment. It would be replaced again soon by the feeling that came next. Irritation, to begin with, imagining the words on the screen spoken aloud. Something about that fantasy never failed to set Blair's teeth on edge.

Blair used to think it was the sound of the voice itself. Too high. Jarring. Juvenile. There was something slightly off in the pitch or cadence, some indefinable flaw that had never quite done justice to the perfect bone structure of the face. Such a shame, really. Some people were better as a silent image, caught on film—seen and not heard. A physical specimen, perfectly preserved, without all those inconvenient words to mar the visual.

It wasn't just the sound of the voice though. Blair understood that now. These DM conversations made it clear. It was something in the words themselves and the thoughts they represented. Ever since Blair began following their correspondence, the feelings went far beyond mere irritation. Something deeper, darker. An undying anger. A fury at them both.

But mostly at the interloper.

The obstacle.

The one who needed to be removed. Erased. Blotted out, like a bad dream.

The one who didn't deserve to be in the picture in the first place.

Soon, Blair thought, with eyes slowly drifting closed. *It would happen. Soon enough.*

21

PRIVATE PARTY

ERIC STOOD OUTSIDE the Trail Dust Honky-Tonk Saloon beneath the emblazoned marquee:

Happy New Year's!

Closed for Private Party

Of course, the sign didn't say just how private the party would be. Eric couldn't help but chuckle to himself at the absurdity. Even before he got his record deal, he'd never played a live show for an audience quite this small. He'd be flying solo tonight without his usual crew. No backup singers. No hip-hop dancers. No elaborate concert pyrotechnics. Just a single pair of eyes staring back at him as he took the stage alone, with her therapist lurking somewhere in the shadows.

Eric rubbed his dampened palms against his jeans. It must be almost six by now. She should be pulling up any moment.

Maury had really outdone himself with the choice of venue tonight. Admittedly, it couldn't have been easy to find an empty club on New Year's Eve, but still… Was this really the best that Midland, Texas, had to offer? A dilapidated roadside club on an abandoned stretch of highway, miles from anything that could even pass for a downtown? Eric had seen a grand total of one big-rig truck pass by in the entire time he'd been standing out there. Otherwise, no sign of another living soul as far as the eye could see. Was that an actual tumbleweed rolling around in the parking lot?

He wrapped his arms around himself, wishing he'd worn something warmer than a thin leather motorcycle jacket. He'd expected mild weather. The temperatures had hovered in the midsixties since he rolled into Texas this morning, but he could feel a change in the air tonight. Must have been some late-December cold front blowing in. He could see the dark storm clouds gathering overhead.

Maybe it was a good thing that Maury had chosen this dump. Eric should consider it a stroke of luck. He usually had to contend with gate-crashers when he gave a private show. Somehow, the location always leaked, and the local fans showed up in droves. But not out here in the middle of Nowhereville.

Everything was going according to plan, Eric reassured himself. It was just a matter of a few more moments before the car would pull into the parking lot. The door would pop open… and he would finally catch a glimpse of the face he'd been waiting to see for months.

So why did he feel this urge to run away and hide?

It must have been the silence out there, playing on his nerves.

It was getting downright eerie now that night was falling. Tessa should have been there by now. Something must have happened to delay her. Eric stuffed his hands into his pockets, straining to see down the empty span of highway that stretched out in both directions. He heard the faint rumble of an engine in the distance. He held his breath as he listened to the sound approach.

The vehicle came into view, and Eric scuffed the bottom of his shoe against the pavement. Not Tessa. Just a rundown-looking Greyhound bus, speeding down the highway in a cloud of dust…

Eric reached for his phone. Had he misunderstood the plan somehow? He pulled up Twitter and ran his eyes once again over the DMs from this morning.

> **Time Stamp 12/31/2016, 9:23 a.m.**
> **Taylor:** We're still on for tonight, right?
> **Tessa H:** I'll be there. I'm starting to get excited now.
> **Taylor:** Awesome. Excited to meet Eric?
> **Tessa H:** More scared to meet Eric. Excited to meet you. Or maybe the other way around? I honestly don't even know. This whole thing is surreal.
> **Taylor:** Don't be scared. It'll be OK.
> **Tessa H:** You don't think it'll be crowded, do you?
> **Taylor:** What are you talking about? It's a

private show. Just you and me, and some douchebag up onstage, serenading us for our first dance.

Tessa H: But what if other fans find out and try to crash? It could be a total mob scene.

Taylor: Tessa, stop. You're catastrophizing.

Tessa H: I know, but should we have some kind of signal so I can recognize you? Just in case?

Taylor: Whatever makes you feel safe. You want me to wear some hot-pink bunny slippers?

Tessa H: Perfect :P

Taylor: If only I knew someone who could lend me a pair…

Tessa H: I know. How about a hot-pink rabbit's foot?

Taylor: Where am I supposed to get one of those?

Tessa H: They sell them at the service station. Exit 54. It's just a couple miles down the road. Will you do that?

Taylor: Of course. Rabbit's foot. Good idea. I'm gonna need all the luck I can get.

He'd dutifully picked up the rabbit's foot on his way into town that afternoon. The pit stop had raised a few eyebrows, although not for the usual reasons. The men loitering around the service station barely gave him a second look once they caught sight of his car. The baby-blue Ferrari stuck out like a sore thumb among all the tractors and rusty pickup trucks. The mechanic behind the counter even had the nerve to offer him $50,000 cash, right there on the spot, to take the car off his hands. Eric couldn't quite tell if the guy was kidding.

"Nice try," Eric had laughed back nervously. He didn't bother to say it, but they both knew his car was worth four or five times that much. The guy had merely shrugged in response and taken Eric's $3.99 for the rabbit's foot without another word.

Eric glanced down at the piece of pink fluff that dangled on a chain around his neck. The pop of neon color stood out starkly against the black leather of his jacket. How exactly would Tessa react when she laid eyes on it?

He had his opening line all planned out, complete with choreography. Maybe it would come across a little cheesy, but he didn't want to wing it. This particular meet-and-greet was way too important to leave to chance. He rehearsed it one more time inside his head. He knew exactly what he would do. The moment she stepped out of the car, he'd saunter over and hold out the good luck charm for her to see.

"I'm looking for a girl named Tessa who's really into rabbits' feet," he'd say. And then, before she could breathe a single word, he'd hit her with his most handsome, charming, lady-killer smile.

"Guess what," he'd say. "I'm Eric *Taylor* Thorn. And today's your lucky day."

"Showtime."

Tessa murmured the word aloud as her hand came to rest on the bedroom doorknob.

She couldn't procrastinate any longer. Dr. Regan would arrive in a few minutes to pick her up, and Tessa intended to be ready. Nothing would stop her. No triggers. No flashbacks. No panic episodes. She wouldn't bail out at the last minute. Not this time.

This was it. December 31. New Year's Eve. The final day of what had to be the worst year of her life. Tonight she would shut the door on all the irrational fears that had held her prisoner for so long. She would leave her home and make the twenty-minute journey to the concert venue—even if it killed her.

Tessa gritted her teeth as she pulled the bedroom door open and made her way to the bathroom in the hall.

Eric one…Eric two…Eric three…

She'd kept her mind clear for most of the day by focusing on the superficial details. What shoes would she bring out of storage? Which purse would she carry? What clothes would she wear? She must have tried on every single item in her closet before she finally settled on the perfect outfit: dark-washed skinny jeans, paired with a sparkly V-neck top that skimmed her hips and revealed a hint of cleavage.

She took in her appearance in the bathroom mirror. Too much skin? She didn't want to look like she was trying too hard, but she didn't want to hide her assets either. Tonight, Taylor would lay eyes on her for the first time. She wanted him to like what he saw.

Tessa stared at her reflection, forcing a too-bright smile on her face. Happy. Excited. That's how a normal person would be feeling. The boy she loved had come all the way to Texas just to meet her. Her heart should have been thudding with anticipation, not with fear.

Eric Thorn…Eric four…Eric five…

Forget the outfit, Tessa told herself. She was running out of time. The clock was ticking, and she still hadn't done her hair and makeup. Her wavy, brown hair had grown out during the months of her self-imposed confinement. She normally kept it tied back in a braid, but she'd left it down tonight, a shimmery cascade that fell below her shoulders. Hopefully, Taylor wouldn't notice the split ends.

Eric six…Eric sucks…Eric seven…

Then there was the question of makeup. She hadn't worn a drop since the day she fled from New Orleans. Her old beauty supplies never made the trip back home, long since abandoned in her temporary dorm room. She would have to ransack her mother's makeup stash. Tessa knelt down and sifted through the contents of the cabinet beneath the sink. Her eyes landed on a black leather satchel, and she quickly snapped it open, but it didn't contain cosmetics. Looked like a spare set of medical supplies that her mother had brought home from work: needles, rubber tubing, antiseptic wipes…

Tessa pinched her lips together. Maybe she should have asked before her mother left for work. But that would have meant explaining *why* she needed makeup.

Tessa hadn't breathed a word to her mom about the contest or the boy she was leaving the house to meet. Some guy she met on Twitter? A total stranger? She knew her mother would disapprove. It came as a stroke of luck, really, that Tessa had won a show on New Year's Eve. Her mom was working another double shift. She'd left for the hospital a couple hours ago, and she wouldn't be back until morning. Tessa would be home by then, safely tucked in bed, and her mother never had to know she'd left.

But first Tessa needed makeup. Her hands shook slightly as she pawed through the mess below the sink.

Eric eight…Eric nine…Eric ten…

Nervous jitters, she told herself, as she released the knot of tension with her breath. Anyone would feel some nerves on a night as big as tonight.

She still couldn't quite believe that it was happening. It didn't feel real—this whole scenario with the Twitter contest. More like the plot of some fanfic she might have written. What were the odds? A private Eric Thorn show, here in Midland, twenty minutes from her home. Things like that didn't happen by chance. It had to be a sign. The universe was trying to tell her something. This meeting with Taylor was meant to be—the miracle she needed to get her life back on track.

"Aha!" She let out a cry of triumph as she pulled open a plastic grocery bag full of cheap cosmetics. She didn't have time for anything elaborate, but she didn't need too much. The complexion of her heart-shaped face was naturally smooth and unblemished, if a bit pale from lack of sunlight. Tessa mostly wanted to play up her hazel eyes, large and almond shaped, ringed with thick lashes. Mascara was a must. Maybe a smudge of eyeliner?

Now for the lips.

Tessa sifted through the crusty, old lipstick tubes, wrinkling her nose. She held up a dark red shade in front of her mouth, but she set it back down again unused. Too easy to smear. It was New Year's Eve, and Tessa knew what that meant. Just the thought of it made her stomach do a flip-flop. Where would she be at midnight? Dancing in Taylor's arms? And at the stroke of twelve, perhaps their lips would meet…

Her mouth curved in a secret smile, and this time it wasn't forced. No lipstick, she decided. Just a coating of clear gloss. She probably didn't need any blusher either, from the looks of the bright-pink color flooding her cheeks.

She slicked the gloss across her lips and puckered at her reflection.

Ready.

Tessa turned briskly toward the stairs. Her ride would be there any minute. No time to dwell on any lingering anxieties. She began the long journey down the corridor, even as the nervous fluttering in her belly gave way to something darker.

"Eric. Eric Thorn," she whispered like a chant as she took a slow step forward. "See," she told herself. "It's all in your head."

But it didn't feel like her imagination. More like a physical sensation—an external force that grew more powerful by the second. Like she had a rubber band tied around her waist, growing tauter with every step she took. Soon the tension would become unbearable. The elastic would snap. And then what? Then she'd find herself flung back to the starting place, back inside her bedroom door.

Tessa lowered her head and plowed on. She had to keep going this time. Even if she fainted. Even if she had to roll herself down the stairs. Tonight was too important. She couldn't give in to her phobias yet again. She *wouldn't*.

She'd made it halfway down the stairs before she pulled up short. Tessa patted at the pocket of her jeans and realized it was empty. Her phone. She couldn't leave without that. What if Taylor tried to message her? She had to go back for it and do the whole trip downstairs all over again. With a small cry of frustration, Tessa bounded back upstairs and grabbed the phone from where she'd left it by the sink. She was just about to slip it in her pocket when a notification lit the screen.

Her heart skipped a beat.

Taylor? Had he run into some delay? Was he backing out? Her stomach dropped, weighted down by an emotion she couldn't quite name: disappointment mingled with relief.

But the message wasn't even from Taylor. Instead, Tessa found herself staring at a DM from an account that she hadn't interacted with in months.

MET: Hey, ur gonna send me pics from the
show, right?

A wave of vertigo washed over her, and Tessa gripped the
bathroom door to keep from falling. The show? The Eric
Thorn show? What other show could MET possibly mean?

Tessa H: Huh?
MET: Private show in Midland!

MET knew she'd won the contest? She knew where Tessa
lived? But how? Another new DM popped onto the screen.

MET: Are you gonna send me pics, or do I
have to get them myself?
Tessa H: I have no idea what you're talking
about.
MET: Tessa, I know EVERYTHING ABOUT
EVERYTHING in this fandom. Haven't you
figured that out by now?

Tessa thrust the phone into her pocket. Black spots danced
before her eyes as she made her halting way to the bottom of the
stairs. Her stomach rolled, and she pressed a clammy hand across
her mouth. She'd spent the whole last week clinging to the idea
that the concert would be private. No one else would be there,
aside from the short list of people that mattered in her life:

Taylor.

Dr. Regan.

Eric Thorn.

No one else was supposed to know about it. Not even her mom. So how did MET know? How many other people had she told? What if Tessa found a whole mob of rabid fans lined up outside the club? What if security let them in, and Tessa ended up in some overcrowded room, packed shoulder to shoulder?

Strangers jostling…hands groping…cameras flashing…

"No!"

She couldn't let that happen. She sent back another frantic DM.

> **Tessa H:** No pictures. Guest list closed.
> Security SUPER tight. Don't waste your
> time.

It was unreal to think how her feelings about MET had changed in a few short months. She'd felt downright honored when Eric's most popular superfan first followed her account. Now Tessa wished the other girl had never noticed her. There was a line somewhere between fangirling and stalking, and MET had crossed it long ago.

But Tessa couldn't let some stranger spoil this experience. She had to put it out of her mind. Relax. Focus on her breathing, in and out, just the way Dr. Regan had taught her…

Tessa heard the crunch of tires on the gravel road outside. She opened the front door and saw Dr. Regan's silver SUV rolling up the driveway.

Time to go.

With one last deep breath for courage, Tessa stepped over the threshold and pulled the door closed in her wake.

Blair shuffled down the edge of the empty highway, staggering under the weight of the duffel bag. So much for traveling light. The damned thing must have weighed thirty pounds. How much farther was it?

Blair had asked to pull over in front of the club just now, but the surly Greyhound driver had refused. They'd finally rolled to a stop at an abandoned bus shelter, a quarter mile farther down the road. Now Blair needed to hustle if the plan was going to work. No time to stop and redistribute the bag's unwieldy contents.

Why was it so heavy? Blair had only meant to pack a few supplies: a camera, a telephoto lens, a flashbulb… Somehow it had multiplied. One camera turned into three or four, but it couldn't be helped. Every item was essential. The chance had come at long last—a second chance that most people never got. Blair couldn't risk botching it again.

Not like the last time.

Blair couldn't quite suppress the momentary flare of irritation at the thought. The memory still rankled—walking away with nothing but the photos to show for it. So many photos, and not one of them had been right. One image slightly out of focus. Another poorly lit. Even the ones that achieved technical perfection hadn't proven satisfying. Something was missing from all of them: some essence of that inner human fire, so difficult to capture in a single frame.

Blair didn't want to leave it to chance this time. The right equipment could make or break a shot. That meant a few different cameras. A folding tripod. A variety of filters and diffusers. Some rolls of cord and duct tape. And don't forget a good, sharp knife…

The weight of the bag dug into Blair's shoulder, but it would all be worth it. The club had come into view at last. Now all that remained were a few well-timed DMs. Some might say that was a step too far, but Blair couldn't see a way around it. All's fair in love and war, right? None of it would matter in the end. True love would prevail, and a few bumps and scrapes along the way would soon be mended.

The time had come to put all the careful planning into action. Blair broke into a gleeful smile at the thought. Tonight would mean redemption. After the months and months of waiting, things would finally be set right. Two lovers would stand face-to-face, just like the day they first met. Only this time, the eyes looking back wouldn't be blinded by concert lights. This time, those beautiful eyes would see the truth.

But first, Blair needed to clear the field of any inconvenient distractions. This Twitter infatuation had gone on long enough. How had it even started in the first place? How could someone be so misguided? How could you have your soul mate staring you in the face and look away? Turn to someone else, someone so thoroughly undeserving, who could only cause you heartache in the end?

Blair had been over it a million times in the intervening months, and only one answer made any sense. It was a lot like taking a photo, really. Happened all the time, especially with less experienced photographers. Sometimes the subject looked directly at the flash and wound up blinking in the shot. That must have been what happened. A mistake that only lasted for an instant. Eventually, the eyes reopened and the vision cleared.

Tonight it would all be corrected. Blair would make sure of that.

And the other one? The interloper? A mistimed flashbulb. Nothing more. It was unfortunate, of course, but there wasn't any choice. Tonight that light would have to be extinguished, once and for all.

L-O-V-E

"WAIT. STOP. TURN around. I want to go back home."

Tessa whispered the words, and Dr. Regan darted a glance in her direction from behind the wheel of the car.

"You're doing wonderfully, Tessa. We're almost there now. Remember your breathing."

Tessa nodded. She made an *O* with her lips and sucked the air deep into her lungs. She'd felt relatively relaxed earlier, getting ready, but that disconcerting DM exchange with MET had thrown her into turmoil.

It was no use. All the breathing exercises in the world couldn't quiet the chaos going on inside her head. "It isn't working," she said. Her voice sounded high and tight to her own ears.

"Don't give in to the anxiety," Dr. Regan responded calmly. They reached the highway entrance ramp, and Tessa felt the car's acceleration as her therapist pressed down on the gas. "Think about your other tools."

What else? Tessa cast about in her mind for the other relaxation techniques that Dr. Regan had taught her. Meditation? Biofeedback? Yoga?

"Make a list?" she asked aloud.

Her therapist rewarded her with a nod. "Very good, Tessa. Sometimes, just seeing your worries written out can make them feel less insurmountable."

Tessa didn't have any paper, but at least she had her phone. She opened up her Notes app and started to write.

Worries:

I'm not inside my house

I'm 10 minutes away from my house

I'm going to be 20 minutes away from my house

I'm going to a concert

There's a chance it could be crowded

Eric Thorn is going to see me

I'm going to meet Taylor

Tessa stopped, her finger shaking too badly to continue. Maybe she just needed to concentrate on the last one. That was the heart of it, the thought that made her more anxious than all the others and the reason she knew she had to go.

She was going to meet Taylor.

She couldn't back out. Not now. Not after what he'd said to her last night. Maybe she just needed to remind herself exactly how he phrased it.

Tessa opened Twitter and scrolled backward, searching through the thread:

> **Time Stamp 12/30/16, 11:23 p.m.**
>
> **Tessa H:** Taylor, I'm scared. I'm not sure I can go through with it.
>
> **Taylor:** OK, don't freak out. Just talk to me. Tell me why.
>
> **Tessa H:** Agoraphobla?
>
> **Taylor:** I know, I know. But, Tessa, I still don't know what triggered it.
>
> **Tessa H:** I can't.
>
> **Taylor:** Tessa, what happened to you last summer?
>
> **Tessa H:** I should probably say good night now.
>
> **Taylor:** No, no, wait. Forget I asked. Talk to me about something else. It doesn't have to be that. Just keep talking to me right now.
>
> **Tessa H:** I'm not really in the mood.
>
> **Taylor:** Will you dance with me tomorrow?
>
> **Tessa H:** Maybe. I don't know. Which song?
>
> **Taylor:** You tell me. What songs are you hoping Eric will play?

Tessa couldn't help but smile at his transparent attempt to distract her. It was funny, really. Taylor still didn't fully understand why she'd agreed to meet him tonight. He thought it had to do with Eric Thorn—that the prospect of seeing her idol in person was enough to lure her out of her house. Not that she didn't love Eric. She did, in a way. But she didn't *love* him. She knew the difference between fantasy and reality.

Eric Thorn was just a fantasy. But Taylor... He was real.

Tessa flicked her eyes sideways to take in the passing landscape. It was after nightfall now. The sun had sunk below the bank of thick clouds at the horizon. Dr. Regan clicked on the SUV's headlights to illuminate the road. A sign came into view in front of them: Exit 54.

The last chance to turn around before they came upon their final destination.

It wasn't too late. The wheels were in motion, but Tessa could still bring the whole thing to a screeching halt. She could go back home. Unfollow Taylor. Deactivate the account. She could disappear on him without a trace. That would probably be the safest thing to do.

But could she? Could she really live the rest of her life never even knowing his last name? After everything he'd said to her last night?

She lowered her gaze to her phone and resumed where she'd left off.

> **Tessa H:** As long as he does "Snowflake,"
> I'll be happy.
> **Taylor:** The new single? Do you like it?
> **Tessa H:** Are you kidding? I'm obsessed

with that song. You know he's never used the L-word in a song before.

Taylor: Is that really true?

Tessa H: I just want to see the look on his face when he sings it. That's all.

Taylor: Me too.

Tessa H: You do? I thought he was a douche nozzle. What happened to #EricThornSucks?

Taylor: I want to see the look on your face when you see the look on his face.

Tessa H: I don't know. It might make me sad. If it looks like he's really, truly in love…

Taylor: What? You'd be jealous?

Tessa H: Not jealous exactly. It's more complicated than that. I guess I just wish someone would write a song like that about me.

Taylor: Goddammit, Tessa.

Tessa H: What?

Taylor: Tessa……

Tessa H: What?? Now you're scaring me again.

Taylor: I really want to tell you something right now.

Tessa H: What????? Is there something you're not telling me?

Tessa felt her pulse quicken yet again as she reread it. She remembered the way her breath had caught in her chest last night as the moment dragged on and on. She'd felt so certain that all her fears were justified. He'd been hiding something all along, and he was about to make a confession.

Taylor: One more day. Then you'll understand. You have to trust me, OK?

Tessa H: Please tell me. I can't take the suspense. I really can't. It's killing me.

Taylor: You really want the truth? Right now?

Tessa H: TELL ME

Taylor: OK. Truth... I don't know about Eric Thorn and his cheesy-ass songs, but I do know that I love you.

Taylor: Do you hear me, Tessa?

Taylor: L-O-V-E

Taylor: And I need you to remember that tomorrow. Whatever else happens, just remember I said that, and I meant it. Because it's TRUE.

Taylor: Are you there?

Taylor: OK... I guess I'll just see you tomorrow.

Tessa H: No, wait. I'm here. I'm crying.

Taylor: Don't cry.

Tessa H: I'm crying because I love you
too—

"Tessa? Earth to Tessa?"

Tessa's eyes had grown misty, but her head jerked up at the sound of Dr. Regan's voice.

"Huh? What? Did you say something?"

"What are you up to on that phone of yours?"

"Nothing. I was just—"

"Are you ready for this? We're almost there."

"No. No, stop. Wait."

"What is it?"

"Wait," Tessa said again. "Pull over."

"Tessa, you can do this. Remember your breathing—"

Tessa waved an arm to cut her off and motioned toward the shoulder of the road. Her eyes were glued to the phone again, but not to the same place in the conversation.

A new message had just flashed across her screen, added to the end of the thread.

"Pull over," she said to Dr. Regan. "Something happened. Change of plans. Taylor just DM'ed."

Eric rubbed his palms together briskly. He could feel his fingers growing numb. He cupped his hands around his mouth and blew in a puff of air to warm them.

It must be one hell of a cold front blowing in. The temperature had plummeted by twenty degrees in the ten minutes since the sun sank below the horizon. A stiff wind blew steadily across the parking lot, whipping up the dust.

He longed to return inside the shelter of the club. Maybe someone in there had a warmer coat that he could borrow. Maybe Maury? Eric could hear the faint sound of his manager's voice on the other side of the door, yapping away on his cell phone.

But Eric couldn't quite bring himself to peel his eyes away from the abandoned two-lane highway. Not even for a moment. He didn't want to miss her.

He blew into his hands again and stamped his feet against the cold.

Cold feet.

The words came to his mind unbidden, and he frowned as he stamped again. She should have been here by now. It must be after six.

"Come on, Tessa," he whispered. "Don't back out on me now."

He'd spent all day planning how this meet-and-greet would go, but he hadn't seriously considered that she might not show. Not after the talk they'd had last night.

He hadn't meant to tell her just how much he felt over DM. He wanted to say it in person, standing face-to-face, but he couldn't hold back in the end. He simply didn't have the strength to keep the words inside for a second longer. It must have been the song request that did him in.

As long as he does "Snowflake," I'll be happy.

A thrill coursed through him when she'd said that—a trail of icy heat that prickled from the nape of his neck to the tips of his toes. She had no idea how much it meant to hear her say she liked the song. And not just that she liked it. *I wish someone would write a song like that about me.*

A lopsided grin sprang onto Eric's face as he remembered.

Tessa, I DID write that song about you.

He'd entered those words into his message bar, and then he'd sat there staring at them for a long moment with his finger over the Send button. So tempting to come clean and get it off his chest.

Maybe he should have sent that message after all.

Maybe then she would be here now.

He hadn't gone through with it though. He'd settled for telling her how he felt instead—and that confession had been terrifying enough, until she said the word back to him: *L-O-V-E.*

God, he would have given anything to be with her at that moment. He would have given every single cent he had, and every last breath in his body, and every drop of blood running through his veins just to be there, wherever she was. Just to put his arms around her and cry with her, instead of what they had to settle for: two solitary souls crying in the artificial glimmer of their phones.

She'd talked to him for hours afterward. They both stayed up half the night. He'd finally found the magic words to make her trust him, and then the real breakthrough had happened. The whole story had come pouring out of her. That awful story. It made him want to wrap her in his arms even more and take that ugly memory away so she never had to think of it again. He'd felt so powerless, sitting there in silence, watching as she sent him DM after DM. Every sordid detail of her four weeks in New Orleans.

Now he finally understood. It all made sense. The phobia, and all those triggers that she'd mentioned over the months…

Crowds.

Being followed.

Eyes watching her while she slept.

He realized, at that point, that the concert might not be such a good idea. It might be more than she could handle. He'd brought it up before they both signed off, and the memory of those final messages swam inside his head.

> **Taylor:** Tessa, are you sure you want to do this? We could skip the concert. I could come to your house instead.
>
> **Tessa H:** But you don't know where I live.
>
> **Taylor:** That could be rectified.
>
> **Tessa H:** No.
>
> **Taylor:** Really? After everything you just told me, you still won't trust me with your address?
>
> **Tessa H:** No, no, it isn't that. I just need to do this for myself. It's my New Year's resolution. I need to leave my house.

Taylor: But it doesn't have to happen tomorrow. Small steps, right?
Tessa H: Small steps aren't getting me anywhere. If I can't leave my house for something as big as this, then I don't know that I'll ever get out of here.

She'd seemed so certain—so bound and determined to come. But now here he was, all alone again. Just a pathetic, lonely guy with a girl who said she loved him, but not enough to let him see her face.

With a sigh, Eric turned to go inside. He reached out toward the double doors of the club, but he paused at what he saw reflected in the glass. A sudden flicker of movement.

Was someone out there after all? A fan?

Eric squinted into the darkness, but he couldn't see much from this distance. He could barely make out the silhouette of a human form. Medium height. Skinny. Downright spindly, in fact, with the arms and legs of a spider or a praying mantis. There was something odd about the head. No hair? Eric shielded his eyes with his hand and leaned forward into the wind to get a better look. No neck either, at second glance. Maybe that was a hood. A hoodie sweatshirt… Male or female? Facing toward him or away? Eric couldn't tell. Just a solitary figure, standing still, with one foot in the parking lot and one foot in the shoulder of the road.

There was no way it could be Tessa, right?

No. Definitely not. Tessa wouldn't be standing out there all alone. She was supposed to be with her therapist. And when she did show up, she wouldn't be on foot. She'd told him this morning that she would be riding in Dr. Regan's silver SUV.

So where the hell were they?

The fan started moving, but she still didn't turn to face the club. She made her way over to the far corner of the lot, and then she started walking down the side of the road.

Eric craned his neck to watch her, unsure if he should do something. It couldn't be safe. She'd be nearly invisible to any passing cars, dressed as she was in dark clothing. Did she need some kind of help? Should he call out to her? He hesitated, watching the figure's slow progress, until her shadow disappeared around the bend.

Not a fan after all, apparently. No gate-crashers at all tonight? Not that he was complaining. Eric jammed his hands into his pockets and kicked his foot at a loosened stone, sending it skittering across the pavement of the parking lot.

The *empty* parking lot…

Or mostly empty, at any rate. The handful of cars scattered before him belonged to the club's staff, plus the rental car that Maury had driven there from Dallas. Eric's own car didn't occupy a space. When he arrived a few hours ago, he'd pulled around to the service entrance at the side of the building and ditched his Ferrari back there. He didn't want to draw too much attention to its presence, just in case some aggressive fan decided to stake it out and follow him after the show.

Follow him. What a joke. There were no fans here tonight. He could've ditched his car on the side of the road with a big, red "For Sale" sign in the window, for all it would've mattered. No passersby at all, except for that one weirdo.

Eric turned his head to look in the direction she had gone. Or *he* had gone? Was it a man after all? Some kind of drifter, perhaps, trying to hitch a ride into town? Eric didn't have much time to speculate. His ears perked up again, detecting the faint but unmistakable hum of a car engine.

"Here we go." He took his hands out of his pockets and stood up tall, straightening the rabbit's foot that hung around his neck.

Two beams of light came into view. Eric leaned forward expectantly, waiting for the SUV to emerge from the shadows, but he only saw the headlights peeping out from around the bend. He watched, holding his breath, until finally the two lights moved again. They still didn't come closer. Instead, they seemed to swing around in a wide arc. For a moment, the white beams were replaced by the faint red flicker of taillights. And then the total darkness fell again.

That wasn't Tessa either. Eric's face fell with disappointment as he listened to the fading sound of the engine. That guy out there must've gotten a ride. Someone just picked him up and did a U-turn.

"Dammit, Tessa," he said.

This was getting downright irritating now. Suspense was one thing, but the warm glow of anticipation had all but faded as Eric resigned himself to the truth. Nothing was going to happen. Not tonight. After all that, she wasn't even coming. After he'd spent this whole long day imagining the moment—imagining what she would do and say, and the way her face would look.

And now here he was, standing alone in an empty parking lot, freezing his ass off.

Eric wrapped his arms around himself as another powerful gust of wind buffeted him. Maybe if he DM'ed her, he could still wheedle her address out of her. He had to try, right? Tomorrow night he had another tour stop in Santa Fe, and then Denver the night after that. Whatever happened tonight, he would have no choice but to leave town in the morning. He only had one chance to meet her. He only had tonight.

He pulled out his phone and hung his head at the sight of his Twitter home screen. No little blue flag to indicate an unread message. She hadn't DM'ed. Twenty minutes late now, and not one word of explanation.

He flicked onto his messages and began to compose a text.

Taylor: What happened? Are you—

But he broke off in midsentence. His eyes registered the last message on the thread, and he squinted at it in confusion. Wait a minute. Not just one DM, he saw as he scrolled up. A whole back-and-forth exchange.

Which could only mean—

His brows drew together slowly as he struggled to make sense of the words:

> **Taylor:** Tessa, there's a million other fans here. Wayyyy too crowded. Pull over and pick me up.
> **Tessa H:** Hold on. Pulling over. Where are you?
> **Taylor:** Look up, dummy. I'm the one with the rabbit's foot walking toward the car.

OTHER FISH IN THE SEA

ERIC REREAD THE DMs, his mind spinning. Messages to Tessa. From him. But not from him. It could only mean one thing…

> Username: @EricThornSucks
> Password:

A coldness clenched around his chest, squeezing the breath out of his lungs. How had he not seen it coming? All this time, he'd focused on what happened to Dorian Cromwell. How many times had he looked back over his shoulder to see if someone was following him? And someone had been! Not walking down the street perhaps, but following him just the same. Some hacker stalking his Twitter from afar…

Or had he laid eyes on her before? Could it be the same one who jumped onstage in Seattle? Green eyes. Dark hair. Maybe five foot nine…The memory of her shrill voice still echoed in his mind: *Wait! He knows me! I'm telling you—he follows me on Twitter! He's followed me for years!*

Delusional. Convinced of some secret relationship that only existed in her own imagination. How many times had he tried to warn his record label? He knew it was only a matter of time.

What had happened to Dorian was horrifying enough. But this…this was unimaginable. This fangirl hadn't gone after him. She'd gone after the one he loved. She'd gone after Tessa.

And Tessa had no idea.

Eric's hand leaped to his throat. Would Tessa go with her? Would she fall into the trap? Would Tessa think…

His mind raced back over old conversations, hopelessly jumbled inside his head.

Maybe I've seen Catfish *too many times*, she'd told him, not so long ago. *Pretty much the same plot twist every time. Are you secretly a girl?*

Tessa. No!

That damned pink rabbit's foot. There were only two pink ones left on the little hook next to the gas station cash register. Eric had purchased one this morning and left the other one hanging.

He should have bought them both. Hell, he should have bought all the other colors too. Cleaned out the whole rack. He should have bought every last rabbit's foot in the entire state of Texas. He'd just left it there, dangling on the end of the hook. And someone else had bought it. Someone else had held it out to her. And Tessa must have fallen for it, hook, line, and sinker.

The seemingly innocuous events of the past twenty minutes took on new significance. The spindly-legged figure in the parking lot… The pair of headlights that stopped just before the final bend in the road…

That must have been her. Eric had stood right there and watched the whole bait and switch go down. The car had idled briefly, just long enough for introductions. Then it swung around in a U-turn and went—went where, exactly?

They could be anywhere.

Did they go back to Tessa's house? But where was that? She'd never given him the address. And now she was out there some-where with…with…

Eric felt the bile rise in his throat, and he swallowed hard. He couldn't lose it. Not now. He needed to think.

He only had one hope—one way to reach her. He double-tapped the Caps Lock and began firing off DMs:

Taylor: STOP!
Taylor: TESSA, THAT WASN'T ME!
Taylor: I'M STILL AT THE CLUB!
Taylor: TESSA, GET OUT OF THE CAR!

She would see the notifications. She had to. She always did. How many times had he messaged her at some random hour of the day or night only to be rewarded with an instantaneous reply?

"Come on, Tessa," he whispered hoarsely. "Answer me, goddammit!"

Tessa's fingers itched to check her phone, but she didn't want to be rude. It was just a nervous tic—not like she would have any messages worth reading. She was already sitting next to the only person whose DMs mattered, right here on her living room couch.

The conversation had once again faltered into silence. Tessa chewed her nails, racking her mind for something else to say. She hadn't expected her first meeting with Taylor to turn into such a horror show. How could it be this painful? They always had so much to talk about over Twitter. They could go on and on for hours. But here, in real life, it was almost like sitting face-to-face with a completely different person.

Tessa didn't know why she felt so awkward, exactly. Taylor seemed nice enough. Or Blair, Tessa mentally corrected. That pretty much summed up the entire conversation on the ride back to her house.

"Are you Taylor?" Tessa had asked, despite the rabbit's foot held out in confirmation.

She hadn't caught the answer. She'd locked eyes with the stranger who approached the car, and she'd felt the weirdest sensation. Not a panic attack, but even more disturbing in a way. It was almost as if her whole brain shut down for a moment.

She didn't pass out, but her mind went kind of numb—like when your hand falls asleep, and you know it's still attached to the end of your arm, but you've lost all ability to control it. Could that happen to a person's brain?

She only spaced out for thirty seconds, and then the sight of the rabbit's foot brought her back. Blair must have handed it to her. They were seated side by side in the backseat of the car at that point. Tessa had clutched the lucky talisman in her lap, struggling to catch up on the missing fragments of conversation.

"Wait. So, Taylor—"

"No, I'm Blair. Blair Duncan. You know who I am, Tessa." The rabbit's foot glowed pink, as if for emphasis, in the light of a passing streetlamp.

"Yeah," Tessa had stammered in reply. "Obviously. Sorry, I'm kind of nervous."

Blair had merely shrugged. "So is this…OK? Do you still want to talk and stuff?"

"Sure." Tessa had tried for a friendly smile. She'd worked out that Blair must've lied about the name, but big deal. Tessa could live with that. And that picture of man feet attached to a pair of well-muscled calves? Oh well. She wasn't all that surprised. Maybe Blair wasn't exactly what Tessa had pictured all those lonely nights falling asleep by her phone, but Tessa had promised herself to keep an open mind. If all she got out of this was a friend, that wouldn't be the worst thing—still a lot more than she had going in.

"Are you sure we shouldn't go to the concert?" she'd asked.

"Definitely not. It's a total circus back there. There's got to be somewhere quieter we could go."

Tessa had cast her eyes uncertainly in her therapist's direction.

"That's very thoughtful of you to consider Tessa's feelings, Blair," Dr. Regan had said from behind the steering wheel. "My advice would be to go where Tessa feels most comfortable. Your own house would make sense, Tessa."

"Home?"

A part of her had wanted to protest. She'd gone to so much trouble to avoid telling some online stranger where she lived. She'd left her house for the first time in months just so the two of them could meet in a public place. But Tessa held her tongue. If her therapist thought it was safe, then her fears must be irrational. And she'd already left her house. She'd shown herself that she could do it. What else did she have to prove?

Now she and Blair sat alone together in her living room. Dr. Regan had left them a few minutes ago to wait outside in the car, in spite of Tessa's whispered protestations. "What if I start to panic?"

"Do you have your pills with you?"

Tessa had set them on the coffee table, and Dr. Regan nodded in approval, issuing her final instructions to Blair on her way out the front door. "If she starts to hyperventilate, give her two pills with a glass of water. You can text me for help from Tessa's phone."

"But why don't you just stay?" Tessa had argued.

Her therapist murmured something about giving them space to get acquainted. No doubt Dr. Regan found the awkward silence too unbearable to withstand for more than a few minutes. Tessa couldn't blame her.

Blair shifted restlessly on the couch, and Tessa fought the urge to cover her nose. With every movement Blair made, Tessa caught another whiff of the overwhelming scent: some kind of flowery fragrance, so intense that it stung the inside of her nostrils.

Tessa snuck a sidelong glance. Blair was leaning to adjust the oversize duffel bag, still slung over one shoulder.

"Do you want to put that somewhere?" Tessa asked.

"No. It's OK. I'll just keep it—"

"Here," Tessa said, helping to ease the bag onto the floor. "Wow, that's ridiculously heavy. What do you have in there?"

Blair's eyes darted away for a brief instant. "Just…stuff. Maybe it's my Eric Thorn CD collection."

"CDs? But he only has three albums."

"Right. Well, I brought along my CD player too. You can never be too prepared."

Tessa's forehead furrowed as she eyed the bag. Who traveled with a CD player? Who even *owned* a CD player nowadays? "Don't you have iTunes?"

"I'm kidding, Tessa. It was supposed to be funny."

"Oh."

"Whatever. Can I use your bathroom?"

Blair stood, and Tessa breathed a sigh of relief. This had to be the most excruciating conversation ever. It was almost like Blair was holding back, waiting for something—some signal. Tessa didn't know what any of it meant. The long silences. The weird jokes. The overpowering cologne. And that bag… There had to be something juicy in there. Something important enough to carry all the way to Texas. She hadn't missed the way Blair dodged the question, and it only served to fuel Tessa's curiosity.

Tessa glanced up at the bathroom door. Still closed. No sound yet of a flushing toilet. She could take a tiny, little peek, right? No harm in that. How bad could it possibly be? With one eye on the bathroom, Tessa crouched down next to the bag.

She slowly zipped it open, bending her head close to look inside.

"Oh my God."

The words came out as a breathless whisper, but Tessa didn't hear the sound of her own voice. Her mind had slipped its groove again. Her eyes widened, but they didn't see. Her heart stopped beating, but she didn't feel afraid. She didn't feel a thing. She only whispered the same words over and over, repeating her mindless chant. "Oh my God. Oh my God. Oh my God. Oh my God. Oh my God…"

Taylor: TESSA I'VE BEEN HACKED.

Eric stared at the useless words, cursing each second that ticked by with no response. 6:23 p.m. now. How much time had passed since that car drove off? Tessa must have put her phone away. Must be busy getting acquainted—getting acquainted with "Taylor." Taylor, the first stranger she dared let back into her life. The one she thought she trusted. The one she thought she loved.

Eric nearly threw his phone across the parking lot.

He had to do something. But what? Should he call for help? Call the police? Eric flipped away from Twitter and began dialing 9-1-1. His finger hung suspended over the Call button, but he hesitated. Call 9-1-1 and tell them what, exactly? He winced as he played out the imaginary conversation inside his head.

"9-1-1. What's your emergency?"

"I'd like to report a missing person."

"Male or female?"

"Female."

"Age?"

"Eighteen."

"When was she last seen?"

"Never."

"I'm sorry?"

"I've never actually seen her. But she was supposed to meet me here twenty minutes ago."

"She was supposed to meet you where?"

"At the Trail Dust Honky-Tonk Saloon."

"A woman was supposed to meet you at a bar? A woman you've never met?"

"Right, but then she—"

"I'm sorry, sir. Are you calling to report that your blind date stood you up?"

Eric clicked the phone keypad closed. He'd never be able to explain the situation to some operator—someone who'd probably never even heard of Eric Thorn or catfishing or Twitter itself for that matter. The story would take hours to untangle. And even if he could explain it, even if he could somehow convey the danger that Tessa was in, then what? What could they do? Where would they send the squad car? He had absolutely no idea where she'd gone or where she lived. He didn't even know her last name.

Another precious minute ticked by. 6:24 p.m. Eric shifted his weight from foot to foot, staring at his phone. He was breathing hard now but getting nowhere fast. What else could he do? He was just about to send another useless DM when a hand clapped him on the back.

"Hey, kid, I just got off the phone with—"

"Not now, Maury!" Eric brushed his manager's arm away with a violent shrug.

"Texting again with the mystery girl? She's got you reeled in pretty tight, my friend."

"I said not now!" Eric strode down the sidewalk, desperate to get away from Maury's prying eyes, but he heard his manager's footfalls scuffle after him.

"Kid! Wait up! Trust me, you're going to want to hear this."

Eric turned on his heel, glaring daggers in Maury's direction. "Whatever it is, it can wait."

"What happened?" Maury asked with a nod toward Eric's phone. "Caught the little lady stepping out on you?"

"Maury, I swear to God—"

"OK! OK, keep your pants on. You'll like this. I just put in a call to publicity. The show's off for tonight."

Eric blinked. "What do you mean?"

"Canceled," Maury said. "Take the rest of the night off. Go deal with your text message situation. Ring in the New Year however you see fit. Just get yourself to Santa Fe in time for sound check tomorrow."

Eric shook his head, confused. "But what about the show? What happened to Tessa?"

"Who?"

"The concert winner! Tessa!"

"The fan from Twitter?" Maury cocked an eyebrow. "Since when did you start caring about—"

"I care, OK! Where is she?" Eric took a step closer, fighting the urge to grab his manager by the neck and shake the information loose. "For God's sake, Maury, will you stop joking around for once in your life!"

"Take it easy!" Maury stumbled backward. "What do you want me to say? She flaked out. She bailed. She's a no-show. I thought you'd be happy."

"But did you talk to her?"

"Don't take it personally, kid. You've got enough fans to spare." Maury reached out to pat Eric on the arm, but he dropped his hand again at Eric's harsh intake of breath.

"Dammit, Maury! DID YOU TALK TO HER?"

"No!" Maury shouted back, his own voice rising in defense. "Don't take it out on me! I haven't heard a peep. She's not answering her phone."

THE INTERROGATION
(FRAGMENT 8)

December 31, 2016 9:17 p.m.
Case #: 124.678.21–001
OFFICIAL TRANSCRIPT OF POLICE INTERROGATION

—START PAGE 8—

INVESTIGATOR: Tessa, I have some bad news. My partner just spoke with your therapist, Dr. Regan.

HART: Is she coming soon?

INVESTIGATOR: I'm afraid she won't be able to join us.

HART: What? No! She was right behind us. The officers took me here in a police car, and she said she would follow us to the station. Did she get lost or something?

INVESTIGATOR: It appears that she had second thoughts.

HART: What do you mean?

INVESTIGATOR: When Detective Newman spoke to her, she referred him to her attorney and declined to speak any further.

HART: I don't understand. Why does she need an attorney?

INVESTIGATOR: Her malpractice attorney.

HART:	She's worried about malpractice? Are you kidding me? My single worst fear in the entire universe just came to pass, and she's worried about getting sued?
INVESTIGATOR:	She provided Detective Newman with a 1–800 hotline you can call if you're in crisis.
HART:	I'm supposed to call some stranger on a hotline? Did she miss the memo where I have an irrational fear of strangers?
INVESTIGATOR:	Would you like me to call your mother? I'm sure the hospital can get someone to cover her shift.
HART:	No!
INVESTIGATOR:	Is there anyone else?
HART:	I can't believe this is happening.
INVESTIGATOR:	Maybe a cup of tea or coffee? Is there anything I can do to put you more at ease right now?
HART:	Yeah, you know what? There is something you can do. You can arrest that animal, put him in jail, and throw away the key.

HIM

TESSA'S EYES FLITTED around the living room, unable to comprehend the meaning of her surroundings.

Chairs…couch…coffee table… The familiar furnishings of her childhood home. And yet something wasn't right. Something she couldn't quite remember…

Her gaze came to rest on an object sitting on the floor. Black and shapeless. Heavy, she knew, without reaching to pick it up.

A bag. Duffel bag. Whose duffel bag was that?

It didn't belong there. Tessa knew that much. It belonged to… It belonged to…

The realization hit her all at once. A wave of nausea rolled through her, and the air in her lungs burst upward from her chest, but the scream died inside her throat. The sound came out as nothing more than a whimper.

Her mouth… There was something wrong with her mouth. She could only breathe through her nose. Her cheek muscles strained, and she felt a pop in the joint of her jawbone, but her lips remained closed tight.

Sealed, she realized. Sealed shut.

The truth came back to her in full then—the moment of sheer panic, just before the world went fuzzy gray. Dr. Regan had left her alone in the living room with Blair. Tessa had stooped to look inside the bag, and she'd understood everything the instant she unzipped it.

Cameras, lenses, tripods. A spool of thick white cord. A roll or two of duct tape.

The cord, she saw with a downward glance, now bound her wrists together. Long strands of it looped around her torso and upper arms, fastening her securely to a straight-backed wooden chair. And the duct tape… She could sense the sticky backing against her lips now. He'd plastered it across her face from cheek to cheek.

A low moan escaped from behind the gag as Tessa's eyes made another rapid circuit around the room. Her captor had disappeared somewhere. She could hear his footsteps puttering around overhead. If she listened closely, she could just make out the sound of him creeping from room to room: closing windows, drawing blinds…

Tessa remembered how he came up behind her before. He'd caught her red-handed, looking inside the duffel bag. She'd opened her mouth to scream, but he'd clapped a heavy palm across her mouth. His other hand had reached around her and emerged from the bag holding a long, sleek blade—a butcher's knife. He'd brandished it in front of her face.

She could only remember bits and pieces after that. Her mind kept going vacant, drifting in and out of focus. She couldn't recall being bound and gagged—only the way he hauled her over to a chair. She'd felt him reach inside the front pocket of her jeans, and she'd kicked her legs with all her strength. He hadn't kept his hand in there for long though. He'd pulled it out again, and she'd felt the glide of an object against her outer thigh—her cell phone. He must have pocketed it before he tied her up.

Tessa flexed her arms and strained forward with her chest. She had to get out of here before he returned. If she could only make it to the front door… She knew Dr. Regan must still be sitting in her car. Tessa pressed her weight forward, but the cord barely flexed. It cut painfully into the flesh of her arms and across her ribs. No way could she loosen it enough to slip out. Maybe if she tipped the chair over… Maybe she could try to crawl…

The sound of a creaking floorboard interrupted her. Too late.

Tessa squeezed her eyes shut as she heard the steady footfalls on the stairs.

Eric stared in bewilderment as the meaning of his manager's last words sunk in. *I haven't heard a peep. She's not answering her phone.*

"Wait a minute," Eric said, his eyes suddenly going round. "You have her phone number?"

"Sure, I tried calling. Don't worry about it, kiddo." Maury gave him a tentative jab in the arm. "It's just one fangirl. You've got fourteen million others where she came from."

"But...you have her cell phone number? Do you have her last name?"

Maury nodded. "Sure, I have a copy of her driver's license too. Full background check. The works. I know you like to complain about security, but they're not actually so reckless that they'd stage a whole concert for some—"

"Wait," Eric cut him off. "Wait, wait, wait. You have her address?"

"Why are you so hung up on this?"

"Answer the goddamn question, Maury! Do you have her address?"

Maury shrugged and began patting around the pockets of his jacket. "Yeah, sure. Got it here somewhere. Some rural area about twenty minutes' drive from here."

Eric felt something click inside his chest. Not quite relief, but at least a ray of hope. He turned on his heel and ran toward the side of the building where he'd left his car. "Text it to me!" he called over his shoulder. "I'm on my way."

He didn't stop to listen to his manager's voice, trailing behind him. "Eric, wait. You gonna do the concert there? I mean, that's... I appreciate the initiative. Don't get me wrong. But that's not what we agreed. At least take a guitar or something. What about hair and makeup? Eric!"

Eric reached for the handle of the car door when another

thought flashed through his mind. He looked back over his shoulder at Maury, waddling around the corner of the building in pursuit. "Call her again!" Eric shouted to him. "Keep trying to get through! Tell her…tell her that girl isn't who she says she is!"

"What? Who isn't?"

"Just call her back and tell her!"

Maury stopped running and watched in utter bafflement as Eric wedged himself into the driver's seat.

Eric tried again. "The catfish! The one with the rabbit's foot! She's lying! Tell Tessa not to take the bait!"

"The catfish—"

"The other one," Eric yelled. "Not me! The *other* catfish!"

"The other… Eric, have you been watching MTV again?"

But Eric didn't hear the question. He'd already pulled the car door shut. His manager's bemused words were lost in the sound of squealing tires as Eric slammed his foot down on the accelerator and sped away.

"Still asleep?"

Tessa froze at the sound of her captor's voice as he stepped off the stairs and entered the living room. She'd closed her eyes when she first heard his approach. Now she didn't dare open them.

"Gosh, you're sleepy, Tessa. You should get more rest. This is what happens when you stay up all night DM'ing some loser on Twitter."

He clucked with disapproval, but Tessa thought she heard a trace of humor in his voice. Was he making a joke at his own expense? She supposed he must be. He must find it all rather amusing. She'd stayed up almost every night for months, and the whole time she'd been talking to… How was it possible? Why hadn't some instinct warned her? How had it never occurred to her—not once in all that time—that the person on the other end was him?

Him.

Tessa kept her eyes shut tight. She couldn't bear the thought of looking at him.

"That's all right, love. You go ahead and sleep. Just hold still, OK? I'm going to start with some close-ups."

Tessa heard the noise, barely audible over the sound of his voice, but to her it resonated louder than a peal of thunder. That *click, click, click* of a camera shutter. She'd spent her whole time in New Orleans hearing that faint rhythm at every turn. For weeks, she'd thought she was only imagining it—hallucinating, hearing things. It was only on that final night that she understood the truth.

Tessa's eyes popped open at the ugly memory, only to be blinded by the sudden blaze of a flashbulb.

"Goddammit!" he cursed. "You blinked! I told you not to move! Why do you always have to ruin everything? I swear, Tessa, if you would just listen to me for once—" He broke off angrily, adjusting some setting on the back of the camera.

Tessa fought for breath. She recognized the familiar feeling starting up: the vise grip of anxiety tightening around her chest. Her usual deep-breathing tricks couldn't help her now. Not with a piece of duct tape over her mouth. She couldn't get enough air in through her nose.

"I'm sorry, Tessa," Blair said without looking at her. He lifted his camera and took a test shot of the wall. Then, with a grunt of satisfaction, he began edging around the room, viewing her from different angles through the lens.

Tessa darted a glance from the corner of her eye. He didn't look the way she saw him in her nightmares. Not handsome but not exactly a monster either. He looked ordinary enough, with a sallow complexion and greasy, light-brown hair that might have been blond if it were clean. She could just detect the stale body odor that emanated from his clothes, concealed beneath the cloak of overpowering cologne.

He spoke in a low monotone as he moved about the room. "I didn't come here to fight with you. Don't look at me like that. You know why I had to do this. You left me no choice."

Tessa struggled to follow the rambling speech. Her breath came faster now, despite her efforts to control it. She could feel her nostrils flare.

"You can look indignant if you want, love, but you know I have a point. It wasn't very nice, what you did. Not a nice way to treat someone." He paused to examine the picture he just snapped, but he shook his head. "Try not to do that thing with your nose, please. It's not the most flattering look."

Tessa barely comprehended. The buzzing sound had started

in her ears. Soon it would be followed by the thick, black clouds at the edges of her vision. Would she zone out again? And then what? What would he do once he finished with the pictures? She blinked hard and forced as much air as she could manage into her lungs. His voice grew more forceful now, ranting, but she was too preoccupied with her own breathing to focus too closely on the words.

"Women! Why are women so stupid? Huh? Can you explain that to me? You're all the same. You want the same ridiculous thing. Some asshole who treats you like garbage. Am I right? Calls you a bunch of disgusting names? And you talk to *him*. You say you love *him*. A guy who doesn't even deserve to lick the bottoms of your feet! And meanwhile, a nice guy comes along—a genuinely nice person—who wants nothing but to love you and cherish you like you deserve, and how do you treat him? How, Tessa?"

Tessa blinked again. An asshole? Someone who called her names? Who was he talking about? Scott? But she'd broken up with Scott months ago…

She shook her head from side to side in confusion, and that was when her eyes landed on the coffee table just off to her left.

"He calls you a bloodsucking leech, and you follow him. You *fall* for him. And me? Not even a follow back. Honestly, how stupid are you?"

Tessa didn't even register his words—too consumed with the bottle on the table. She suddenly remembered Dr. Regan's final instructions before she left the house:

If she starts to hyperventilate, give her two pills with a glass of water.

If she could just get to that prescription bottle. Tessa shifted in her chair, awkwardly extending her leg as far to the left as it would go. So close. Just a few more inches…

"What are you doing?" he snapped. "Stop that! Stop leaning. You're ruining the shot!"

Tessa lowered her leg and sat up straight again, planting both feet on the ground. She paused for a moment to suck in one more noseful of air. Then she jerked sideways with her full body. The chair legs screeched against the living room floor as she scooted an inch to the left.

"Cut it out, Tessa! What the hell?"

He took a step in her direction, but Tessa didn't pay him any heed. She stuck out her foot again. This time she made contact with the tip of her toe. The bottle fell sideways, its contents rattling against the coffee table, and Blair stopped in his tracks. His whole face changed, so suddenly that it might have been comical under other circumstances. The anger evaporated, replaced by a mask of puppyish devotion.

"Your pills?" he said softly. "Oh gosh, are you OK, love? Are you hyperventilating?" He set down his camera and rushed to her side, grabbing the medication off the table. "Tessa, are you having a panic attack? Just say so. Just nod if you need your pills."

She nodded vigorously.

"Anxiety disorder," he muttered. "You know, you never would've had this problem in the first place if you'd stuck with me." Tessa flinched at the flare of disapproval that crossed his face, but he patted her knee reassuringly. "Don't worry. There's no need to panic, Tessa. You did me wrong, but I forgive you. I love you. I'm here to be a good boyfriend to you now." He opened the bottle and shook out a few pills onto the table. "You take these with water, right?"

Tessa nodded again. He stood and headed for the kitchen, and she slumped forward in relief.

Now what? Her mind reeled with scattered thoughts. She needed a plan. She didn't have much time. He would have to take the tape off her mouth when he gave her the pills. Should she try to scream then? Would Dr. Regan hear it from the car?

Tessa shook her head. She couldn't take the risk. If she screamed and no one heard…

She let out a tiny whimper. No, she couldn't scream. Not from here. She tried desperately to focus, but she could barely summon the energy to put together a coherent thought. Her mind kept going back against her will, like a swimmer fighting against the current. Back to that other time…the time before. Last June.

She hadn't screamed that night either. She'd somehow had the presence of mind to swallow her terror. She'd woken in the dark in an unfamiliar room, and she'd known she wasn't alone. She'd sensed his presence beside her. He'd stirred, and she'd whispered soothingly, barely louder than a breath:

"Shhhhhhh. Go back to sleep."

He'd rolled over in the bed, and she hadn't stopped to look at him as she'd stumbled for the door.

THE INTERROGATION
(FRAGMENT 9)

December 31, 2016 9:17 p.m.
Case #: 124.678.21–001
OFFICIAL TRANSCRIPT OF POLICE INTERROGATION

—START PAGE 9—

INVESTIGATOR: Tessa, I need you to stay as calm as you possibly can right now, so that I can take your complete statement. Let's talk about Blair Duncan.

HART: If you want me to tell you what happened last summer, I can't. Anything but that. I can't talk about that.

INVESTIGATOR: That's all right, Tessa. We have a full account from the direct messages you sent over Twitter last night. I've just been reading through them. If you like, I can go ahead and read your messages into the record. All you have to do is listen and confirm whether you want to make them a part of your official statement. Can you manage that?

HART: I think so.

INVESTIGATOR: Let the record show that I'm looking at a series of multiple direct messages sent from the Twitter account @TessaHeartsEric to the Twitter account @EricThornSucks. The first time stamp is December 30 at 11:56 p.m., and the messages continue without interruption until 12:17 a.m. The messages begin, and I quote:

"I'm not completely sure when it started. I think it might have been the first weekend of the program." End of message.

"It was a summer fine arts program sponsored by the university. Really hard to get into. People came from all around the region for different things. Creative writing, music, painting, film-making, photography..." End of message.

"We were all staying in the empty dorms. I didn't do a lot of sleeping...or creative writing either. It was pretty much partying every night." End of message.

"We went out a lot that first weekend, club-hopping different places. I think that's where he first saw me. At one of those clubs." End of message.

INVESTIGATOR: Tessa, I'm going to break here for a moment. The events you're describing took place in New Orleans?

HART: Yes.

INVESTIGATOR: Can you remember the name of the club where you first encountered this individual?

HART: I don't know. There was a bunch of places. I can visualize what it looked like inside, but I don't know the name.

INVESTIGATOR: To the best of your recollection, was it more of a dance club? Or would you describe it as more like a venue for a music concert?

HART: More like a concert. A bar with a live band.

INVESTIGATOR: OK, thank you. I'm going to continue now with the next message in the thread. The time stamp is 11:59 p.m. And I quote:

"It was super crowded, and I kept feeling this guy creeping up on me." End of message.

"I shrugged it off at the time, but I started having this weird sensation afterward. Like this nagging feeling that someone was following me." End of message.

"It went on for the next four weeks. I would walk down the street and feel sure there was someone behind me. But when I turned to look…nothing." End of message.

"I told myself I was just being paranoid, but it kept getting worse and worse. It started happening in my dorm room too." End of message.

"I would get this weird feeling like someone was watching me through the window. But when I went to look outside, I didn't see anyone." End of message.

"So then I really started to lose it. I started keeping my blinds shut all the time, but it didn't really help." End of message.

"I would go to bed and wake up with this feeling that someone had been watching me while I slept." End of message.

"I started having trouble sleeping. So that's when I started drinking a lot more. Just to take the edge off." End of message.

"I guess that was a mistake. The drinking. I still don't know for sure if it was just the alcohol that night or if he slipped something in my drink." End of message.

HART: Stop. That's enough.

INVESTIGATOR: OK, Tessa. We're almost done. Just a few more messages to go now.

HART: Do you really have to read the rest out loud? We both know what it says.

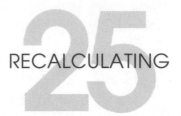RECALCULATING

"9-1-1, WHAT'S YOUR emergency?"

Eric gripped the steering wheel so hard that his knuckles turned white. He'd pushed his Ferrari's engine as fast as it would go, but he eased off the gas slightly as he leaned into the speakerphone.

"Send the police! There's a girl—a break-in! Someone's trying to break into a house."

Not exactly but close enough. He didn't have time to explain the truth. They'd sort it out once they got there. Right now, he needed to say whatever it took to get the police to Tessa's door. The text from Maury had just come through moments earlier.

"Three Sycamore Lane," Eric said into the phone. "Hurry!"

"Sir, did you get a look at the suspect? Could you describe him for me?"

"It's a girl. A teenage girl!"

"A female? Acting alone?"

"Yeah, but…but she's armed. Definitely dangerous. I think she might have a gun. Seriously, hurry up!"

"Police are on their way, sir. Anything else you can give me by way of a description?"

"Maybe five foot nine. Green eyes. Dark hair. Skinny legs. Wearing a dark hoodie sweatshirt."

He clicked to end the call and drove down the deserted road in silence, trying not to think. Failing. At least Tessa had her therapist along for the ride, he reassured himself. She wouldn't be alone.

Would she? Would Tessa even go along with it, when she saw that it was a girl? Maybe not. Maybe it was all a big false alarm. He was freaking out over nothing. Tessa was way too paranoid to bring some stranger back to her house.

But then why wasn't she checking DMs or answering her phone? Maury had texted him Tessa's phone number, but the call went straight to voice mail. Something had to be wrong. Seriously wrong.

Dangerously wrong.

Eric glanced at the clock on his dashboard. Nine minutes had passed since he left the club. He needed to concentrate on driving. He couldn't afford to dwell on all the horrifying possibilities. Not if he had any hope of getting to Tessa in time. With an effort, he forced himself to focus on the directions coming from his GPS.

In one half mile, take ramp on right…

Proceed on the current route…

Left turn ahead…

Recalculating…

"Shit," he swore, brakes squealing. He'd missed a turn in the darkness. Hadn't they ever heard of streetlights around here? He swiveled his head, straining to make out anything that could pass for a sign. Long stretches of black nothingness flanked the poorly lit back road, with a few scattered houses set far back from the curb.

Tessa shrank down in her chair as the unbearable memories crashed over her in surging waves. She'd be neck-deep in the flashback soon. She couldn't let that happen. Blair was coming back, and she still hadn't figured out a plan. She needed to stay focused—concentrate on getting out of here and let the terror overtake her afterward. She closed her eyes, and her thoughts drifted back to their usual safe harbor.

Eric. Eric Thorn.

"No," she moaned inside her head. She couldn't afford to start projecting now, even if it helped to ease the panic. She didn't have time for this! But she couldn't shake the old, familiar image that she saw behind her closed eyelids: Eric's face, looking over his shoulder, frozen with fear.

Tessa's eyes snapped open.

"Eric," she tried to whisper in spite of the tape that covered her mouth. A new thought had just struck her. The answer to a question that had haunted her for months—a question that her therapist had reflected back to her time and time again:

I just don't understand why I chose him. Why Eric Thorn of all people?

You tell me, Tessa. Why do you think you've fixated on him?

The answer was so obvious. How had she failed to see it before? She knew exactly why she'd obsessed over Eric. Not because she liked the way he looked or the sound of his voice. Because she identified with him. When she looked at his picture and saw fear on his face, she recognized herself. It wasn't just projection. She understood firsthand where his anxiety came from—the same source as her own worst fears.

The fans.

That's what she had in Blair, when she came right down to it. A fan. A fanatical follower who loved her too much, like the fangirls who stalked Eric's every move. Not one of the casual fans, who were content to buy his music and reply to his tweets. No, she had one of the dangerous ones—the fans who wanted their crush to love them back so badly that they convinced themselves it was true.

She heard a different voice inside her head now. Not Dr. Regan. The memory of a reporter's voice, crackling from her TV.

Such a class act. That could have turned ugly so easily...

You can tell he's had his share of run-ins with overeager fans...

How did Eric deal with the obsessed ones? Tessa knew the answer. She'd seen it with her own eyes. She remembered the whole scene now, the way it had played out on her TV screen in blurry cell phone videos.

He'd looked deep into that girl's eyes, and his lips had formed the magic words—words that Tessa couldn't hear, but she could guess their meaning. The words that his pursuer wanted to hear above all others. The lies that every fangirl dreams of hearing from her idol:

"I see you… I notice you… I know that you exist… I love you back… I love you too…"

Tessa heard the kitchen tap turn off, followed by the sound of Blair's hurried footsteps. He was coming back, but she felt her fear receding. She sat up and squared her shoulders. She knew what she needed to do.

"OK, Tessa. Ready?"

Ready, she confirmed inside her head.

"I'm going to take off the duct tape now, but you have to promise me you won't do something stupid. No screaming. Do you promise?"

Tessa nodded calmly.

"Good girl." He set the water glass down on the coffee table and peeled away the tape with one hand. In his other hand, all the while, he gripped the butcher knife in a tight fist.

"There now," he said gently as he eased away the tape. "Sorry it's so sticky, Tessa. Am I hurting you?"

"No," she answered once her lips were free. She forced her mouth to curve into a smile. "Thank you. I'm OK now. I feel so much better."

"You do?" His brow crinkled with concern. "You're not having a panic attack anymore?"

"No, no," she said, smiling even brighter. "I think it was just the tape making me hyperventilate. I wasn't scared. Why would I be scared?"

He tilted his head to one side, examining her face. "You were going to scream before, when I caught you snooping in my bag. I had to put my hand over your mouth. Don't lie to me." The knife flashed in front of her face. Tessa bit back a gasp and forced herself to laugh instead.

"Of course I was going to scream, Blair. I just realized who you were! I was excited. That's what all girls do when we're excited. We scream!" She laughed again. "You're so funny. I can't believe you tied me up. I'm not afraid of you. I love you."

His eyes narrowed, and Tessa held her breath.

"Then why did you run away from me last summer?" he asked. "Why did you leave me in the middle of the night like that, Tessa? You just left. You didn't even say good-bye."

Tessa's smile faltered slightly. Her mind raced for an explanation that would convince him. "That's true," she admitted. "I was scared of you in New Orleans. I think you just came on a little too strong. But that was all before...before I really knew you. You were still a stranger to me then. I know you so much better now!"

"Bullshit."

The word hit her like a gut punch. It wasn't working. Tessa blinked and looked down at her knees.

"That's bullshit, and you know it," he said, his voice low and intense. "Before you really knew me? What's that supposed to mean, Tessa? We were together! I loved you. I treated you right. And you…you loved me too." His voice rose higher and higher as he continued. "And then all of a sudden, out of nowhere… *poof!* Gone. Not one word of explanation. Like I meant nothing to you. Like I never even existed!"

"Blair," she whispered. "It wasn't like that."

Tessa saw her mistake now—a slight miscalculation. She hadn't realized just how deeply his delusions ran. He must have concocted a whole fictional love affair inside his head and convinced himself that it was real. She was in too deep now to backtrack. Her only hope was to go with it. Play along, just like Eric had done. He'd held that girl in his arms and whisked her around the stage, and she'd let him waltz her right into the hands of his waiting bodyguards.

Tessa gave up trying to smile and schooled her features into a coquettish pout. "You say you love me, Blair, but I know it isn't true. Don't lie to me."

His eyes went wide, incredulous. "Of course I do! How can you say that?"

Tessa shook her head. "Actions speak louder than words. This was supposed to be a special night for us, and you tied me to a chair. How is that supposed to make me feel?" She lifted her eyes and gazed up at him through veiled lashes. His face changed at the accusation in her words. He lowered the knife to his side.

"Tessa, I'm sorry."

She glared at him indignantly but not with the true disgust she felt—more like the kind of look she used to cast at Scott in the middle of some petty argument.

"Tessa," Blair tried again. "Don't be mad. I have to do this after the way you treated me...after you ran away. You see that, right?"

She nodded slowly, pretending to agree. "I know. I'm sorry I acted that way. Blair, please." She raised her eyes to him again, imploring. "We were so good together before. I just want things to go back to the way they were."

"That's what I want too!" He dropped to his knees in front of her and wrapped his arms around her legs, resting his face in her lap. "That's all I want, Tessa. Just like it was before."

Tessa ignored the bitter taste rising in her throat. She awkwardly positioned her bound wrists beside his head and stroked her fingers through the clumps of unwashed hair. "It's not too late," she said softly. "Don't you remember what we said last night?"

"Last night?" He lifted his head from where it rested on her knees. "Who? Me? When?"

"Over DM!" she went on. "We said we would dance. Remember?"

"No, you said that with—"

But Tessa plowed on before he could protest. She was so close now. She could sense his resolve crumbling with each new lie she told. "I want to dance with you, Blair. Just you and me. It's not too late. Untie me so we can dance."

THE INTERROGATION (FRAGMENT 10)

December 31, 2016 9:17 p.m.
Case #: 124.678.21–001
OFFICIAL TRANSCRIPT OF POLICE INTERROGATION

—START PAGE 10—

INVESTIGATOR: We're almost done, Tessa. I'm resuming with the next message in the thread. Are you OK to continue?

HART: Please just get it over with.

INVESTIGATOR: I'll go as fast as I can. I know this isn't easy for you. The next time stamp is 12:09 a.m. The message reads, and I quote:

"The last thing I remember, I was drinking at some party, and then I woke up in a room I didn't know." End of message.

"I don't know how long I'd been lying there. It was pitch-black outside, and I couldn't find the lights. I was still pretty woozy." End of message.

"But I felt...him. I felt his presence. He never actually touched me, I don't think. But I could hear his breathing next to me. Slow and even. I could tell he was asleep." End of message.

"He had a very distinctive odor. Kind of like

chemicals. It's hard to describe." End of message.

"That's what I remember most about him. The smell. When I have flashbacks, it's always with that smell." End of message.

INVESTIGATOR: Tessa, can you give me any more details about the odor you were describing? You said it was a chemical smell?

HART: I don't know. I think it might have been photo-developing chemicals, but I only realized that afterward. After I found the lights.

INVESTIGATOR: So you woke up in this dorm room, and you switched on the lights, and you saw—

HART: I don't want to talk about the rest. I really, really don't.

INVESTIGATOR: There are just a few more messages here that I need to get into the record. I'll skip to the important ones. I'm resuming with the message at time stamp 12:15 a.m. The message reads, and I quote:

"Every single square inch was covered with photos. Just photos, everywhere, floor to ceiling. I couldn't even guess how many. Thousands of them." End of message.

"Pictures of me." End of message.

"Dancing at the clubs…" End of message.

"Walking down the street…" End of message.

"And in my room too. In my own room. In my underwear. Asleep." End of message.

"It wasn't just my imagination. It was him. That whole time, he'd been—"

HART: Stop! Stop it. Please. Please stop. I don't want to hear anymore.

INVESTIGATOR: OK. I have most of what I need now. Take a deep breath. I just have a few more details I need you to confirm. Am I correct that after you saw the pictures, you then fled the premises?

HART: Yes.

INVESTIGATOR: You did not get a good look at the perpetrator's face. Is that correct?

HART: No. I mean, I don't…I don't think so. Maybe. I don't know, OK? I don't remember.

INVESTIGATOR: You never went to the authorities?

HART: Can we please stop? I don't feel good.

INVESTIGATOR: We're almost done, Tessa. Are you certain that the individual in New Orleans was the same person who held you captive tonight?

HART: Yes!

INVESTIGATOR: But you didn't recognize him when he first approached you tonight?

HART: He had the rabbit's foot. I didn't know... I didn't think... How is that possible? How could I not realize?

INVESTIGATOR: No one is blaming you for what happened, Tessa. You're the victim here. I need you to remember that.

HART: I know. I'm trying.

SEE YOU LATER

BLAIR CUPPED TESSA'S elbow to keep her upright as she rose from the chair. He'd used his knife to cut through the cord around her upper body, but he left her wrists tied together. She looked up into his face, plotting her next move.

She could try to make a run for it, but she doubted she would make it to the door. No, she needed to bide her time, wait for the right moment. If he figured out she was lying to him before she could get free, he might lose it completely. And he still had the butcher knife clutched in one hand.

"Blair," she said, glancing down at the eight-inch-long blade. "Do you think you could put that down? It's really big."

His face had softened before, when she told him she wanted to dance, but now she saw him tense and pull away. "I don't think so, Tessa."

She hadn't won his trust. Not yet. She still needed to tread carefully. Tessa kept her voice light and cheerful as she took a tiny step in his direction. "Well, try not to stab me by accident, please. My mom will kill me if we get blood all over the upholstery."

He chuckled, but he still held the knife as firmly as ever. "I would never hurt you, Tessa. You know that."

She nodded and forced herself to smile. Now what? Maybe she could get her phone somehow. He must have slipped it into his own pocket after he took it from her. Was it that bulge in the front pocket of his jeans? But then the only way for her to get it would be to… No way. She couldn't even finish the thought. Just the idea of dancing with him made her skin crawl.

"Should we put on some dance music?" he asked, grinning at her playfully. "A little bird told me you like 'Snowflake.'"

"No!" Tessa drew back at the suggestion. *Not "Snowflake,"* she prayed silently. She couldn't bear to ruin that song with this memory. Not that she'd be in a position to remember much of anything if she didn't get help soon.

If she couldn't get the phone, then she would have to scream for help. But not in here. Somewhere Dr. Regan would be sure to hear her. Outside somewhere. How could she get him outside?

Blair eyed her skeptically. "I thought you liked that song."

He reached out to touch her hands, and she shied away in spite of her best efforts. "Sorry," she said, stumbling a step backward. "I do. It's just… I'm just… I think I'm going to sneeze!"

The new idea came to her, triggered by the overpowering fragrance that swirled in her direction. Tessa covered her face with her hands and faked a sneeze. Then another, and another.

"Are you OK?"

"I think it's allergies," she said, sniffling. "It might be all the cologne."

"Cologne? I wore this for you!" The knife blade glinted dangerously as he threw up his hands in frustration. "I went and bought a whole bottle of this stuff. Honestly, I can't win with you!"

"No, no!" Tessa backpedaled, keeping one eye on the knife. "I love it. That was so sweet and thoughtful. It's just a little strong." She sneezed again. "I think fresh air might help. Maybe we should dance outside? Under the moonlight. Oh, Blair, it'll be so romantic!"

She sighed and batted her eyelashes like a fairy-tale princess with her handsome prince—all the while watching his reaction. Would he go for it? Was he so delusional that he'd forgotten Dr. Regan was out there? Tessa doubted it somehow. But it didn't matter, even if he refused. She was already one step ahead of him.

"No," he said at last. "We can go upstairs if you want, but not outside. We're going to need our privacy tonight."

Tessa ignored the leer that had crept onto his face. "Not out front, silly! Out back! The back deck. It's totally private back there. Come on. I want to show you!"

Eric hit Reverse and peered out the back windshield into the inky darkness behind him. The GPS had to be wrong. He'd been up and down this stretch of road three times now, and he still hadn't seen any trace of the turnoff onto Tessa's street.

In one quarter mile, turn right…

Recalculating…

"Shit! Shit! Shit!" Eric slammed his fist against the dashboard. Useless piece of crap. He'd made good time driving here from the club—hadn't paid much attention to all those pesky traffic lights and speed limits—but now he'd just wasted four precious minutes trying to make the final turn.

Sycamore Lane. Where the hell was Sycamore Lane?

It had to be nearby. Maybe he hadn't gone far enough. He gave up on reversing and threw the gearshift into drive.

Turn right…

Recalculating…

Perform a legal U-turn…

Eric drew in a sharp breath at that last GPS instruction. A U-turn, huh? Where had he heard that before? For some reason, it brought to mind another voice buzzing uselessly in his ear—a slightly different choice of words, that night in Seattle, but the meaning was the same.

ERIC! ERIC, TURN AROUND!

He'd done his best to put that whole incident out of his head. His manager assured him that the situation was being handled. Security would make the necessary adjustments. They were raising the railing and doubling the number of guards around the stage for all upcoming shows. It would take a military special ops unit to breach that barrier again. In any case, the girl that night was harmless. Maury had repeated it enough times that Eric had started to believe him.

Harmless. Just a fan.

He should have listened to his gut. He knew that girl was a menace the moment he met her eyes. Green eyes at first glimpse, but the longer he looked into them, the more the pupils dilated…until by the end of the dance, the eyes that stared back at him had turned completely black.

Evil eyes. Nothing harmless about them. He knew it at the time, but he'd let other voices drown out the doubts inside his head. And now look what had happened. Of course she came back. The figure he saw on the edge of the parking lot had to be the same fangirl, haunting him again. She'd somehow hacked his phone and found the second Twitter account, and it was the single worst thing she could have seen. His DM chain with Tessa would only drive her closer toward the brink of violence—watching those words of love she wanted for herself directed at another girl instead.

He should have handled it differently that night in Seattle. He saw that now. He'd reacted out of pure instinct, with no other thought than to save his own neck. He'd pulled the girl into ballroom dance position to subdue her thrashing arms, but that wasn't even the worst of it. He'd looked at her. For those brief moments, waltzing around the stage, he'd given her his full attention. Not just eye contact. He'd talked to her too. Anything to buy himself some time. He'd fed her the lies she longed to hear, and she gobbled them up like a shark smelling blood in the water.

"You need to calm down," he'd said. "Calm down, sweetheart."

"I love you!"

"I love you too."

How could he have said that? How? Did he have a death wish? Eric tried to force the memory from his mind—concentrate on the road instead—but the echo of that fleeting conversation still reverberated.

"I love you too," he'd told her.

"You do? Really?"

He'd nodded earnestly. "You're special. I can tell. You have the prettiest green eyes I've ever seen."

"Oh my God! Do you really think so?"

"Beautiful. But I need you to go now. I have a concert to finish for all these other people. I'll see you later, OK?"

"See, Blair?" Tessa said softly. "Isn't it so nice and peaceful back here?"

Tessa let the air out of her lungs with a long, controlled breath. The night had grown colder since the sun went down, with a steady wind whipping her hair against her face, but she didn't mind the chill. The crisp air only served to sharpen her senses and steel her resolve. Her legs had gone rubbery before, when she first stood up from the chair, but they felt solid beneath her now. It didn't hurt that the night sky had grown overcast with thick, black storm clouds blocking the moonlight. The only source of illumination was the dim yellow light filtering through the living room curtains.

It was too dark back here to see more than a few feet from the house. The rest of the backyard remained shrouded in shadows. Anyone unfamiliar with the terrain would have no way of knowing how the ground beneath the deck sloped steeply downward. Tessa herself hadn't been out here in ages. She only knew what her mother had told her months ago—the last time she'd suggested a visit to the back deck:

No one's used that deck for years. The railing's completely rotted through. Only a matter of time before someone falls and breaks their neck…

Tessa looked down for a moment at her balled-up hands, still bound at the wrists as they rested against Blair's bony chest. He stood a few inches taller than her, but his shoulders were narrow for a guy. Scrawny. Not much muscle on him anywhere, from what she could feel beneath his baggy sweatshirt. Even his face appeared emaciated, with sunken eyes and hollowed-out cheeks that only added to the impression of a hungry wolf stalking its prey.

She shuddered, and his arms tightened around her waist.

"Are you cold, love?" Blair asked as they swayed together awkwardly. Tessa could tell he didn't have much experience dancing—not exactly as graceful as Eric Thorn waltzing around the stage. The knife blade in his hand pressed against her back. "Tessa? Should we go back in?"

"No," Tessa said, forcing her posture straighter. "No, let's dance. This is nice."

"This is all I ever wanted," he whispered. "Just to hold you in my arms like this."

"That's what I want too."

His eyes drifted closed. Tessa watched his lips part with a faint sucking sound as he leaned in for a kiss. *No*, she thought, stiffening. *No way.* She couldn't stomach it. Not on the lips. Even Eric hadn't gone that far...

Tessa turned her face away and rested her head against Blair's shoulder. His breath tickled her ear as his mouth grazed her temple, and Tessa gritted her teeth. This dance routine had gone on long enough. She couldn't keep the pretense up much longer before she gave the whole game away.

"Blair," Tessa said, leaning her weight against him heavily. "Blair, I'm dizzy."

"What's the matter?"

"It's the meds," she said, with a tremor in her voice. "My anxiety pills. They make me dizzy sometimes."

Tessa felt him shake his head, and she cringed as she realized her mistake. The pills...

"But you didn't take any pills," he said suspiciously. "You said you didn't need them."

I'll see you later, OK?

Eric choked on the sour aftertaste of those words—his parting blow when he delivered his attacker to security. He hadn't thought about the consequences at the time. He had no one but himself to blame if she'd come back. He'd invited her, after all. *I'll see you later.* His lies may have soothed her at the time, but they'd only fueled her obsession in the long run.

He saw the truth so clearly now, as his car crept down the road and his eyes scanned across the darkened Texas landscape.

He never should have trusted security to deal with her. He should have ignored those guards. Handled it himself. Eric knew what he would do differently if he could hit Rewind… relive that night again. They probably wouldn't have played the video on the morning talk shows the next day. Or if they had, the viewing public wouldn't have LOL'ed. They probably would've called for his arrest. Put him in jail and thrown away the key. But he'd do it anyway, without a second thought, if he had the chance.

He could see the whole dark fantasy play out in his mind's eye. He held the girl in his arms once more and danced her around the stage. And he spoke to her again. He said every single line the same, except the parting words. He altered those just slightly. Not: *See you later.* Not this time.

This time, he gazed straight through her ink-black eyes to the depths of her deluded soul. "I'll see you in hell, OK?"

Then he glided her over to the edge of the stage and pushed her.

Let her fall and break her skinny, little neck.

Tessa blinked. He'd almost caught her.

But you didn't take any pills. You said you didn't need them.

She pressed her face into Blair's shoulder to cover her wince, but she didn't lose her nerve. Maybe it was the cold night air or maybe the adrenaline coursing through her veins, but her mind remained clear and calm. Another lie rolled smoothly from her tongue. "I took a whole bunch before though. In the car on the way over. I was so nervous to meet you!"

He let out a huff. "You dummy. You took too many, didn't you?" His voice dripped with disapproval, but Tessa heard an undercurrent of affection as his arms squeezed around her. She felt the tip of the knife blade prick the skin of her back. "Stupid girl," he said. "What am I going to do with you? Will it pass soon, do you think?"

Tessa took a few fluttery breaths for good measure as she nodded against his chest. "Soon," she said. "Really dizzy now. Can we just lean against the railing for a sec?"

She lifted her head and tilted it toward the far edge of the deck.

"Of course." Blair smiled at her condescendingly, smoothing a strand of wild hair away from her face. "Just relax and lean on me."

He shuffled backward in the direction of the railing, pulling her along by the waist. Tessa rested her forehead trustingly against him. She didn't lift her head again until she knew they must be close. She felt him crane his neck around to watch where he was going, and she closed her eyes to gather her courage.

It all came down to this. No room for second-guessing.

Her one and only chance. She prayed what felt like a hundred prayers at once: that she had the strength inside herself to fight…that the knife he held wouldn't slash her…that the railing was as weak as her mother claimed…

The railing. She could sense it right behind him now. The time had come to act.

With a single fluid motion, Tessa reared backward and stamped down hard on top of his foot.

She felt his arms go slack. He took one more step backward, his head snapping around to look at her in surprise. Tessa kept her eyes fixed firmly on his chest as she closed the distance between them. She drove her fists into his stomach—and she channeled every last ounce of fear and anger, hatred and disgust into the blow.

He reeled, arms flailing.

Tessa heard the clatter of the falling knife and the groan of wood as it gave way with a crack.

She met his gaze one final time. His eyes stretched wide with panic as he sensed the open space behind his back.

Then all at once, he vanished—the monster who had haunted her, the memory that had held her hostage for so long. He disappeared into the pitch-dark void below. Only a gaping hole remained where he had stood.

DARKNESS

"THERE!"

Eric leaned forward in his seat as his eyes landed on what looked like a narrow driveway. That had to be it. Sycamore Lane. He hit the gas, and the Ferrari's engine roared as the car shot around the corner of the unmarked intersection.

Proceed on the current route. Destination is ahead...

Well, at least the GPS lady seemed confident. Eric didn't quite share her enthusiasm. If anything, this road was even darker than the last one. Eric couldn't see a thing beyond the arc of illumination provided by his headlights. Was this even a real street? The pavement left off after a few feet, and he felt the crunch of loose gravel beneath his tires. No sign of any houses yet. Just a clump of trees off to one side.

Eric hoped to God that they were sycamores. If this wasn't Tessa's street, then he'd have to give in to the thought that made his stomach churn with fear. He might not get to her in time. He was lost.

⟳

Blair lay still in the darkness, unwilling to open his eyes for fear that he might lose the warm glow in the pit of his stomach. He'd been having the most satisfying dream.

What was it about again? The details had already receded. He could only remember the sensation—that delicious prickle of desire, the anticipation of sweet fulfillment. Why did his dreams always end before he got to the good part? It was maddening, really. Just when he had his object within reach…

He sighed and cracked his eyes open, blinking to clear his vision. He couldn't see a thing. A cold wind blanketed him as he felt around with his hands. In some dim corner of his mind, he expected to feel the splintery surface of a wooden deck, but his fingers only encountered frozen ground. A few clumps of dried-up grass. Mostly rocks and hard-packed earth.

Blair propped himself up on his elbows, ignoring the waves of dizziness. He must have hit his head. His eyes adjusted slowly to the dark of the moonless night, and a few indistinct memories filtered through the haze. He'd been on a deck in his dream. A wooden deck. At least, he thought it was a dream. When he looked up now, he could just make out the slats of the deck railing looming overhead. He must have fallen. But why was he up there? He had the vaguest recollection of

standing and…swaying. Dancing. Slow dancing. Slow dancing with…

Tessa.

Blair sat bolt upright as it hit him. Tessa's house. Tessa's deck.
Where was Tessa? Had she fallen too? Was she hurt?

He got to his knees and groped around in a wide circle for
any sign of another body. A burst of pain shot from his left
shoulder, but he ignored it. "Tessa," he whispered hoarsely.
"Tessa, where are you?"

He gave up after a moment. If she was down here, he couldn't
find any sign of her. She'd disappeared on him again. Just like
the last time.

Blair let out a yelp—the sound of a wounded animal, sick
with rage and pain. Why was she always vanishing on him?
Why wouldn't she ever stay where he put her? He could never
seem to keep her still, no matter how he tried. Even with all the
pictures, it never felt like enough. Never satisfying. He wanted
to freeze-frame more than just her image. He wanted her body
and her soul that way—forever fixed in place—so he could
enjoy her at his leisure.

Had she abandoned him again now? If so, he'd make her live
to regret it. One mistake he could forgive, but twice? Three
times? No. For that she had to pay…

He stood, swaying unsteadily on the sloped ground as he
surveyed his surroundings. No way could he climb back up
to the deck from there. Not with a bum shoulder. He'd have
to scramble up the slope and go around to the front of the

house. Cradling his bad arm to his chest, Blair began the slow trudge uphill.

Eric thought he heard a siren, ever so faint. He slowed the car and rolled down his window to listen. There. He heard the sound again more clearly. His eyes took in a faint glimmer of flashing lights.

He hit the gas, and the car lurched over a rise in the road. At last the scene came into view below. Three cars? Maybe four? They were arrayed in an arc around a white clapboard house, reflecting pink in the rotating glow of the police cars' beacons.

Tessa's house. It had to be. Had they gotten there in time?

His eyes were fixed in the distance, straining to make out more details. He didn't see the dark shape come up before him until it was inches from his front fender.

"Jesus!" Eric slammed the brakes.

The figure stood in front of the car, one arm raised against the glare of the headlights. Their eyes locked through the windshield glass—and in that instant, Eric understood.

Medium height. Hoodie sweatshirt. Spindly arms and legs. It was the same figure that Eric had seen lurking in that wide, empty parking lot. But the eyes that stared back weren't green.

Brown eyes. Crooked nose. Sunken cheeks, darkened with five o'clock shadow. Not a fangirl after all.

Eric's jaw dropped open. How had he not seen it earlier?

Tessa had told him the whole story over DM last night. He knew exactly who stood before him now.

The other boy's face registered recognition at the exact same moment. He side-stepped the car and ran.

"Oh no you don't!" Eric cut the engine and flung his car door open.

He nearly made it back to the main road, huffing and puffing with exertion, by the time he finally caught up. If not for the sound of panting, Eric might have run right past the fleeing figure in the pitch-black night. Instead, he took a flying leap and tackled his prey to the ground.

"Oomph!"

Eric expected to overpower those toothpick limbs easily, but the other boy surprised him with his wiry strength. No match for Eric's more muscular frame but enough to give Eric a run for his money. They rolled on the ground, locked together, and Eric gagged slightly at the overpowering stench that emanated from the boy's clothes: a putrid mixture of sweat and flowery perfume.

"Over here!" he shouted over his shoulder when he could manage to spare a breath. "Help! Police!"

Eric turned his head back toward the figure locked in his embrace, and he felt something hard graze his temple. A rock. A glancing blow. One inch to the left, and he might have gotten his skull bashed in. This was getting out of hand. With one final burst of strength, Eric brought his fist down against the center of his adversary's face. Then he flipped the other body over and caught hold of both wrists.

"You disgusting piece of shit," he growled as he pressed his weight down, pinning the bony frame to the ground.

The boy only moaned in response. He stopped struggling. Had Eric knocked him out cold? Or was he merely playing dead, hoping Eric would relinquish his grasp?

Eric pressed down on the wrists more firmly and called over his shoulder once again. "Police! Over here!"

At last he heard their footfalls. He couldn't see a thing out there in the darkened road, but the two officers came up over the rise with flashlights blazing. The beams swung over his shoulder and illuminated the form that lay on the ground beneath him.

Eric turned again and met a pair of dazed eyes staring back. The voice began to mumble, half-intelligible. Eric could just make out a few disjointed words:

"She's mine… She said it…said the words…said she loved me… Tessa…"

At the sound of her name, something inside Eric snapped. For a moment, the whole world went black and then bright crimson. The shouts of the police officers barely penetrated from somewhere far away.

"Tessa…" the voice moaned beneath him. "I'll never let her go… I'll never let her forget…"

Eric picked up a jagged rock and slowly raised it overhead.

THE INTERROGATION
(FRAGMENT 11)

December 31, 2016, 9:17 p.m.
Case #: 124.678.21–001
OFFICIAL TRANSCRIPTION OF POLICE INTERVIEW

—START PAGE 11—

HART: Oh God, I'm going to be sick.

INVESTIGATOR: Tessa, you showed tremendous presence of mind tonight. You should be very proud of how you handled yourself.

HART: But it was all my fault. I brought the whole thing on myself.

INVESTIGATOR: Listen to me, Tessa. I hear that kind of nonsense all the time from victims. It's absolutely not true.

HART: Yes, it is true! I invited him here! Don't you understand? I DM'ed with him for months!

INVESTIGATOR: No, Tessa—

HART: Months and months! It never even occurred to me that it was him.

INVESTIGATOR: Tessa, the individual you've been talking to on Twitter was not the suspect.

HART: Yes, it was! I'm sure now. I'm sure it was him!

INVESTIGATOR: Oh, I don't doubt that Blair Duncan was the indi-
                     vidual who stalked you in New Orleans. He was
                     enrolled in the same summer program, for photog-
                     raphy. We found numerous pictures of you on his
                     cell phone camera roll. We've got him dead to rights
                     on unlawful surveillance and abduction charges. He
                     should be going to prison for a long time.

HART: But you just said—

INVESTIGATOR 2:   I don't think she knows who she was talking to,
                     Chuck.

INVESTIGATOR: She didn't see him at the scene?

INVESTIGATOR 2:   I believe the responding officers already had Ms.
                     Hart in the squad car when he arrived. He fol-
                     lowed them back to the station in his own vehicle.

HART: No, no. He came with us in Dr. Regan's car. He
                     didn't have a vehicle.

INVESTIGATOR: No, Tessa, I'm not referring to Blair Duncan. He
                     was arrested at the scene.

HART: Wait. Then who are you talking about?

INVESTIGATOR: Tessa, the person you've been chatting with on
                     Twitter was not Blair Duncan. We believe that Mr.
                     Duncan began following your Twitter account at
                     some point during the time that he was stalking
                     you. He was still following you when you left
                     New Orleans and changed your username from
                     @TessaHart to @TessaHeartsEric. He changed
                     his own username at one point to @TheRealEricT

and tweeted at you repeatedly in an attempt to engage you in conversation.

HART: I remember that. That weird Eric Thorn impersonator account. I muted it. That was him?

INVESTIGATOR: From what we can gather, he became frustrated when you didn't follow him back and then even more enraged when he saw you followed @EricThornSucks. However, he was not the owner of the @EricThornSucks account.

HART: But he knew everything we talked about. He knew so many details.

INVESTIGATOR: We believe he became aware of your private messages with @EricThornSucks in September. If you recall, on September 20 at 11:25 p.m., @EricThornSucks tweeted publicly, and I quote: "@TessaHeartsEric I swear I'm not a bad guy. Talk to me? Please?" You then exchanged a few more public tweets, culminating with another tweet from @EricThornSucks stating, and I quote: "@TessaHeartsEric what happened? Follow me back so we can DM."

HART: And then I followed him.

INVESTIGATOR: That public exchange apparently alerted Mr. Duncan to your ongoing private correspondence with @EricThornSucks. Mr. Duncan then hacked into the @EricThornSucks account.

HART: But wait. Then why…why didn't he just hack my account to begin with?

INVESTIGATOR: He was able to guess the password on the @EricThornSucks account. You know, you should really have a talk with your boyfriend about cybersecurity. You would think someone in his position would know better—

HART: What are you talking about? What boyfriend? Do you mean Scott?

INVESTIGATOR: I apologize. He described your relationship as romantic in nature.

HART: Who? Blair? He's delusional!

INVESTIGATOR: No, I'm sorry. I meant—

HART: I'm so confused. You're telling me there's actually a Taylor. A real Taylor? You've actually talked to him?

INVESTIGATOR: He's here in the station. Who do you think alerted the authorities tonight? In fact, we owe him one for intercepting Blair Duncan fleeing the scene. Roughed him up pretty good, probably more than necessary, but—

HART: Wait. He's still here? Right now? He's here in the station?

INVESTIGATOR: Yes. He gave us a lengthy statement. He's anxious to speak with you.

HART: Is his name really Taylor?

INVESTIGATOR: No.

INVESTIGATOR 2:   Chuck, go easy. She's had a long day already.

INVESTIGATOR: Well, this should be interesting.

HART: What? What should be interesting?

INVESTIGATOR: Tessa, would you like us to bring him in here to meet you?

HART: Yes!

INVESTIGATOR: OK. I'll go get him. But, Tessa, I think you'd better sit down.

—END OF TRANSCRIPT—

FANGIRLING

TESSA SAT ALONE in the empty interrogation room, her mind whirring with unanswered questions. One of the police officers had given her a scratchy gray wool blanket, and she clutched it tight around her shoulders. How was it possible, she wondered, that she wasn't completely overcome with panic right now? She'd just stood face-to-face with her predator. How was she not a mass of quivering jelly on the floor?

Maybe the shock would hit her later. She probably shouldn't be alone…but she wouldn't be alone for long. Tessa's stomach fluttered at the thought. Taylor would be with her soon. Or whatever his name was… It didn't really matter. What mattered was that he existed.

Tessa's leg bounced nervously beneath the table. Something else still niggled at the back of her mind. Some detail didn't add up in the story the police told her. She couldn't quite put her finger on it, but she felt a tingle of misgiving mixed in with the anticipation. They'd overlooked something. She knew they had. But what? What could it be…

She gasped as it hit her. "They said Taylor sent the police to my house, but he couldn't have. I never told him where I lived!"

A voice sounded behind her, and Tessa turned in her chair.

"Yeah, I think that creep was counting on it that I didn't have your address."

Tessa's grip on the blanket slackened as her eyes focused on the face that had spoken. Her mouth fell open and then formed soundless words: *Oh my God.*

"I got it from my manager. He had your contact info."

"You're Eric Thorn," she whispered in response.

He stood uncertainly in the doorway, waiting for her to speak. He had one hand jammed in the pocket of his leather jacket, and he ran the other hand through his shaggy mop of hair, smoothing it away from his forehead. He took a hesitant step in her direction. "Hi, Tessa."

"You're Eric Thorn," she said again, a little louder.

"Eric *Taylor* Thorn," he corrected with a trace of a cocky grin on his lips. "You'd think a superfan like you would know my middle name."

"What… Why…why are you… I don't understand."

He pulled out the metal chair beside her and took a seat at the interrogation table. She watched him, still confused. He fished for something in his jacket pocket. At last he took it out and set it on the table.

A pink rabbit's foot.

At the sight of it, Tessa felt the familiar choke hold of anxiety closing around her throat. She hugged the blanket tighter, her thoughts scattering. Why did he have the rabbit's foot? Had the police given it to him? Was he here for publicity right now? Still part of the contest?

"Tessa, don't you get it?" His hand flitted to her shoulder. "*I'm* Taylor. I'm the guy you were talking to all this time."

"No, you're not," she said. "You're Eric Thorn."

"I used my middle name."

"No!" She shrugged his hand away. The tight feeling spread to her chest now, and she forced herself to breathe.

Eric one...Eric two...

Tessa shook her head. It wasn't working. "You're Eric Thorn. You're not a real person."

Eric's smile faltered. "What does that even mean?"

"Where's the real Taylor? They told me there was a real Taylor."

She turned toward the entrance of the room, expecting to see someone else, but the doorway stood empty. She cast her eyes wildly about the room, searching for answers to the questions rushing through her head. Had it all just been a game, then? She hadn't been talking to a real guy after all? A guy who wanted to be with her? Just a pop star who liked to amuse himself by playing tricks on unsuspecting fans?

"No, Tessa. You're not hearing me..."

She stopped listening as her gaze landed on his face. The corners of his mouth kept twitching. Was he laughing?

"No," she whispered. "It isn't true. Please tell me this is a joke."

"It's not a joke," he said, even as his smile deepened.

"You're laughing. You think this is funny?"

"No!" His lips straightened, but his eyes still danced with amusement. "Well, maybe just a little," he confessed. "You have to admit, Tessa, it would've been the *Catfish* episode to end all *Catfish* episodes."

She just stared at him, unable to believe what she was hearing. All that time on Twitter…all those months and months…

As the truth sank in, the panic left her, chased away by the bitter taste of anger.

"No?" he added, still smirking. "Come on! You have my poster hanging above your bed. You wrote a story about me called 'Obsessed'! And now it turns out that *I'm* the one you've been talking to?"

Tessa's head reared back, and the metal chair screeched against the floor as she sprang abruptly to her feet. She watched in disbelief as he grinned up at her and laughed.

She let go of the blanket and slapped him hard across the face.

NOT FANGIRLING

ERIC RAISED A hand to his cheek, more from the shock than the pain of the blow. It wasn't the reaction he'd expected. He'd waited patiently from the moment he entered the room for the full impact of the truth to register. He knew what would come next—or he thought he did at any rate. The unintelligible fangirl scream. Just like when he'd followed her and she'd tweeted in response: "*OMGGGGGGGGGGGGGGGGGGGGGGGGG!*"

But the expression on her face didn't look like fangirling. If anything, she looked like she was going to throw up. Eric tried his best to school his features into an expression of concern, but he couldn't quite manage it. The corners of his mouth seemed to have a mind of their own.

He couldn't help it. How could he not smile? He was finally here, meeting Tessa. *Seeing* Tessa. And damn if it wasn't a sight worth waiting for. He couldn't see her body, shrouded beneath the oversize police blanket, but her face was more than enough:

heart shaped, with almond eyes that only seemed to grow larger the longer he stared.

She looked like she'd been through hell, of course. She'd pulled her long, brown hair away from her face in a messy ponytail. Her makeup was hopelessly smudged, with dark rings around both eyes from rubbing away her mascara. But none of that mattered. None of it could hide what he saw in front of him.

Beautiful. More beautiful than he'd ever dared to hope.

But now her eyes narrowed dangerously, and her whole body quivered like a cat about to spring. He cradled his stinging cheek, all trace of humor wiped away. "Tessa, what the hell?"

She sank back down into her chair and buried her face in her hands. "I want the real Taylor. Where's the real Taylor?" Her shoulders ceased trembling and began to shake in earnest. "There was supposed to be a real Taylor!"

"I'm here!" he said. "Listen to me. I'm right here!"

Eric put a tentative arm around her. He tried to pull her toward him, but Tessa turned in her chair and pushed violently against his chest. "Don't touch me!"

"Sorry!" He let go and held up his hands. "I'm sorry. Are you OK? Should I get someone?"

She looked back at him at last, with eyes so full of disappointment, it made him want to crawl inside a deep, dark hole. "There's no real Taylor, is there?" she whispered.

"Tessa," he said softly. "I should have told you sooner. I just... I wanted to tell you face-to-face. That's all. That's why I'm here.

I staged this whole fake contest just to come here and meet you."
He scooted out of his chair and squatted down beside her, forcing
her to maintain eye contact when she tried to look away. "Tessa,
it's me. Do you hear me? I'm real. You're real. This connection
that we have is real. When you're the only person on earth who
can make me smile anymore, that's real. That's the only thing
that's real. It's everything else in my life that's fake as hell."

She didn't answer. Tears spilled silently down her cheeks. She
swiped at her eyes, but she only managed to smear her mascara
even more. Eric reached into his pocket—he'd have given his
life to hand her a tissue—but he came up empty.

"Tessa," he tried again, desperate to get through to her. He
took her hands in his. "Tessa, listen to me. You know me. Even
before we started talking, you saw me better than other people.
You could sense that something was wrong. I'm not sure exactly
how. Maybe because we were going through some of the same
things. Or maybe you're just really intuitive. But you really saw
me. And you listened to me. You're the only one who listens
to a single thing I say anymore. The only one, Tessa. And I listened to you too. I know you too. I know how scared you must
have been tonight."

She snatched her hands away. "You have no idea."

"Tessa—"

"You have *no* idea how I felt tonight! You have *no* idea what
I just went through!"

"OK." He backpedaled, retreating to his chair. "No, that's
true. I don't. I can only imagine—"

"Did you think I would be excited now?" She let out a harsh breath. "Did you think I would scream and cry and fangirl all over you, and it would all be OK?"

Eric looked down sharply. "I don't know. I guess I hoped... I don't know what I hoped. I guess I did think that. A little bit. And obviously I was wrong. And I'm sorry."

She leaned forward once again and rested her head on her arms. Eric longed to reach out and comfort her, but he didn't dare touch her again. Instead, he looked across the room toward the horizontal mirror built into the opposite wall. A two-way mirror, no doubt. He'd seen enough cop shows to know that much. Were those police detectives watching right now from the other side? Did they find this show entertaining?

He met eyes with his own reflection: Eric Thorn, in the flesh—just a little worse for wear. He could see a dark bruise forming on his forehead, where he'd been struck earlier, rolling around on the ground with Tessa's stalker. And now he had a new red splotch across his cheek, from where Tessa herself had just slapped him.

Slapped him. After all that. Really?

He took a breath and squared his shoulders. "I'm sorry you're disappointed, Tessa. I really am. But I don't think I deserved to be slapped."

She looked up in surprise at the firmness of his tone. "Sorry," she whispered.

"Thank you."

She tried fruitlessly to wipe her eyes again. "Look, I shouldn't have slapped you. I'm sure you're not a bad person," she said with a loud sniff. "I love your music. You know that. It's just that today was pretty much the worst day of my life, and I'm not... I'm just not in the right frame of mind for a meet-and-greet—"

"This isn't a meet-and-greet!"

"I just thought there was going to be someone here at the end of all this who actually wanted to be with me."

"I do!" Eric threw back his head and looked up at the ceiling in helpless disbelief.

Tessa avoided his eyes. She addressed her words to the table-top, her forehead resting against her hand. "No, but like, I thought someone was going to come in here and be my boyfriend now. Someone normal. I didn't even care what he looked like. Just someone...just someone nice who could love me and talk to me and be with me. That's all I wanted. But instead everyone left. Everyone just bailed on me again. Even Dr. Regan—"

Eric turned back toward her. "What? What do you mean, she bailed on you?"

"It doesn't matter. I'm sorry I slapped you, OK?" Tessa pushed back her chair from the table. "I really just want to go home now."

Eric's shoulders slumped. There was no use trying to argue with her further. He'd had his answer from the moment her heavy palm made contact with his cheek.

"OK," he said dully, rising from his chair. "Let's go. I'll drive you home."

"No."

"My Ferrari's right out front."

"The police will take me."

"I'll take you," he insisted. He shrugged off his jacket and draped it around her. "Wear this. It's cold outside."

She shook her head, but she clutched the jacket tightly around her shoulders. They met eyes for a long moment, his own heartache reflected back in the misery he saw on her face.

So this is it, he thought. The night he'd been anticipating for so long now. Of all the times he'd played it out in his head, he'd never imagined it quite like this. Total rejection. Complete and utter disappointment. He'd been living in some kind of dream world apparently. Some fantasy land, where Tessa would fall into his arms, be his girl for one magical night, and then go back to talking him to sleep over Twitter every night afterward.

But that was his fantasy, not hers. She didn't want Eric Thorn. Not in real life. Not for anything outside of music videos and fanfics.

He couldn't say he blamed her. She wanted something normal. How many times had he wanted the same thing? A normal job. Normal friends. Normal house. Normal bills to pay. A normal girl to take out on normal dates. Someday, a normal wife. Maybe a few normal kids to drive around in their normal minivan. He could have had all of that if he hadn't been so dead set on fame. Maybe he could have had Tessa.

"I'll just drop you off," he said, his voice barely above a whisper. "I won't even get out of the car. I'll let you go, OK? You can say good-bye, and walk away, and unfollow me, and go about your life. Forget I ever existed. That's fine, if that's what you really want. But, Tessa, please—"

He paused and swallowed hard against the lump inside his throat.

"Please, just this once. Just let me be the guy that takes you home."

A COLD NIGHT IN HELL

ERIC HUNKERED DOWN behind the steering wheel of his parked car and wrapped his arms around himself for warmth. How cold was it tonight, anyway? It must have dipped below freezing outside, judging by the way he could see his own breath.

A violent shiver overtook him, and he looked longingly at the Ferrari's red push-button ignition. Maybe he should idle the engine for a few minutes. His fingers twitched, but he resisted the temptation. Not yet. He only had a quarter tank of gas left, and he needed to make it last all night.

Eric glanced at his phone to check the time. Just past eleven thirty now. He assumed he'd still be sitting here at midnight, counting down the New Year all alone. An hour had passed since that silent car ride back to Tessa's house. She hadn't uttered a single word until he pulled into her driveway, but he'd stopped her with a question before she got out.

"What time is your mom coming home?"

She had her face turned away from him, but he saw her shoulders draw upward at the sound of his voice. "What do you care about my mom?"

"You shouldn't be alone in there," he said. "Not tonight."

She'd cracked the car door open. "Thanks for the ride."

"I'm not leaving," he'd called after her.

"If you think I'm inviting you into my house—"

"I'll just sit out here in the driveway," he'd interrupted, striving to keep the desperation out of his voice. "Just in case. I'll keep an eye on things until your mom comes back."

"Well, that should be around nine tomorrow morning."

"Then I guess I'm sleeping in my car tonight."

She'd exited without another word.

Now he trembled against the cold and swore under his breath. Damn, it was frigid. He'd thought it was bad outside the concert venue earlier, but the temperature must have dropped another twenty degrees in the hours since. He expelled a steaming breath, fiddling with his phone to distract himself from the impending hypothermia, and his thumb landed on its usual destination.

Twitter.

The police had frozen his second account—they needed it for evidence—but they'd left his @EricThorn account untouched. Eric stared down at his profile. He'd told Tessa in the police station that she should unfollow him, and he couldn't help but wonder if she'd done it. Had she blocked him too? Deactivated her account? He couldn't bring himself to check.

Instead, for some unfathomable reason, Eric clicked to compose a new tweet.

He didn't know what he hoped to achieve. Tessa wouldn't be on Twitter tonight. Not after what had happened. Eric didn't bother aiming his message @ her, or at anyone in particular. Fourteen million followers would see it, minus one. He entered the words anyway, driven by a force he couldn't explain. There was a pain in his chest—the last ember of a fire that hadn't quite died. He had to give it one more try before the flame went out for good.

He hit Tweet, and his notifications lit up with the inevitable blizzard of replies. In the past, he would have viewed those messages with contempt, but now he couldn't summon up more than a numb indifference.

Who was he to judge, anyway? He wasn't so different from all those fangirls after all. In the end, he wanted the same thing they all did. A like. A reply. Maybe a follow back. Some sign of acknowledgment from an account that probably couldn't hear him. Some tiny gesture that told him the words he craved: "*I see you… I notice you… I know that you exist… I love you back… I love you too…*" Anything to know that his message had been heard by its recipient and not shouted into an empty void.

Eric rested his forehead against the steering wheel, staring at his useless phone, but a sharp knock on the window interrupted him. He looked up, startled, and his body temperature spiked a few degrees at what he saw: Tessa, with her hands cupped round her face, peering at him through the glass. She hadn't left him for dead out there after all. He cracked the passenger door back open.

"Do you have frostbite yet?" she asked.

Eric couldn't help but grin at the sight of her. She'd changed from before. Taken a shower, twisted her hair into a thick braid, and scrubbed her face free of makeup. She'd decked herself out in a pair of mismatched pajamas covered by a ratty flannel robe. And on her feet, of course, she wore a pair of hot-pink bunny slippers.

"Nice slippers," he said with a nod toward her feet. "Those are even hotter in person."

She glowered at him as she climbed into the passenger seat and tucked her feet beneath her, out of sight. "Here," she said, shoving a thick down comforter in his direction.

He took it greedily and wrapped it around his shoulders. It was big enough to go around him twice, but he held out the excess in her direction—a silent offer to share. For a moment, he thought she would refuse. Her eyes darted to his face and back away. Then she shimmied an inch closer and wrapped her side of the blanket around her arms.

Eric cleared his throat. Did she see the tweet just now? He couldn't quite summon the nerve to ask. He had a million different things he wanted to say to her, but he didn't dare speak. He knew that one wrong word could send her scurrying into the house for good.

Tessa broke the silence, and Eric choked at her chosen topic of conversation. "I'm not going to sleep with you."

"Now that's an understatement," he said with a dry laugh. "Trust me, I wasn't expecting you to."

She looked down at her lap. "I just wanted to make that completely clear."

"Message received." He knew he should leave it at that, but he couldn't quite manage to bite his tongue. "To be fair, Tessa, I did just spend the past five months texting with a girl who wouldn't even send me a selfie."

"So what?" Her head snapped up, and her eyes flashed with defiance. "That means I'm obligated to sleep with you?"

"No! I'm just saying, if I wanted to get laid, I can think of easier ways."

Tessa pressed her lips together. Her gaze lingered, and Eric turned his head to give her a better view. Even in the darkened car, he could see the way new color stained her cheeks when he looked her full in the face. Was she thawing toward him? Just a little? He rocked his body toward her and knocked his shoulder lightly against hers. "Hey, look at you, outside your house again. Twice in one day!"

She slid down farther in her seat, pulling her shoulder out of range. "It's not like I feel safe in there anymore," she said. "Not after *he* was in my house."

Eric scratched his nose, unsure how to respond. "Do you want me to take you somewhere else?"

"No." She shrugged. "Nowhere else to go, really." She sounded matter-of-fact, but Eric couldn't quite read the expression on her face.

He paused, waiting for her to say more.

She let out a noisy breath. "Shouldn't I be better now?" Her mouth scrunched sideways, and her voice tightened with frustration as she spoke. "I mean, logically, I was afraid to leave my house because I could feel him out here. Somewhere. Somehow. I could sense that he was still watching me. Now that he's locked up, I should feel safe. That seems only fair, right?"

Eric raised an eyebrow. He had a feeling it didn't work that way. A phobia was an irrational fear. It didn't respond to logic. It had no sense of fairness. And he could tell from her expression that Tessa knew it too. He longed to reach out and squeeze her hand, but he didn't want to spook her. He ventured a hesitant smile instead. "So I guess that means you can come to my show tomorrow in Santa Fe?"

"If you think that's happening, then you're the one with mental problems."

She met his eyes, striving for a withering glare, but she couldn't quite manage it. He broke into a grin, and he saw her cheeks flood with color once again. She turned away, but not fast enough to hide the involuntary smile that popped onto her own face in response.

"So that was really you?" she asked. She kept her eyes averted, plucking stray feathers through the comforter's outer shell. "All that time? That was actually you texting? Not some publicist or something?"

"Nope. All me."

"I'm just trying to process it."

"Take your time."

She stole another look, and he forced his face into serious lines. No more cocky grin. Her forehead crinkled as she studied him. "Tell me the truth," she said. "How many other fans did you have this going on with?"

"None. Tessa, I'm telling you, it wasn't like that. It was only you."

She shook her head. "It doesn't make any sense," she said. "Why would you even talk to me in the first place?"

Eric thought back to that morning when he first became aware of her account. He'd been a total mess that day, driven by unchecked anger and the thinly veiled anxiety that lay beneath. He hadn't yet learned how to control it. Only her calming influence had taught him how to cope.

He shrugged, suddenly self-conscious. He turned away from her and looked straight out through the windshield. "Talking to you helped me. You helped me through a lot of things."

"But why?" she asked, incredulous. "You're Eric Thorn. Why would you need help from someone like me?"

"You already know all this, Tessa. It's nothing we haven't talked about before."

"When? In the police station?"

"No! Tessa, you know me." He leaned toward her, his eyes growing more intent. "I'm not a stranger. We've been talking every night." She opened her mouth to respond, but he continued before she could speak. "You know all those times we were talking about Eric Thorn, and I said some theory about him, and you accused me of projecting? Remember? Well, it turns out I wasn't projecting, Tessa. I was telling you things about myself. Real things. Stuff I couldn't tell anyone else."

"Like what?"

"I don't know. Hating what I do? Feeling trapped? Getting locked into a bad record deal and forced to act like a male stripper? Does any of this ring a bell?"

She nodded slowly but didn't answer. For a moment, her eyes went far away, and he thought he might be getting through to her. Then she returned her attention to the comforter's frayed seams. "But what about all the other stuff?" she asked. "Like you told me how some coworker got stalked. What was that? Just some story to make me feel like we had something in common?"

"No!" He reached for her arm, but he let his hand drop without making contact. "Tessa, I didn't even know about Blair. That was true. All of it."

She looked up, blinking rapidly.

"Dorian Cromwell," he explained. "I was a total wreck last summer after Dorian got killed."

"Did you know him?"

"No, that's not the point!" Eric's voice rose, and he took a deep breath to control it. "I just felt like a sitting duck. It only takes one copycat, you know? It's only a matter of time before the same thing happens again."

Her eyes went wide, but her expression softened as she scrutinized his face. "That fangirl in Seattle," she said. "You said you didn't sleep a wink after it happened. That was true?"

He nodded, holding his breath. It took every ounce of self-control not to reach out and touch her face. He could sense her presence beside him now—the sensitive girl he'd fallen in love with over Twitter, not the ice princess from the car ride home tonight. She was still in there, just beneath the surface. He just needed her to thaw a little more…

Maybe he should show her the tweet he sent before. She clearly hadn't seen it. Eric reached for the phone in his lap, but his attention was distracted by a flutter of movement in front of him. He sat up in his seat and pointed toward the windshield. "Look!"

SNOWFLAKES

TESSA WATCHED IN puzzlement as Eric's whole face changed. In the blink of an eye, his expression went from shuttered darkness to a look of childlike delight. She followed the direction he was pointing and saw the reason why. The night sky had filled with snowflakes, dancing through the air in all directions.

He reached toward the windshield and touched the glass where one of the snowflakes had stuck. Then he glanced back at her face with a silent question in his eyes. She knew what he was asking. The same question he'd asked her over DM last night. She'd reread that conversation enough times to commit it to memory.

> **Taylor:** What songs are you hoping Eric will play?
> **Tessa H:** As long as he does "Snowflake," I'll be happy.

It was strange to think she'd written that to Eric. The person beside her felt like a total stranger—and yet somehow, she knew him well. She'd felt a small jolt of recognition just now when he mentioned Dorian Cromwell. She knew the expression that crossed his face: that glimmer of fear. She'd seen it before in videos. She'd frozen that frame a thousand times. He normally concealed it with a fake smile or a come-hither look straight into the lens. But this time he didn't bother hiding behind a mask. He let her see the truth.

Tessa suddenly remembered the rest of what she said to him last night. *I just wish someone would write a song like that about me.* But he hadn't, of course. He couldn't have...

She didn't have time to think about it further. She gasped at the sound of his voice beside her—so strange and yet so achingly familiar. Eric skipped over the song's opening and came in on the second verse.

> *The wind, it started whipping.*
> *It slammed my window shut.*
> *My snowflake left a teardrop.*
> *I guess she'd had enough.*
>
> *But I won't forget my snowflake.*
> *Can't melt her from my mind.*
> *I'll watch here from this window.*
> *For the love she left behind.*

Tessa listened to his rich, full tenor voice, but she didn't look at him. She kept her eyes glued firmly to her lap. She felt the gentle pressure of his hand against her elbow, and she shuddered at his touch. Even through the layers of flannel, she could feel his fingers, freezing cold.

What was she doing out here? She hadn't meant to stay and talk. She hadn't even intended to get in the car. Just drop off the blanket and leave.

"I'll keep an eye on things," he'd said when he dropped her off earlier. She had to admit, it was kind of sweet. Especially after the cold shoulder she'd given him on the ride home. Not the kind of behavior she would have expected from a famous pop star meeting a fan. More like something a guy might do for his girlfriend after getting in a fight.

Tessa shook the thought out of her head. *He's not your boyfriend*, she silently reminded herself. *He's Eric Thorn.*

But what was he doing, parked there in her driveway for hours on end? What exactly was he trying to prove?

He took a breath before he hit the chorus, and Tessa swept a glance in his direction. He looked back at her with fierce determination that sent a pulse of heat rippling through her. She couldn't bear the scrutiny. She interrupted, her voice terse, before he could let out another note. "What do you want from me?" she whispered.

"I want to be with you."

"Why?"

"Because I'm in love with you."

At his words, the tiny spark kindled stronger. She pressed

her palm below her rib cage to smother it. She refused to meet his eyes, but he caught her wrist and pulled her toward him. "Tessa, last night you said you loved me too."

She twisted, wrenching free. "I said that to Taylor. Last night I was talking to Taylor."

"I *am* Taylor!"

"No, but—"

"Tessa, look."

He pulled out his phone, and she squeezed her eyes shut at the sudden flash of blue.

Twitter.

Really? After everything that had happened? Tessa couldn't bear the sight of it. The detective had suspended her account in the police station, and she hadn't protested. She never wanted to lay eyes on that little bird logo again.

"Look." She heard Eric's voice in her ear, low and raspy. "Please look. Tessa, I need you to see this. Please."

Tessa could hear the urgency in his voice. She didn't know what it meant—what he could possibly need to show her so desperately. She sucked in a deep breath and forced her lids to open. He'd pulled up his own profile, and her eyes fell on the most recent tweet.

Eric Thorn @EricThorn
I love you, snowflake. This is real.

Tessa's vision blurred. She slammed her eyes closed again and covered them with her hand.

"Tessa," he said, pulling at her wrist. "C'mon. Don't do that. I'm sorry, OK? I'm sorry I'm Eric Thorn. But why does that change everything?"

She didn't know how to explain it to him. So many words had passed between them—all those months of endless direct messages—and all of it had now been cast in a new light. Different fragments of their conversations kept springing to her mind, and she gave up trying to suppress them. She merely spoke the words aloud, a different set of words that she'd long since learned by heart. "You know what Eric Thorn would see if he ever noticed I existed?"

Eric peeled her hand away from her eyes, and Tessa cast a quick look at his face. She couldn't tell if he recognized the quote. The next line would do the trick.

"How did you put it, exactly?" she asked. "A leech? With no point to my meaningless existence except to suck?"

"Tessa, don't." He rose to his knees in the car seat and grabbed her by both shoulders, forcing her to turn toward him. "I didn't mean that. I didn't even know you yet!"

She shrugged beneath his hands. "It was kind of true though. I'm a fangirl. I have a thousand pictures of you on my phone. I started a whole hashtag about you called #EricThornObsessed."

"Right," he said slowly, his eyes boring holes straight through her. "Which I kind of interpreted to mean you were—you know—kind of…maybe…into me?"

She looked away. "It's just really embarrassing. Try to imagine how you would feel."

"You're embarrassed because you're into me?"

"No," she said, cringing. "Because I know how you feel about fangirls! Tell the truth. You don't love us. We're not snowflakes to you. We're leeches."

He slumped forward and scrubbed his hands across his face. For a long moment, Tessa thought he wouldn't bother to reply. But he gathered himself again. With a sigh, he turned back toward her. "OK," he said in a flat voice. "I get it."

"You do?"

"Yep. Loud and clear." He nodded firmly. "You're a fangirl. You're embarrassed. Now get over it."

"I can't just—"

"Here," he interrupted. "Give me your phone."

"What? Why?"

He held out his hand. "Just do it. Trust me. Just this once."

Tessa wasn't even sure she'd brought it out here, but she dug into the pocket of her robe, and her fingers closed over the phone's familiar form. She handed it to him without meeting his eyes. In her mind, all she could think of was the picture on her lock screen—the first visual he'd see, the moment he flicked it on. She'd changed it the other night to the new single cover for "Snowflake": Eric Thorn, riding a snowmobile, naked to the waist.

"Please, don't look at the camera roll," she whispered.

"Nah, I'm familiar with what I look like."

Tessa didn't watch him, but she could sense his smirk. She waited for him to make some snide remark. Instead, she felt him thrust something back into her hands. She looked down to see her red leather cell phone case, now empty. "What's this?" she asked with a frown.

He didn't answer. He merely cracked his car door open and chucked her phone into the darkness, as far as he could throw.

Tessa's eyes flew open wide. "My phone! What did you just do?"

"There." He wiped his hands back and forth to say good riddance. "All gone. No more pictures."

"But that's my phone!"

"I'll buy you a new one."

She looked at him in silence, too stunned to speak.

"Tessa," he said, his face dead serious. "It's really not that complicated. If being my fangirl embarrasses you, then stop being my fangirl. Be something else instead."

"Like what?"

"I don't know. Like, you could be my girlfriend, for example."

He took her hand again.

"Tessa, I love you. Do you understand that? I'm in love with you. I'm freezing my ass off in your driveway for you. I'm sitting here singing a whole sugary-sweet love song that I wrote for you. Just for you. Not for anyone else. The song isn't called 'Snowflakes,' plural. It's 'Snowflake.' Just one snowflake. How many more ways do you need me to say it?"

She ducked her head.

He squeezed her hand. "Look at me."

"I can't," she said. She could feel her heart thumping. Her

throat was starting to constrict. She knew she should do her breathing exercises, but the Eric five count wouldn't have its usual effect.

She didn't want to have a panic attack, sitting here in front of him—or worse, that terrifying blankness that had happened earlier with Blair. That nothingness when her mind switched off, like a cell phone running out of batteries. Tessa didn't know where she went exactly when that feeling overtook her, but the mere idea of it made her break out in a sweat. She dug her nails into her palm, focusing on the sensation to keep herself anchored in the here and now. "I'm such a mess," she said. "You don't even know the half of it."

"Yes, I do." His voice was strong, unflinching. "Tessa, look at me. I know you. I know your weaknesses, and you know mine." He edged closer as he spoke. "And I also know how special you are. That's what I remember from the first conversation we ever had. I didn't know you yet, but I could tell that you were special. And the more you let me see you, the more I couldn't get enough. Because what I saw inside you has got to be"—his voice cracked, but he plowed on—"has got to be the bravest, strongest, most beautiful person I've ever known."

Tessa covered her face with her hands. Her throat felt thick, but not from panic. She recognized the ache that came from trying to hold back tears. "Stop," she begged. "Please stop!"

"Why? You're embarrassed?"

"No."

"What, then?"

She whispered the answer, barely louder than a breath. "I'm scared."

Eric's face relaxed. He took her hand and cradled it gently as he began to sing again.

> *Just one snowflake.*
> *She thought that no one cared.*
> *Perfect snowflake,*
> *I'll catch you. Don't be scared.*

Tessa knew she shouldn't look at him, but she couldn't help it. She needed to see. She gazed helplessly at those ice-blue eyes, that chiseled jawline, those perfect lips… She knew his face better than her own, and yet he wore an expression she didn't recognize. His cheeks had turned a shade darker. His eyes were hooded but soft. She'd never seen him look that way before. Not once, in all the screenshots she'd collected.

She realized what it meant: the answer to all the questions she didn't dare to ask. Eric Thorn had never turned that look upon a camera lens. His fans had never seen his face in love.

He reached out one finger and touched the corner of her mouth. Tessa didn't realize she had a tear running down her cheek until he made contact with the damp spot. He leaned toward her then and kissed her, softly, his lips just barely grazing hers.

Tessa gasped at the sensation. His fingers were freezing, but his lips melted a path straight through her icy core. She felt a crack in the numb exterior—a fissure that slowly spread until she crumbled.

They broke apart, and she looked up. His face was inches from hers, their frosty breath comingling. "You'll freeze to death out here," she whispered.

His arm went tight around her waist as his lips sought hers again. "Maybe," he whispered back. "But I'll die happy."

Tessa could see him shivering badly though. She pulled away from him again and popped the passenger side door open.

"Where are you going?" she heard his voice call after her.

She turned and looked back over her shoulder with a ghost of a smile on her lips. "Come on," she said, nodding toward the house. "It's OK now. You can come inside."

U.S. DEPARTMENT OF JUSTICE
FEDERAL BUREAU OF INVESTIGATION

OFFICIAL MEMORANDUM

DATE: *1-03-2017*

FROM: *Special Agent Donald J. Peterson, FBI*
TO: *Charles D. Foster, Lieutenant, Midland Municipal Police Department*

The Federal Bureau of Investigation asserts investigative authority in the matter of Case ID # 79-SA-1337, pursuant to Title 28, U.S. Code, Section 540A0. We hereby confirm receipt of a total of eleven (11) excerpted fragments from the interrogations conducted by the Midland Municipal Police Department on the night of December 31, 2016. Full data records of the online Twitter history for accounts @EricThornSucks and @TessaHeartsEric have also been obtained at your suggestion. Forensic crime scene analysis is currently underway, and results will be made available to your department forthwith.

Please find enclosed a transcript of our recent conversation conducted in the FBI San Antonio Field Office. Thank you for your department's full and speedy cooperation in this ongoing investigation.

Case ID #: 79-SA-1337
TRANSCRIPT OF ELECTRONICALLY RECORDED INTERVIEW
DATE: January 2, 2017, 12:17 p.m.

—START PAGE 1—

AGENT: Lieutenant Foster, thank you for coming in today.

As you know, you're being interviewed as the last known person to speak with the victim in our case. This interview is being recorded.

FOSTER: I understand.

AGENT: For the record, I'm Special Agent Donald Peterson with the FBI San Antonio Field Office. Today is January 2, 2017. Could you please identify yourself?

FOSTER: Lieutenant Charles Foster. I'm an investigator with the Midland, Texas, Police Department.

AGENT: Thanks, Charles. You were the lead investigator conducting your department's inquiry into the Blair Duncan–Tessa Hart stalking case. Please describe to me the last time you saw Ms. Hart.

FOSTER: After the interrogations. I put her in a room with Mr. Thorn.

AGENT: In the Midland police station?

FOSTER: Yes, in one of the interrogation rooms. It was consensual. We recorded video footage of their interaction from behind the two-way partition, but unfortunately no audio. I sent you a copy of the tape.

AGENT: I reviewed it. Can you provide any insight into Ms. Hart's state of mind that might have led her to strike Mr. Thorn across the face?

FOSTER: I couldn't say. Not with any certainty. At the time of the incident, I put it down to shock.

AGENT: Did Mr. Thorn at any time give you reason to believe he might be fearful of Tessa Hart?

FOSTER: No, but he appeared paranoid in general. He was clearly concerned about a fan becoming violent. He spoke at some length about the Dorian Cromwell murder case and his concern that a deluded fan might attempt a copycat crime.

AGENT: A fan, but not Tessa Hart in particular?

FOSTER: No. It was such a strange dynamic. He didn't see Ms. Hart as a fan. He came across as a bit delusional himself, in my opinion. To hear him talk, the two of them were in a mutual relationship. He viewed her as his girlfriend. And yet when I interviewed her, she had no idea the person she'd been talking to was him.

AGENT: Did you get the sense that Ms. Hart might pose any kind of threat to him?

FOSTER: Not really. We interviewed her as the victim in our case. We never considered her as a potential perpetrator. I don't know, Don. It seems pretty tenuous.

AGENT: We have physical evidence at her place of residence.

FOSTER: What kind of evidence are we talking about?

AGENT: Track patterns in the snow, fingerprints on both their cell phones, a butcher knife that may have been the murder weapon, and multiple bloodstains in her bedroom.

FOSTER: His blood?

AGENT: The final DNA report is still pending, but the
               initial blood type analysis looks like a match for
               Thorn.

FOSTER: And the body?

AGENT: No body just yet. From the tracks outside the
               house, it looks like the suspect managed to drag
               the body into the victim's vehicle. It'll probably
               turn up somewhere once the snow melts.

FOSTER: Can't rule it a homicide without a body.

AGENT: We're still treating it as a missing persons case
               for now. We were called in by state police in New
               Mexico after Thorn failed to appear for a show in
               Santa Fe.

FOSTER: Can't even say for sure there was foul play
               involved, if you ask me.

AGENT: You think Thorn could've staged it?

FOSTER: Depends. What does Tessa Hart have to say
               about it?

AGENT: Nothing. She's long gone. We believe Ms. Hart
               made it across the Mexican border. The victim's
               car turned up this morning at a chop shop outside
               Del Rio. Our analysts are checking it over now.

FOSTER: Damn. That car must've been worth a few hun-
               dred grand.

AGENT: Yep, we're guessing it may be a while before she surfaces, with the amount of cash she would have obtained for it.

FOSTER: Well, that doesn't look good for her. She told us she didn't leave the house. Agoraphobic.

AGENT: We have reason to question the credibility of certain statements she made to you.

FOSTER: You never can tell, can you? I've been on the job twenty-five years now, and I wouldn't have pegged her for a killer. You'd think Thorn would've seen it coming, the way he obsessed about that Cromwell case.

AGENT: Love is blind, right?

FOSTER: You can say that again.

AGENT: Just one more thing, Charles. Could you take a look at this and tell me if it means anything to you?

FOSTER: What am I looking at here?

AGENT: The final tweets sent from Mr. Thorn's Twitter account. He tweeted just before midnight on December 31, and I quote: "I love you, snowflake. This is real." And then he tweeted this one on the morning of January 1—

FOSTER: That's impossible. We froze that account, pending our investigation.

AGENT: No, I'm not referring to the @EricThornSucks account. This was tweeted from @EricThorn.

FOSTER: My mistake. I just assumed because of the reference.

AGENT: What do you mean by that?

FOSTER: It's a reference to a direct message that Eric Thorn sent to Tessa Hart from the @EricThornSucks account. Hang on while I look it up… [pause] I'm guessing you're going to want to enter the whole thread into evidence, Don. This tweet right here's your smoking gun.

AGENT: Let the record show that we're discussing a tweet sent out on January 1 at 7:26 a.m. from the account with username @EricThorn. The tweet states, and I quote: "Sleep with a leech, and it just might bleed you dry."

ARE YOU
#EricThornObsessed?

CAN'T WAIT FOR THE NEXT BOOK?

Visit books.sourcebooks.com/FollowMeBack and sign up to receive exclusive content, insider info, and more!

And follow these REAL Twitter accounts to hear directly from the author and your favorite characters:

@TessaHeartsEric
@EricThornSucks
@av_geiger

ACKNOWLEDGMENTS

I WOULD LIKE to thank each and every Wattpad user who read the first draft of this story online. Your feedback inspired me to keep writing when I felt like giving up. This book would not exist without your constant encouragement.

To Lydia Shamah, my agent, who had the vision to see this story's potential, thank you for your insight and wise counsel. Thanks also to my wonderful editor, Kate Prosswimmer, and to the entire team at Sourcebooks, including Elizabeth Boyer, Alex Yeadon, Katy Lynch, and Annette Pollert-Morgan. I am forever grateful for your leap of faith and your tireless efforts on my behalf.

To Caitlin O'Hanlon, I-Yana Tucker, Aron Levitz, and all the incredible people at Wattpad HQ who work so hard to nurture budding authors, thank you for all that you do. I'm proud to call myself a member of the extraordinary community you have built.

Finally, a word of gratitude to my family, whose love and support never waver: Helene, Alex, Ted, Debbie, Allan, Gail, Jeanne, my children, and above all, David. Thank you for your patience, for the hours of effort you've put in, and for following me on this journey into the unknown. You know that I will always follow you back.

ABOUT THE AUTHOR

A. V. GEIGER is an epidemiologist who spends far too much spare time on social media. By day, she studies women's psychiatric and reproductive health. By night, she can be found fangirling, following people back, and photoshopping the heads of band members onto the bodies of unicorns. Her writing career began with celebrity fan fiction, and her work draws extensively on her own experiences with online fan culture. Her original teen fiction has received millions of hits on the story-sharing website Wattpad, ranking as high as #1 in the mystery-thriller genre. She lives in New Jersey with her husband and twin boys. Visit avgeiger.com.